THE ALLIANCE

THE ALLIANCE

THE HYBRIAN SERIES BOOK TWO

L. WOOD

The Alliance: The Hybrian Series Book Two

ISBN: 978-1-7374846-4-6 (Paperback)

ISBN: 978-1-7374846-5-3 (Hardcover)

ISBN: 978-1-7374846-6-0 (Hardcover)

Cover Design by Miblart

Character Art by Kalynne_Art

www.authorlwood.com

To those who love fudge brownie mint ice cream—this is the way.

Content Warning

Mild torture, suicidal thoughts, and PTSD. As the characters grow and experience life changing situations, the story grows with them. This novel is rated upper young adult.

CHAPTER ONE

T HE CHILLED FALL AIR leaked through my leather jacket, sending shivers down my spine. I leaned against the chipped wooden railing overlooking the Willamette River, the moon reflecting off the water's calm surface. A strong arm wrapped around me, catching me by surprise, but the gesture was welcomed. I glanced over at Miles, his hazel eyes fixated on me. I guess he wasn't ready to say goodbye either.

Tomorrow I would leave with Liam and the others to go into hiding, leaving Miles behind. I had no clue if that involved moving from place to place or if they had another building off the radar similar to this old run-down fishery currently being used as a temporary base for Alcorp. Doctor Alan Roulings—who I had known as Frank in the Vault—was the CEO of Alcorp, and they had resources to prevent me from being found.

Ringing resonated from Miles' phone in his pocket, and he fished it out. Kat's name flashed across the screen. As a Portland police officer, Miles had been assigned to work with FBI Agent Katrina Foster to solve the case behind my captivity in the Vault. Now, she knew the truth and was currently collecting clothes from my shared apartment. I hadn't been allowed to go back after being attacked, and the temporary base wasn't supplied with extra outfits.

Miles hit the answer button and held it to his ear. "Hello?"

I used my heightened hearing to listen in.

"Officer MacLand. I have a message for you," a familiar voice said. A shiver—not from the cold—ran down my spine, and my heart thrummed against my chest.

Miles stiffened. This was bad. *Very* bad. The voice wasn't Kat's—it was Avery's, the traitor who had attempted to attack us.

"Agent Foster is safe—for now. Harper has until midnight to turn herself in at the trainyard on the river in exchange for Kat's life," Avery continued. "She must come alone or Kat is dead."

Miles and I shared a glance, not needing words to understand the severity of the situation. What I feared had become reality. The plan to go into hiding was so no one would get hurt. My DNA contained something special that could be used to turn Hybrians—genetically altered super soldiers created with the Hybrian serum—into more of a weapon than they already were.

My true identity hadn't been revealed, and only those involved in the investigation were known to have been associated with me. I would have never thought an FBI agent would've been targeted, and Miles and his partner, Brandon, were both cops. It was only their families we had been truly worried about.

We have twenty-seven hours to figure out how to save Kat and not let Doctor Killian Krauss get what he wants: me.

CHAPTER TWO

ONE OF THE THREE large bay doors opened as Miles pulled into the garage on his motorcycle, parking next to the black SUVs. He took off his helmet and started this way, his brown cowboy boots clanking on the concrete floor. I immediately noticed the dark circles under his eyes, matching his black hair. He wore a different pair of jeans from last night, and his dark brown leather jacket opened up to one of his simple navy blue t-shirts.

Miles had gone early in the morning to the precinct. He informed his captain that Kat had been taken. Anyone who knew Kat wouldn't know the finer details. No one besides Alcorp, or anyone that already knew the truth, should get involved. All Hybrians were dangerous—I was dangerous.

"What'd you bring us?" Travis sat up from the couch and shook out his shaggy blond hair. His eyes narrowed in on the white paper bags clutched in Miles' hand.

"Carbs." Miles walked over and set them on the coffee table by the couches.

Travis immediately opened one of the bags and pulled out a bagel.

"I call dibs on raisin." Chloe grabbed the bagel from his hand.

"Gross." Travis gave her a disgusted look and began rummaging through the bag.

After Miles had filled everyone in last night, we had spent the next few hours trying to come up with a solution that ensured everyone's safety. Our eight minds combined hadn't been able to form a solid plan that didn't involve me stepping foot in the trainyard.

"Where's Frank?" I asked.

"I'm here, dearie." Frank emerged from the hallway in a heather-grey V-neck sweater vest overtop a white collared shirt and matching pants. His brown-streaked grey hair was feathered back. "We have a big day ahead of us. Adam, have you found anything?"

Adam hit a few buttons on the keyboard. "Nothing on the agent."

I walked over to the computers and looked over Adam's shoulder. "You know how to hack cameras?"

"Alcorp taught me a few things, but I'm not the best at it. We have connections. It's a part of the training we can choose if our bodies don't accept the change or if we don't want to be a Hybrian. Hybrians can go through it too."

"Why don't I start a pot of coffee and then you can inform everyone about the plan," Frank said to Miles, catching my attention.

Miles nodded as Frank pivoted and headed toward the small, old kitchen. Travis started pestering him with questions as soon as Frank left.

"Harper?" I turned. Adam sat facing me.

"Yes?" I asked, narrowing my eyes as he stood, still unsure of him.

"I wanted to apologize for the Vault. It was an awful way to treat you. You didn't consent to the training." His Scottish accent was barely noticeable as he frowned. His cheek indented where his teeth gnawed at the inside as if he was nervous, and I wasn't used to seeing this side of him.

"You were doing your job and following orders." My voice came out unintentionally flat.

"That doesn't make it any better." Adam rubbed his short, russet brown beard.

"You were supposed to train and prepare us for the next phase, right? Well, isn't that helping?" I refrained an eye roll.

"Didn't make it any easier." His voice dropped.

Ugh. Why was I feeling bad for him? His job was intense, but he hadn't needed to be so harsh.

"That day we fought, you had wanted me to give up." I thought back to the Vault, remembering his hands around my neck as the darkness danced at the rims of my eyes. "You wanted me to pass out so the fight would be over." My gut twisted as the puzzle pieces assembled.

"I alone wasn't enough to initiate the change. You needed more motivation—you all did." He sighed. "I didn't like hurtin' you, but these guys we're facing are brutal. You never knew before entering the program like the others had." The guilt gleamed in his dark green eyes.

"I can probably bring myself to forgive you." I forced a small smile and turned to join the others. Adam had been responsible for his own actions even if he had only meant to help. Frank could've told the truth, even after the temporary memory loss occurred. My memory of the last five years hadn't come back yet.

Frank walked back with two steaming cups of coffee and held one out to Miles. "You, my friend, look like you need a cup," he said. Miles glared at him and hesitantly took the cup.

Everyone finally took a seat except for Miles and me after a few minutes.

"Alright, Doc. Boss. What's the game plan?" Travis looked between Frank and Miles.

"Our acquaintances in the FBI are going to help us, and I recruited other members from Alcorp," Frank started.

"They'll arrive in the city later today—some are already in the area," Liam added. Frank gave Miles a nod. The three of them must've talked about it after most of us went to bed.

"I'm going to lead a team of two others in the water. We'll use the boat here and anchor it where they won't notice and swim the rest of the way. The water will provide cover. Two teams will be stationed nearby with Travis, Maya, and Adam. Road spikes will be placed, and the trade will happen. We'll be ready to move in and get Harper after the trade. Liam is going to be the only one in the trainyard during the exchange. We can't risk more inside. My team will make sure they won't leave by boat. Dr. Roulings will monitor the computers here, and Brandon will be working with Dr. Roulings' acquaintances with the FBI."

I shared a glance with Chloe, which told me she thought the same thing: Charlotte and Richard—Brandon's parents who owned the café we had worked at—would be sitting ducks. Miles looked between the two of us, reading our concern.

"The Kovars' will be moved to a secure location for tonight while Brandon helps." That must've taken some convincing. There had been no reasoning with them to temporarily close down the café for their safety. "According to Dr. Roulings, only us and a select few from Alcorp know about this safe house. We will be meeting everyone at separate locations. This is to keep the fishery secure." Miles rubbed the back of his neck and held the coffee in the other. He hated having to trust people he didn't know.

"You're actually letting me go?" I gaped. My intentions were to go regardless, but I hadn't expected to be in Miles' plan unless it involved staying at the fishery.

"We thought about having someone similar to your build go with a hood on." Liam glanced at Miles.

"They'd be able to spot that it wasn't you before Kat's cleared. A few of them know what you look like, and there's no good alternative to get Kat out safely. We'll have the place surrounded—they aren't going anywhere with you."

Liam opened his mouth but shut it quickly. A flash of apprehension crossed his face before he masked it.

"I agree," Frank said. "As much as any of us do not want to put Harper in harm's way, this is the only sustainable option to get Agent Foster back."

I highly doubt Frank cared if I was in harm's way. He was just worried about sharing what was inside of me.

"Everyone here will have coms in—except Harper. We can't risk them finding it." Miles sighed. "Any questions?"

"Yes," Chloe piped up. "What about me?"

Miles glanced at Liam before speaking. "You'll stay here with Dr. Roulings."

"What? No!" She shook her head in disagreement.

"We need to keep as many people out of danger as possible," Miles said. Chloe hadn't had as much training as the rest of us, and she couldn't rely on morphing into a Hybrian.

"Harper's been training me, and you taught me how to shoot. I can help," she argued. I felt for her but agreed it was best for her to stay there.

"Someone needs to look out for Doc. If anyone finds this location, we'll need you here. You can put that training and shooting to use." Travis gave her a wink.

"He's right. We'll need someone to protect the base," Miles added.

"Fine," she huffed and tucked a short loose strand of caramel hair behind her ear.

Miles turned to Frank. "Can I borrow a vehicle to pick up the water gear? My truck is out of the way."

"Of course. Take Travis with you to be safe." Frank glanced at Travis, who nodded.

"We leave in fifteen," Miles told him.

When it was clear our little meeting was over, Liam walked over to the kitchen and grabbed a glass of water from the sink. He had been uncharacteristically quiet. I followed and was about to question him on whether or not he should be drinking the water from the tap.

"Are you okay?" I asked instead.

"I should be asking you that." He looked over at me, his dark brown hair still tousled from sleep.

"This is nothing new to me."

"Neither is it for me, sunshine." He smiled, but it didn't reach his eyes.

"Please don't lie." I shouldn't pry, but I cared too much about him to let it go.

"Your life is in danger, again. But this time we're up against a real threat." He shoved his hands in the pockets of his black cargo pants.

"Last time, we thought Frank was the worst of the worst, so it's really just the same." I shrugged. "There's something else bothering you, though."

"This is the best plan that will provide the best outcome for both you and Kat. It's the right thing to do." He paused. "But a part of me doesn't want to do the right thing."

"It's hard to see someone you care about in danger." I placed a hand on his shoulder. "This has to be done, even if it goes against what you believe in. I need to do this."

Liam put his hand over mine and grinned. "Did you know you were my first friend in the Vault?"

I laughed. "Who else would it have been, Adam? You hated him."

"I'm fine with him now." He shrugged, then his face set. "I don't want you at the mercy of Dr. Krauss—of anyone. I don't agree with how Doc took you without your consent."

"That makes two of us."

CHAPTER THREE

"I'M GOING TO DIE." I didn't think my quick healing would save me from this.

"You're about to face an evil doctor and you're afraid of driving a motorcycle?" Miles laughed.

"Uh, yes." I gripped the handles, careful not to engage the throttle and shoot forward again. Luckily, no one was around on the small farming island just north of Portland. "I don't even have a real driver's license, and your morality as a cop is okay with me driving your motorcycle?"

"I think we're past that, and my cop morals say to do whatever it takes to protect you." His gaze briefly met mine and his expression softened. "Try again. Just let up on the throttle."

I exhaled and tried again. My first attempt hadn't gone over well. This time, the bike moved forward at a slower pace. I put my feet on the pegs and went a little faster. It wasn't smooth, but I managed.

After two hours of practicing, I finally got it down enough that Miles was comfortable with ending our lesson. I wasn't great at driving it, but I could escape if need be. Miles took us to a nearby town to get burgers and then to a park on the river to eat them.

There weren't many people at the park, and birds scattered in the trees and across the luscious green grass. We sat on top of a picnic table with our feet propped on the bench. I didn't have an appetite, but I ate because it appeased Miles.

We sat in silence as my mind focused on tonight.

"Thank you for not keeping me on the sidelines," I finally said after finishing my burger.

"Would you have listened if I told you otherwise?" He glanced sideways at me and crumbled up his wrapper.

"No. I suppose I wouldn't have." I held out the bag so he could toss his garbage inside.

"We also said we would do this together."

"We did." I smiled at his words but then frowned at my thought. "If this works, which it has to, what are we going to do until we can stop Dr. Krauss? We can't have agents or Hybrians guarding everyone."

"Let's just worry about tonight." He knew who I meant by *everyone*. Everyone I knew was in jeopardy, and in return, that put everyone they knew in jeopardy.

"You aren't just worrying about tonight," I noted. He was always analyzing and planning.

"That's the SEAL in me." He chuckled softly. "But we also think on the spot and focus on the current mission."

I sighed, unable to stop my brain. "I'm sorry your grandparents are in danger because of me."

"What I do puts them in danger, not you." His hand moved closer to mine on the table, and I became fully aware of the small space between our hands. "You don't ever have to apologize to me. Unless you purposely cause harm, like shooting me in the foot. That would hurt and not be fun."

I let out a small laugh. "There would have to be a good reason for me to shoot you in the foot."

"You're right. I probably would've deserved it." His smile made my stomach flutter. "I have something for you," he said after a moment. He reached in his jacket pocket and pulled out a knife similar to the one he normally carried on him. "It's a tactical knife."

I grabbed it. "Where'd you get this?"

"I have a few lying around." His few was probably twenty.

"Thank you." I examined the knife and pocketed it. "Do you still have that Rogue's switchblade?"

"Yes. It's tucked away on my bike until I can return it." His idea of returning it had to be more cynical than he made it sound. "Come on. We should get back."

Miles stood and held out a hand. I accepted his offer and jumped down from the picnic table. My foot landed on a stone, causing me to stumble. Thanks to years of training, I righted myself quickly, but Miles was also fast to act. His arm was wrapped around me, tugging me closer and bringing his face a couple inches from mine.

Though I was steady, his arm stayed put. His gaze flitted to my lips, and heat crept along my neck. The urge to close the gap beckoned me, and without thinking, I gave in. I brought my lips to his and was welcomed as his parted for mine, as if he had been waiting for it. He gently cupped the back of my neck with one hand as his other found the small of my back, pulling me closer. Our kiss deepened and became more forceful, like a desire finally being fulfilled.

I put a hand on his chest, not to push him away, but to feel him. His muscles surged beneath my hand as his moved up my neck and intertwined with my hair. Our lips moved as one, and I drew in his fresh pine and leather scent. My head swirled with emotions and a small voice told me I wanted more.

A small groan escaped his lips and then the pressure was gone. He stopped the kiss but kept his forehead pressed against mine and dropped his hands. Both of us panted as if we had just run the entire city.

"I've been wanting to do that for a while," I whispered heavily, confessing what I hadn't fully acknowledged to myself yet.

"Me too." He smiled and gently rested a hand on my face. He brought his lips to mine, kissing me more gently this time.

He pulled away and brushed a strand of hair from my face, his fierce hazel eyes holding mine. I blushed even more and glanced down.

"Let's get out of here," he said as he grabbed my hand and led me back to his bike.

We arrived back at the fishery, and I excused myself to the bathroom. The hideous shower curtain canvasing multiple species of trout never ceased to make me laugh. My phone buzzed in my pocket while I was washing my hands, and I fished it out. My finger froze over the screen. It was a message from Kat.

Keep quiet or she's dead.

A picture of Kat came through. Her eye was bruised, her curls lacked their natural bounce, and dark bags under her eyes replaced her glowing bronzed skin. Three more messages filtered in one after the other.

Macleay Park by midnight.

ALONE.

Or she won't be the only one that dies.

A series of photos popped up on my phone. The first was Miles inside the precinct, wearing the same clothes he wore today, the next was Brandon at his parents' café, then Liam crossing a street in the city, then Maya with her silky long black hair. My knuckles turned white as I clutched my phone.

We can find them. They can't hide forever.

Bile rose in my throat and I practically dove at the toilet. My stomach clenched in waves as I hurled up my dinner. I rocked back on my knees and grabbed a wad of toilet paper and wiped my mouth.

I looked back at my phone and scrolled through the photos. They had someone in the precinct; whether or not it was a visitor, someone who snuck in, or someone on the inside. I wanted so badly to tell Miles and Liam, but I couldn't let anyone else get hurt. If I told them, they wouldn't let me go alone. If Dr. Krauss had my number this entire time, why not tell me the initial instructions instead of Miles? He must have planned it as a diversion.

My hands started trembling and I squeezed my phone in an attempt to control it. Static built in my chest and I knew my beast had surfaced. I would go back on the honesty and trust that Miles and I had built, but I knew what I had to do.

I got off the ground and walked over to the sink. I shoved my phone back into my pocket and washed out my mouth before splashing cold water over my face. My blue eyes disappeared as the static retreated and the beast calmed down. I used the towel to dry my face, taking deep breaths, and ran a hand through my blond hair.

Once I thought I was composed as much as I could be, I left the bathroom and emerged in the garage, trying to avoid eye contact. I spotted Chloe on one of the couches and decided talking to her would be the best distraction.

"You okay?" Liam stepped right in front of me, causing me to jump.

"I didn't even see you." I took a deep breath, calming my racing heart.

His eyebrow raised.

"Yes. I'm just worried about Kat," I answered. That part was true.

He held my gaze before relaxing his shoulders.

"We'll get her back and get you out of there," he said.

"We will." I rubbed my hands together. "I'm going to go talk to Chloe. I know she's still bummed about staying back tonight."

"That's a good idea." Liam nodded.

I went to walk around Liam, but stopped and glanced at him. Regret and sorrow hit me. I was going to sneak off on my own tonight to Macleay Park, wherever that was. He had no idea—no one did. The events of tonight were unseen, and who knows if I would make it out of the park alive.

I wrapped my arms around him, catching him off guard—my rare hugs always did. He slowly wrapped his arms around me and rested his chin on top of my head.

"Thank you for being my best friend and always being there for me," I mumbled into his chest. "I wouldn't have survived the last five years without you."

"You would've survived without me."

"Barely." I took in his familiar comforting vanilla sage scent one last time before I pulled away.

"Are you sure you're okay?" Liam's brows knitted.

"Yes... just worried. Frank fears Dr. Krauss, and that's unsettling." I had to secretly say goodbye, just in case. I needed to say goodbye to everyone. "Alright. I should go calm Chloe down." I smiled and left before he could say anything else.

I sank into the seat next to Chloe. "What are you watching?"

"*Bridesmaids*. It's hilarious," Chloe answered, eyes fixed on the TV that the three couches surrounded.

"I am going to let the two of you enjoy the film." Frank wore a smile as he got up from the couch next to us. "It is not for my taste."

"When you and Miles eventually get married, can I please be one of your bridesmaids?" She waved toward the TV as Frank walked away. "I promise it'll be fun and not disastrous like this."

"Married?" I whisper-yelled. "Slow down there."

"I said *eventually*." She looked at me with a huge grin. "Come on! You can't deny the chemistry between you two."

I blushed. She was right about the chemistry. Despite everything going on, I couldn't stop thinking about our kiss, or him.

She became more serious. "Are you and Liam okay?"

"Yes." I lowered my voice and checked to make sure no one was around. "I can tell it hurt him, and I feel awful for that."

Liam had told me he had feelings for me—more than the best friend kind.

"You can't help what you feel." She put a hand on my arm. Despite her fun and humor, she was always benevolent.

"I love them both, just differently." That was the first time that I had admitted to someone that I loved Miles. I guess not knowing my fate tonight increased my bravery at sharing my emotions. "With Liam, I was going through the change and my emotions were going crazy. I don't want to lose either of them."

"I doubt either of them are going anywhere. Liam might not like Miles, per se, but he also respects him and your happiness. And Miles, well, he never really shows any hostility toward Liam more than he does anyone else. He's hard to read." She was right on that one, but the closer I got to Miles, the easier it was to read him. "It could be worse," Chloe continued. "They could be feuding over you."

"That's true." I grinned. "And of course you'll be a bridesmaid if I ever get married, but that's not even in the books right now—with anyone."

If ever after tonight.

"Someday, then, I will be honored." Her familiar smile almost brought me to tears.

"And what about me in yours?" I asked.

"Duh. I may remember my old friends now, but you're number one." She winked, and guilt wrapped around my heart like a string. She had told me that she didn't have many friends from her life before the Vault and was pretty much on her own. Her grandfather had passed away and her grandmother couldn't remember her.

Chloe and I continued talking until Travis joined, and shortly after, Maya and Liam did too. They cracked jokes while I sat back and enjoyed the conversation. It reminded me of the good times in the Vault and felt as if there wasn't going to be a shift in my world tonight.

Almost everyone was there except for Brandon, so I pulled out my phone and sent a quick text to him.

I won't see you before it all goes down tonight, so I wanted to thank you for all of your help. I could use your humor right about now. See you after we win. —**Harper**

Shame on me for having said that last part. I hoped it would be a win tonight, but something wretched twisted in my gut. I was blindsiding all of them but had to cover my tracks in case my message made Brandon suspicious.

CHAPTER FOUR

I T WAS ALMOST TEN when Miles finished loading up the boat. He would be leaving soon to pick up his team at a neighboring dock. Liam and I would be the last to leave.

I stood in the boathouse watching Miles, the old wood groaning with each wave or gust of wind. Little did he know he wouldn't end up needing any of the bags he was packing.

"I have to leave, but I'll see you soon," Miles said as he hopped out of the boat.

I swallowed hard at his words. He noticed and closed the small gap between us, wrapping his hands in mine. The small gesture took me by surprise—he didn't seem like the affectionate type.

"I'll be right there." His eyes never left mine. "I promise."

"I know." I smiled—he would always try to be there for me. "I haven't said this enough, but thank you. I bet you had no idea what you were getting yourself into that night we met."

"I think I had a pretty good idea." He grinned. "You don't normally run into a woman taking down a grown man in an alley in the shape you were in."

"Touché." I chuckled at the thought. He had to have thought I was insane that night he saw me covered in blood, rust, and grime, and dressed in plain pajamas.

Miles pulled me closer, and my breath caught at the fierceness in his eyes. It wasn't threatening, but something more along the lines of longing and desire. He normally held a straight face, but he was opening up to me, sharing his soul through his eyes. The spark in my chest ignited and my eyes radiated blue.

I wanted to tell him that I loved him, but I held my tongue. He knew me too well, and if I expressed my love now, he would know something was up. Even though I had played the scenario of telling him the truth a million times in my head, it always ended with him or someone else in danger.

Miles moved his hands, cupping my face.

"Harper...I never knew someone could do what you do to me." He dipped his head, bringing his lips to mine. I let his lips gently explore mine. The kiss ended and he gently laid one more on my forehead. His arms wrapped around me, and I fell into his embrace. The static from my beast dissipated, and my eyes changed back as I soaked in his touch, his warmth, and his pine and leather scent. Miles slowly pulled away, too soon, as footsteps approached.

"I'm sorry to interrupt. I just got word your team is ready for pickup," Liam said as he entered the boathouse.

"I'll see you soon." Miles planted one more kiss on my forehead before stepping back into the boat. He glanced at Liam. "Thank you for looking after her."

"You don't have to thank me." Liam's gaze flitted to me. "I always will."

Miles nodded and turned on the motor while Liam pulled the tarp back and hooked it to an old rusty nail. He and Miles finished untying the boat, and Miles left.

"Let's finish getting things ready," Liam said when I failed to move.

"Good idea." I faced him, giving him a small smile, and headed back into the garage.

I didn't have a plan for how to sneak out yet. All I knew was that I had to take one of the SUVs and grab the other keys so they couldn't leave right away. I already had the keys to Miles' motorcycle.

"Alright, everyone. It is time," Frank announced from the computers. He waited for everyone to gather before continuing.

"Liam went over this with you earlier, but we are going to brief you again. Liam?"

Liam pointed to the satellite map of the trainyard and surrounding area on the monitors. In less than ten minutes, he discussed where everyone's locations would be. While everyone was paying attention, I noticed a set of keys to one of the SUVs on the table in front of me and discretely snatched them without anyone noticing.

My long-sleeved V-neck and leather jacket suddenly felt hot despite the cool breeze flowing through the opened garage doors. Maya had given me a pair of skinny jeans and a plum shirt so I didn't have to wear my clothes from the day before. They had to have been her backup clothes due to their lack of style, and I was thankful for that—I didn't want to wear leather pants.

"Adam, is your laptop in the Expedition you will be in?" Frank asked.

Adam glanced around the table. "I must've left it in the office when I went to find more coms. I'll go load it up." Adam started toward the office.

"I'll get it," I offered and shrugged when everyone looked at me. "I need to do something. Standing here isn't helping my nerves."

Adam gave me an understanding nod. "It should be on the chair next to the desk."

What I really needed was to get to a vehicle, and luckily, the keys were numbered. The set I had belonged to the one on the farthest end. *Thank you, Travis, for telling Miles what number went with which SUV when I was in earshot.*

I casually walked to the office. Empty crates and a few full bags remained of surveillance equipment and weapons. I saw the laptop and grabbed it but froze when I saw an old blank notepad and pen. I set the laptop back down and picked up the pen and wrote *I'm sorry* on the top piece of paper before ripping it off. I tucked it in the same pocket with my phone and snatched the laptop on my way out.

"Which one?" I asked.

"The second one. Passenger seat, please," Adam replied.

I strode over to the second SUV and set the laptop on the passenger side. I needed to improvise—I didn't have the keys for this one. I peered around the first SUV. Everyone was occupied with the map and asking questions.

The tires caught my attention. *That will do.* I knelt down and pulled out the pocket knife Miles had given me earlier. I summoned the strength from my beast and held my breath as I jammed it into the tire and slowly pulled it out. No sound came from the deflating tire, and I released the breath I had been holding. This wasn't what I thought I'd be using the knife for.

I went over to the SUV next to me and did the same thing to one of the tires. They couldn't see me between the vehicles as I made my way toward the last SUV. Miles' bike was next to it, and I reached into my pocket, pulling out the note and my phone, which Miles could track. I opened up the messages from Kat's phone—deleting only the message that had the true meeting location—and set it along with the note on the seat. I hoped this explained my reasoning for sneaking off and that Miles would forgive me. That all of them would forgive me.

I kept the motorcycle keys and went to the opened hatch of the last SUV. Luckily, this one only had two bags in the back. I grabbed a single handgun from one of the bags and tucked it in the back of my high-waisted jeans. I quietly set the bags on the floor of the garage and shut the hatch.

I hurried to the front and climbed into the driver's seat. It was go time. I bit my lip and turned on the engine. It had to be easier than driving a motorcycle, *right*? Dylan said my driving wasn't that bad.

"Harper?" Liam's shout echoed through the garage and the rolled-down windows.

I put the SUV in drive and hit the gas.

"Harper!" Liam shouted again as I drove out of the garage and down the drive.

I spared a glance in the rearview mirror and saw all of them appear outside, even Frank, who was the last to get there. The pain and worry on Liam's face will haunt me as the mental picture pinned itself to my brain. Liam pivoted toward the other SUVs. Soon he would learn that he wasn't getting out of there, at least not any time soon. I'm sure they had spare tires.

There was no going back.

CHAPTER FIVE

I DROVE FAST TOWARD the city but was careful to not draw too much attention to myself. The last thing I needed was to get pulled over—the others would be behind me shortly.

Miles would have been informed of my little stunt by now, and my chest tightened at the hurt he probably felt when he got the call. This bordered on betrayal after everything we had been through, and I hoped he would find the note and text messages and understand why I did what I did.

"Please forgive me," I whispered to the empty dark space surrounding me in the SUV.

Once I got into the city, I found a wide alley and drove down it. The SUV could be tracked, so I needed to ditch it. The alley was meant to be wide enough for garbage trucks to get through to the dumpsters, not for regular civilians. Although, I wasn't an ordinary civilian.

I parked it, put Miles' motorcycle keys in the cup holder, and attempted to lock the SUV keys inside, but the stupid vehicle wouldn't let me. I settled on chucking the SUV keys under a nearby dumpster so they were out of sight. There didn't need to be a stolen Alcorp vehicle.

I ran a block before I found a taxi and waved it down. I climbed in the back and told the driver to head to Macleay Park.

"Pardon me, miss, but you're going there alone at this time of night?" The taxi driver turned to face me. He was middle-aged with a greying mustache.

"I won't be alone. I'm meeting someone," I clarified, but he didn't start driving. "Macleay Park please."

"Macleay Park it is." He finally began to drive. "Anywhere specific? The park is big."

"The main entrance will do." I hoped that was a good enough answer because I had no clue where I was headed. When the taxi driver nodded and didn't respond, I figured it was. We arrived in less than ten minutes.

"Thank you." I had stashed a wad of cash in my pocket earlier, and thankfully the cost of the ride didn't use it all up.

I kept the gun hidden and started walking up a paved path big enough for one car. Trees lined one side and a small clearing stretched on the other. Fog floated perfectly at the forest's floor and park grounds, and the full moon provided enough light that I could see where I was going. Each breath released a small vapor cloud in the air. Besides the noise from the swaying trees and leaves in the wind, it was silent. It must've been too cold for the crickets to chirp their songs.

I walked a little farther as the road led uphill. I came up short on a small parking lot with a few lit streetlights and a forest on the far side. The road looped around, continuing back down the hill. No one was around, and I had no clue where I was going. Finding Kat wasn't going to be easy.

The engine of a motorcycle roared behind me. I put my hand on the gun and the other out at my side. Electric static thrummed through my body as I morphed, bringing out my electric beast. The air became crisper, the scents became sharper, the hum of the engine grew louder, and my vision became clearer.

The motorcycle reached the top of the hill and I put the gun away. Miles had somehow found me, and so far, he was alone. My beast beacon—similar to when animals sense others nearby—was not picking up anything. Unfortunately, it didn't work on Rogues.

He must've turned the boat around as soon as he found out. I also had his keys, but it didn't surprise me that he knew how to hotwire his motorcycle. The bike came to a halt in front of me and Miles flipped up his visor.

"Get on," he ordered, his voice hard.

"How did you find me?"

"Tracker. Get on," he said sharply.

"What!" I exclaimed and thought about when he would have put a tracker on me and gasped. "Either of the times we kissed..." I trailed off.

"No, Harper. I was a little too occupied then. Now get on."

Dinner maybe? When he put his hand on my back? I don't know, but it didn't matter right now.

"I can't." I took a step back. "They'll—"

"I saw the messages with the threats," Miles said. Of course he did. I had left them on his bike. "We need to leave, right now."

"Miles, I'm sorry." I took another step back, and it felt like my heart was cracking with each step I took away from him.

He flipped his kickstand down, took off his helmet, and got off the bike and then cleared the small space between us in two strides.

"This is not the way." With his left hand, he pressed his helmet into my stomach for me to take, even though his spare was on the bike. "So help me..." he gritted through his teeth. "I don't want to drag you out of here."

He and I both knew that wasn't going to happen despite how much he wanted to. I wouldn't allow it, and he didn't want to, but the fierceness in his eyes told me he wasn't going to let me stay either.

"If I go, they'll kill Kat. Then come after everyone else, including your grandparents." My voice wavered at the truth.

"If you stay, they will torture and use you, and then kill you. We will find another way to save Kat and not let them hurt anyone else." His eyes were bold and begging. "Please."

My gut told me to listen, but my brain said not to. My gut won. I finally nodded and had gone to take the helmet when the sound of a twig breaking in the forest caused us to turn. Miles transferred the helmet to his right hand and pulled out his gun with his left. The electricity was back and flowed through my veins. I held out my hands at my sides, like how the other Hybrians did with their claws—except my hands could be lethal at a distance.

"I see you brought company." A familiar voice came from the other part of the loop. I recognized the man with the scar on his face as he turned to Miles. "We meet again."

"We were just leaving," Miles growled and tipped his head for me to head over to his bike. I slowly sidestepped toward the bike as Miles followed.

"Not so fast—we're just getting started. We brought more gunfire this time." His face twisted into a wicked smile as two men emerged from the forest. Both had also been at the trainyard.

I heard another snap of a twig behind us and less than a second later felt a pinch near my shoulder blade. Miles took a step back, angling himself so he could see in both directions, as I reached my hand back where it stung.

"Son of a gun." I pulled out a tranq dart and tossed it on the ground.

Avery stepped out of the tree line, aiming a gun at us.

"I told you I wasn't going to miss next time," Avery spat. She was too far for my power to reach her this time, so I pulled my gun.

"I wouldn't do that if I were you." She nodded in the other direction as a large black van drove up the hill and pulled up behind the scarred-faced Rogue.

The electricity in my veins started to recede against my will. I pulled one hand off the gun and attempted to create a small bolt, but nothing happened.

"Miles..." I looked at him and knew my blue eyes had faded to their normal brown. It wasn't a tranquilizer per se but an inhibitor.

I looked back at Avery, who holstered the tranq gun and grabbed a different gun. Miles aimed his at the Rogue, and I put my other hand back on my gun, aiming it steadily at Avery. The van's back door opened and a bound Kat was shoved out. She fell to her knees as a man jumped out behind her and yanked her back to her feet.

Kat's mouth was duct taped and her hands were bound in front of her by zip ties. She still wore the black dress slacks and blazer she normally wore to work. A large bruise shadowed her cheek, and she looked exhausted. The Rogue pushed her forward next to the one with the scar.

A second van pulled up and more Rogues jumped out, along with a tall man who caught my attention. His golden-walnut hair was pushed back and fell an inch above his broad shoulders, his square jaw was riddled with stubble that had clean defined edges, and his razor-sharp cobalt eyes perused the area. A shiver ran up my spine when his gaze locked onto me.

"Isa Westbrook, back from the dead." His voice echoed through my bones as he said my real name. He stepped over a puddle, avoiding soaking his brown suede shoes. "I would have thought I was seeing a ghost, but it isn't so. I had my suspicion that this valuable asset of ours was you, but I also had my doubts."

I glanced at Miles, whose lethal stare would have set my hair on end if it wasn't already. His burning glare was locked onto the man speaking in the heather grey suit.

"Oh, my apologies." The man said after a few seconds passed. "How rude of me not to introduce myself." He put a hand over his chest. "I'm Doctor Killian Krauss."

"So, you're the one looking for me?" I wanted to fry the twisted grin off his face. "Kidnapping multiple young blond girls to find me? That's a boastful thing to do."

"I knew I was looking for a Harper and had your description, thanks to my darling Avery. Although, I do wish Dr. Roulings had shared more information about you. It wasn't easy to find you without a picture. I assumed you would have fled Portland. It wasn't until Agent Foster here showed up in Seattle the same time and place Alcorp happened to capture a few of my people that we assumed you had to be near."

"You know about Alcorp?" I kept my gun aimed at Avery. The way he said it made it sound like he knew more about them than I did. It also sounded like he knew Frank—Dr. Roulings—personally.

"Of course I do. There were rumors that there was a favorable person of interest to Dr. Roulings, and I knew that person must have been vital to creating Hybrians. When Damien saw your eyes, he knew it had to be you. Once we figured out the officer you were with was the ex-SEAL helping Agent Foster, it made our targets easier." He grinned wickedly and turned back to Kat, grazing her cheek with the back of his fingers. She recoiled from his touch. "All of my personnel received pictures of Agent Foster and her two agents along with Officer MacLand, but only Avery knew what you looked like until that day at the trainyard. We had no clue you were in so deep, Officer." His gaze shifted to Miles. "You can lower your weapons and slide them this way now that we've been formally introduced."

"You'll let Agent Foster go, and you sure as hell aren't touching Harper." Miles' voice was lethal.

"You and I both know it's a very bad idea to have a shootout. You're out armed, and Agent Foster here would definitely not make it." Dr. Krauss shoved his hands in his pant pockets as if he was untouchable.

Kat shook her head at Miles, warning him not to lower his gun. I admired her bravery. Miles let out a low growl. After a long thirty seconds, he set his gun on the ground and slid it toward them. Dr. Krauss eyed the helmet still clutched in Miles' hand as if it were a weapon. Miles slowly set the helmet on the ground and looked at me, nodding, telling me to do the same. I tightened my grip on my gun and bit my lip. One pull of the trigger and Avery wouldn't be an issue, but then we would have a bigger problem. I grumbled, putting my gun on the ground and pushing it across the parking lot like Miles had.

"We can make the trade now." I clenched my teeth together.

"Come." Krauss waved me forward. "Join us."

"Not until Kat and Miles leave safely." I stayed put, standing my ground.

Dr. Krauss nodded at the Rogue who had a hard grip on Kat's arm. The Rogue let go of her and pulled a knife from his pocket. He cut her zip ties and ripped the duct tape off her mouth, causing her to groan. She glared at him as he shoved her forward.

Kat seemed hesitant as she walked over to us. I slowly made my way toward Dr. Krauss and planted my feet before I was too close, waiting for Miles and Kat to leave. Miles whispered something to Kat that sounded a lot like telling her to take the bike and that help was coming.

"She's not going alone." Miles' words rang from behind me. "I'm going with her."

I turned to face him and opened my mouth to argue.

"We don't need you," Avery said, cutting me off as she made her way across the parking lot.

"Too bad. We're a package deal." Miles' glower never left Dr. Krauss.

"You're not in much of a position to make demands, Officer." Dr. Krauss rubbed the edge of his stubble with his thumb. "Though, you're in luck. I think you can be useful." He looked between Miles and me. "It will help keep her in line, and we don't have to use one of our own to see if the serum is effective and not caustic."

"No!" I couldn't let them use Miles as a test rat. He had helped me cope with that life, and I had a feeling this would be a million times worse.

"Then it's settled." Miles strode over to my side. "I'm going."

"So it is," Dr. Krauss replied.

"No." My voice came out in a plea as I shook my head at Miles.

"I'm not leaving you." Miles urged me forward.

I reluctantly moved, feeling more helpless with each step. I tried to come up with an escape, but we were surrounded and there was no getting out of this.

"Stop there," the scarred-face Rogue ordered. "Clothes off."

"Excuse me?" I crossed my arms at his bold demand.

"You're a feisty one." Dr. Krauss raised an eyebrow. "Yes. Take off your jacket, shirt, shoes, socks, and pants. We aren't risking any trackers, wires, or weapons on your body. We have spare clothes in the van. I do apologize; we only have one pair of pants and one hoodie, as we were only expecting the company of one." Krauss glanced at Miles and gestured toward the Rogue with the scar. "They are Damien's, so the pants should fit you fine, Officer."

When we didn't budge, Damien aimed his gun at my knee. *Right.* They don't need me to be able to walk, just be alive.

"We'll undress." Miles nudged me in the arm. "I'm right here."

I closed my eyes at the contact and wished we were anywhere but there.

CHAPTER SIX

I OPENED MY EYES, glaring at Dr. Krauss, who stood near the van. I wasn't thrilled about stripping down to my underwear and bra in front of everyone, even Miles. The thought made me blush, causing me to glance over at him as he took off his jacket and tossed it on the ground. I shrugged mine off and felt something hard in the pocket. *My kni*fe. I started to slowly set my jacket on the ground. There was no concealing it once I was stripped down, no way I could hurt Dr. Krauss from where I was, and no way Miles and I could make a stand even if he had his too, unless...

I slid my hand into the pocket and pulled the knife out, letting the jacket fall the rest of the way to the ground. I flipped it open and held it to my neck, unsure if I was able to go through with my own threat. *Was I?* I hadn't thought that through.

"He goes free." I pressed the blade against my already scarred throat.

"Harper..." Miles' voice filled with concern.

I ignored him—unable to glance his way—and stood tall as I challenged Dr. Krauss, who stood, unfazed by my action.

"If you could have gotten whatever you needed from me dead, then I wouldn't still be alive. Once he and Kat are out of here, I'll drop the knife." I didn't specify in which manner it would be dropped. I went there knowing two things—number two was that I couldn't let them take me hostage.

"That's bold, Isa." Dr. Krauss merely smiled and waited, as if to see what effect using my real name would have on me.

I pressed deeper, drawing blood, and his smile faltered just enough to show that he did care.

"That's not your best move. If you do that, then what's stopping us from going after and killing them?" He gestured at Miles and Kat.

"I'll be too dead to care. I'm done being an experiment," I said, cutting even deeper and grinding my teeth from the pain. Dr. Krauss may have intel from Avery, but he didn't know me personally or if I was capable of carrying out my own threat.

"Harper. Stop." The distress in Miles' voice caused me to naturally turn toward him. "We'll get through this together. Just like everything else. You and me."

"He'll use you… experiment on you… and if he gets what he wants from me, people will get hurt. People will die." I looked away, unable to take his pleading gaze.

"Remember that night at the hotel in Seattle?" He stared at me with a pained expression and continued once my attention was back to him. "I can't lose you. We'll figure it out."

I moved the knife so it was no longer against my skin but still at my throat. "If they—"

Engines roared behind us, and I lowered the knife as two black Ford Expeditions came flying over the hill behind us. Liam exited the passenger side of the SUV before it completely stopped, gun in hand. Adam stepped out of the driver's seat and rushed around the SUV to Kat. Adam led her to the far side of the front hood where Maya and Travis were, guns drawn.

My beast beacon hadn't alerted me that they were near, but if I focused extremely hard, I could feel the very faint tingle in the back of my head. The inhibitor must've nullified my beacon.

I used the distraction to throw the knife at Dr. Krauss, striking his shoulder. I was aiming for his chest, but pleased as he groaned in pain.

"Harper," Miles warned, and I glanced at him. He nodded at the scar-faced Rogue who had his gun aimed at me.

Crap. Irritation boiled inside me at my failed attempt.

"Let them go." Liam aimed his gun at Dr. Krauss, his eyes glowing a fierce marmalade.

"Ah, you must be Liam." Dr. Krauss waved off the Rogue next to him as he pulled the knife from his shoulder, the pain disappearing from his face as blood dripped from his wound. "We finally meet in person. Avery told me much about you. All of you." His gaze hovered over Maya and Travis then back to me. "Isa, darling, that wasn't very nice, but I suppose it was only fair. We are leaving here with you. I have more men in the woods. They won't kill you, but they won't hesitate to kill your friends. If this turns into a gunfight, people *will* get hurt on both sides. And if I die, then they won't hesitate to kill you either."

"Don't call me darling," I snapped. "My name is Harper."

I couldn't let Miles come with me, and I couldn't let it turn into a shoot-out. Also, how would I know they wouldn't shoot any of my friends as soon as I got into the van?

"We *are* getting out of here. Whether or not we wage a war and people on both ends get killed is up to you, Isa." Dr. Krauss' eyes beamed with excitement.

I glanced at Miles who nodded. "We'll go with you, but you have to let everyone else go unharmed."

"Deal." Dr. Krauss nodded. "Fetch the clothes."

A Rogue climbed into the back of the van and hopped back out holding a pair of black sweats and a black hoodie. He stood by us, waiting for us to continue taking our clothes off. I kicked off my shoes and hesitantly stripped. I wrapped my arms around my body, completely aware that I stood in my bra and underwear in front of everyone. The Rogue held out the pants and hoodie, one in each hand.

"Take them," Miles said next to me.

I glanced at him, forcing my eyes to obey and stay above his neckline. He was stripped down to his boxers. I looked back at the clothes and grabbed the hoodie.

"It's large. It'll cover me fine." It wouldn't be fair if I was covered like a bum while he had to wear only boxers.

I pulled the hoodie over my head and yanked the bottom seam down. It fell just above my knees so it was like wearing a dress and covered more than any shorts I've worn before. Miles waved for me to take the pants.

"Please," I whispered, my voice breaking.

A muscle twitched in Miles' neck as he grabbed the pants, and I was glad he decided not to argue.

I snuck a peek as he donned the sweats. He had a large scar near his right collarbone and a matching one on the back of his shoulder where a rod went through while on a SEAL operation. Multiple scars were riddled over his chiseled abs and chest, along with his back. He had a tattoo on his left shoulder blade, a trident piercing both a military boot and a cowgirl boot. An army helmet rested on top of the trident. I assumed the trident was for him, the cowgirl boot was for his mother, and the helmet was for his fallen father.

When he glanced at me, I held his gaze. He was so young, yet had so many scars.

"Load them up," Dr. Krauss ordered.

Damien gave me a hard shove toward the van and Miles stepped between us, his fists clenched at his sides.

"Stand down, cop," Damien sneered at Miles.

"Damien, let's be a little courtlier toward our new guests." Dr. Krauss' smile was anything but courteous. "After all, they will be giving us what we've been searching so long for."

Damien grumbled and waved us on. Miles walked behind me as we headed to the back of the van. I glanced over my shoulder. Liam had his gun at his side and stood frozen like a defeated wolf watching its predator take away a member of his pack—he wanted to attack but the enemy had the high ground. The pain and hurt on his face when I stole the SUV had been replaced with rage, vengeance, and torment.

Travis stood next to Liam, slouching with pressed lips and doleful eyes. He must have come out from behind the SUV. Maya frowned, and even Adam looked upset. I mustered up a comforting smile for them, but it was nothing of the sort.

Liam lifted his gun at Dr. Krauss and took a step forward. Travis stepped in front of him and put an arm out.

"Not now, Liam," Travis warned. Liam kept his amber eyes on me a moment longer before glancing at Travis and lowering his gun.

I jumped when someone grabbed my wrists, not realizing Damien had moved. He had also acquired zip ties and bound my wrists, fastening them so tight, they would leave bruises.

"Bye, boys." Avery winked at Liam and Travis as she made her way toward the van.

"Move it," Damien barked.

I cast one last glance at Liam before climbing in the empty van with Miles right behind me. I stumbled and he caught my arm with his bound hands, helping steady me. I muttered a quick thank you as I made my way to the side and propped myself against the van's wall. I kept my knees bent at my side as I sat, keeping the hem of the hoodie tucked over them.

Miles sat next to me, careful to be close enough without touching. I imagine he didn't want to make me feel uncomfortable while I currently resided in a man's—who I hated—hoodie with no pants. Whatever he thought about making me feel uncomfortable, he couldn't be more wrong. Yes—I was uncomfortable and livid, but not because he was too close. I inched over, closing the small gap.

Miles looked at me. His walls were up. I couldn't read any emotion on his face and knew he was hiding it from both them and me. I imagined it matched the fear, worry, and despair I felt, except I was also remorseful.

This was my fault.

Miles wrapped his hands around mine—a simple yet strong gesture—as Damien climbed in with Avery, closing the door behind her. I took a deep breath. I hated Damien, but I hated her even more. She was a traitor for her own personal gain. She ducked and made her way to the front of the van, carrying a small pouch wrapped in black fabric. She unwrapped it and pulled out two syringes. I pulled my hands out of Miles' and straightened. I wasn't ready to be a lab rat again, and I sure as heck didn't want Miles to be one.

"Just a little sedative. We have a long trip ahead of us," Avery hissed. "I need your shoulder."

She eyed the fabric that covered it. The collar of the hoodie was large enough to be pulled down, but I didn't move. Damien aimed his gun at me, and Miles' jaw twitched. I knew Miles well enough to know that he wanted to disarm him but knew the risk was too great. When I still didn't move, Damien aimed his gun at Miles, guessing I wouldn't do anything to jeopardize Miles' life. He was right.

"Together." Miles' hands found mine again. I nodded at him before slowly tugging my hands away. I pulled the loose collar down, exposing just enough flesh of my shoulder. She gave me the sedative and then gave Miles his next, and Damien lowered his gun.

"Trouble in paradise, huh?" Avery quipped as she wrapped the syringes back up. "Maya had a point about you having everyone wrapped around your finger. Poor guy. You strung Liam along just to find someone new." She licked her lips as she scanned Miles' bare chest. "Now you're stringing him along so he can suffer too."

Her eyes drew back to me and widened. I swung my feet out from underneath me and kicked her in the gut. She flew backward into the side of the van with enough force to make it swerve and to dent it. The strength of the beast slightly surged inside me, but I never felt the static rise.

Damien drew his gun, but Miles grabbed his arm and smashed it against the roof hard enough that the gun fell to the floor. Avery rolled over onto her side to reach for her own gun. I wanted to throw myself at her, but my body wouldn't move, no matter how much I willed it. My back slumped against the side of the van. Just like my strength had faded, my vision started fading as well.

At my side, Miles was able to get a hold of Damien's gun, but Avery already had hers on me. Miles started to struggle. He must've realized it was over and released the magazine of the gun and dropped it. Someone from the front of the van hollered something, and Avery answered them.

Miles sank down on his knees at my side and looked at me, his face filled with apprehension. I wanted to speak, to tell him to grab the gun before Damien did and shoot them. But he wouldn't risk it. Damien retrieved his gun and aimed it at Miles.

Avery's grin twisted, and my surroundings blurred. I fell against Miles right as the blackness took over.

CHAPTER SEVEN

Whatever I was laying on shook as a cold, hard surface pressed firmly against my cheek and an ache throbbed in my shoulder and hip. I opened my eyes and squinted at a beam of light shining from above. I lifted my head and the shaking ceased.

A metallic odor overpowered a dusty earth scent. I was lying on the floor of a cement block room with a single twin-sized bed. The fluffy red comforter and soft red rug underneath made the room look like it was from a medieval castle, excluding the silver toilet sitting in the corner.

My body ached as I slowly pushed myself off the concrete floor and sat up. The wall across from the bed was made of plexiglass-like panels with a metal-framed door in the middle. The center of the door was the same material as the side panels.

I looked up, shielding my eyes until they adjusted enough to see a small skylight in the vaulted ceiling. Plexiglass stretched between the ceiling and me, creating a box. A giant foil tube protruded above the vent of the makeshift ceiling to the box and connected to the wall above the door.

I pushed up on my hands and stood, rolling my sore shoulders. *They couldn't have at least set me on the bed or the rug?* I went to take a step, but something cold and heavy weighed my ankle down. I looked beyond the hospital gown I wore to see a metal shackle on my ankle, its chain tethered to the back wall.

I attempted to summon my power, but nothing came. My heart started thudding against my ribs as reality kicked in. I knelt and started yanking on the chain, but it wouldn't budge. I walked over to the door and started pounding on it, hoping it would break, but deep down, I knew it had to be bulletproof.

"Miles!" I shouted. "What did you do with him?"

"Harper?" A rough voice echoed from behind me.

"Miles?" I turned but no one was behind me.

"It's me." His voice came through an open vent on the side wall just below the plexiglass ceiling.

"Are you okay? Did they hurt you?" I asked.

I scanned the room. I could move the bed under the vent, but I still wouldn't be able to reach it. My stomach twisted when I noticed the bed was bolted to the floor and metal shackles were connected to each corner of the reinforced bed frame, made to hold someone strong down. Made to hold a beast.

"Don't worry about me—I'm fine. Did they hurt you?" His voice was edged with concern.

"No. I don't think so." I didn't want to know who had changed me into this blue gown. I pulled at the top of the gown and looked underneath, sighing in relief that I still had my bra and underwear on. I slumped against the wall underneath the vent in defeat and slid down to the floor. "I can't feel my beast."

"They gave you another tranquilizer."

"You sound certain," I said. Frank had used an inhibitor on Travis before—it was the same as their *tranquilizer*. Alcohol did the same thing, except it also impaired your motor function and gave you a wicked hangover.

"I heard them," he said with great distaste.

"When did you wake up?" I rested my head against the wall.

"Maybe three hours ago. I'm guessing we've been here a while."

I was surprised he woke up before me. Technically the drugs would have worn off quicker on me because I was Hybrian. Then again, they tranqed me and probably had given me a second dose of the sedative at some point.

"Miles?" I tried to keep my voice calm as I stared at the shackles on the bed and the boxed-in cell. "Does your bed have shackles on it?"

He didn't respond right away. "No—it doesn't."

"Good." I would give up a kidney to be with him right now. "Are you shackled to a wall?"

"Yes. My ankle is." He kept his voice light, but I could hear the faint uneasiness behind it.

I stayed silent for a moment before blurting out the last question. "Are we in a gas box?" I knew the answer, but I didn't want to believe it.

"Yes. It looks like it was built in the last few years." He was going to give it to me straight, and I was thankful for that.

I inhaled and fought back tears. "I'm sorry I dragged you into this."

"Didn't I tell you that you never have to apologize to me?" His soft chuckle echoed into my cell.

"If I didn't cause harm." I banged my head against the wall, but not hard enough to do any damage. "This definitely is causing harm."

"No. Not if you have good intentions. Since I've known you, you've only ever had good intentions." I heard the smile in his voice and pictured his handsome face with pooling eyes of green and grey. "You put others before yourself."

It hadn't felt like I had. I put my head between my knees and watched the silent tears splatter against the surprisingly clean concrete floor. Avery was right. I had gotten him into this, and now he was going to suffer.

"I see you're awake, and you hear that your friend is alive and well." My head shot up at the voice that came through the speaker next to the door.

"Krauss," I hissed.

He stood on the other side of the door, holding down a button that must have been on the same panel the speaker was on. It was built into the glass, and I imagined that was to create full transparency into the cell. Avery and Damien were behind him, and in front of Damien was a wheelchair. Gas masks dangled in both of their hands, and my stomach dropped.

"I apologize that we have to jump right in." Krauss flipped a switch before he put his hands in the pockets of his grey slacks. "We're finally settled in. It's been a while since I've been able to be back here."

"Is *here* a prison?" My teeth ground together.

His head bounced as if he were contemplating. "Technically, yes." He waved his hand in the air. "Sorry for the extensive precautions, but we can't take any chances if your tranquilizer wears off. I also heard you're quite the fighter."

The vent connecting to Miles' cell clanked shut, and the tube connecting to my cell started to shake. A barely detectable faint, sweet odor filled the cell even though I couldn't see anything enter through the vent. I slowly retreated to the back wall, getting as far away from Krauss as I could.

"I do wish when we extract what we need from you, you will become one of us." His face started to blur.

I sucked in a deep breath and tried to hold it, but it didn't matter.

My heavy eyes fluttered open but then shut. I forced them open again and glanced down at the metal restraints on my wrists and then at my blurry feet. My ankles came into focus, and they too were shackled. My waist was even restrained by a leather strap instead of cold metal.

My breathing was slow and heavy as if I were asleep, but I knew I wasn't. I could hear voices nearby, but I couldn't make out any words. My head was so heavy, I could barely turn it to the side. Blood flowed out one of my arms and down into a bag. My opposite forearm burned, along with my thigh. The hem of the gown covered my thigh and my forearm was just out of sight for me to be able to see what was causing the prickling, hot sensation.

A blur of white squatted next to the bag holding my blood, large hands replacing it with an empty one. My eyes focused a little more as I watched the person walk over to a clear refrigerator. I strained to see what was inside. Blood bags—my blood, I assumed. That would explain why I felt like this.

How long had I been out?

Rapid movement next to the fridge caught my eye at the same time I heard faint chirping. A hummingbird was flying in a small cage, its mosaic colors reflecting beautifully. The movement made me dizzy and I glanced away. That poor creature was caged by the same monster who caged me.

My eyes fell shut for a moment and when I opened them, the white blur was at my opposite side. I blinked a few times as his face came into focus like a pixelated TV getting signal.

Krauss held something in his hand.

"Thanks to the Hybrian ability to heal rapidly, we were able to take a quarter more than we normally would have been able to. You'll heal quicker once the tranquilizer starts to wear off, but it will only be a fraction of how you normally heal." He wiped my arm with a brown gauze.

"Why—" I cleared the frog in my throat. "Why are you sterilizing my arm? Does it really matter?" I forced out the words through my dry lips.

"Hybrians seldom get sick, but you're still prone to infection." His gentle smile was anything but warm. "This is to help replenish you. We took a lot from you today. I need you to rest. The samples we took won't last long with my trials, and their viability is unknown."

The unspoken *so we can take more* was implied. It didn't faze me as he placed the IV catheter. Not because I was used to needles, but because I could barely move or speak. If I could, I would protest. Just getting out a few words was too much.

I stared at the clear fluid bag that was supposed to help. Beyond it, another figure in white moved. My eyes grew heavy and I fought to keep them open, but I succumbed to the sleep that called me.

"What did you do to her?" The shouted words were muffled as pounding echoed against glass.

I pried my eyes open to see my arms bound against armrests and straps around my ankles as my feet rested on foot pedals. I was in a wheelchair just outside of my cell.

"Harper!" a familiar voice called out.

I lifted my head and peered through the hair that settled over my face. Beyond Krauss, Miles stood in the corner of his cell against the glass. From this angle, I could only see the small section that he stood in. He wore the same black sweatpants from the night they took us. *Was that last night?*

Avery stood in front of his door, and a red light above it turned on. There was a speaker, a switch, and a button next to the door.

"Put her back in her cell," Krauss ordered to someone behind me.

As I attempted to look to see who he spoke to, my head flopped backward. I guess it accomplished my intentions, as I stared at a white scar etched into the bottom of a chin. *Damien.* I had never realized his scar went all the way underneath his chin.

"Restraints?" Damien's jaw moved.

"No"—a hand rested on my knee while the other tilted my head to the side—"those won't be necessary. Will they, Harper?"

I couldn't respond or spit in Krauss' face like I wanted to. My body sat there as I was wheeled into my cell, and the pressure from the straps vanished. The next thing I knew, I was lying on top of the red comforter, which was surprisingly soft, before I instantly drifted off.

I finally had the strength and propped myself up against the metal headboard. I had no clue how long I had been staring at the dark skylight. My body was sore, my hips ached, and my stomach felt like a shriveled ball. Krauss was already doing a number on me.

A small light above the door helped illuminate my cell so I could make most things out. Cold fluids pumped into my arm and came from a bag hanging on a pole next to the bed. The fluids were to help *replenish* me, but I didn't care. I grabbed the line and ripped it out of my arm. I didn't bother shutting the fluids off, so the clear saline dripped freely onto the floor. For all I knew, it could be laced with the inhibitor.

I looked up at the vent in the sidewall and squinted. My heart thudded when I saw it was open.

"M—" My voice was dry and hoarse. I cleared my throat and tried again. "Miles?"

"You're awake," he said. "Are you okay?"

"I'm fine," I lied. "How long was I out for?"

"A few days."

A few days?

"Did they touch you? Did they hurt you?" My frantic words came out raspy.

"They haven't done anything to me." He kept his voice low and his words were a relief, but the fear inside me stayed.

I looked down at the line I had just ripped out. They weren't going to hurt him unless I stepped out of line. Or so they said.

"Crap," I mumbled and scrambled over to the catheter I had just ripped out. There wasn't a way to put it back in without a new one. Maybe I could use the still sticky tape to put it back on my arm in the meantime and empty the bag under the bed. There was no pump, just a clamp controlling the fluid rate, so it might work.

"What's wrong?" Miles asked, his voice laced with worry.

"Nothing," I reassured him as I fiddled with the tape.

"Harper, what's going on?" His voice was louder, not as if he raised it, but as if he came closer to the vent, and I pictured him leaning against the wall with fierce, dark hazel eyes.

I swallowed. "They were giving me fluids so I would be ready quicker. I yanked them out. Maybe I can play it off that I had just ripped it out after all of the fluids were gone." It was a feeble plan.

I didn't continue to elaborate as silence hung in the air.

"And you're worried that they'll take it out on me," he stated—not asked.

"Yes." Tears began to fill my eyes. *Ugh.* I have never cried so much. I felt so pathetic and weak. I was helpless.

"They're watching, Harper," he said gently.

"What?" I stopped what I was doing and looked at the door, but no one was there. "Where?"

"Look up—one of the corners by the door."

I looked up and sure enough, there was a small blinking red dot. My hand crumpled up the tape and chucked it at the ground. I screamed in anger as I propelled the IV pole into the wall, it barely making a sound at my weak outburst.

"I'm sorry," I panted after a minute had passed.

"Don't worry about me. I'll be fine—I'm worried about you."

"Can they hear us?" I asked, avoiding his comment.

"I'm not sure, but it's best to assume they can."

I walked over to the wall and sat down with my back against it. Physically and emotionally weak, I was no longer able to hold back the tears or the uncontrollable sounds that came out of me as I wept. I pulled my knees to my chest and sunk my head into my arms, trying to muffle the horrible sounds. I had doomed Miles.

"Harper. Breathe."

Nothing he could say would help my panic attack right now, and he knew it too. We sat in silence—besides my pathetic sobs—for what felt like an hour before I was able to calm down. I couldn't think of anything to talk about, and all I wanted to do was to tell him how sorry I was, which wouldn't do justice.

"You're always hesitant to take an elevator." I wanted to think about anywhere but there. When Miles and I went somewhere with an elevator, he would either hesitate or take the stairs. "Is there a reason?"

He let out a soft chuckle. "I was trapped in an elevator when I was a kid. It was only for an hour, but my kid brain was certain it was going to drop and I was going to die."

"I guess that would deter me too." I laughed through my rickety breathing. I didn't think Miles was afraid of anything.

"It's lame, I know."

I didn't think it was lame, but I couldn't find my voice. Another ten minutes passed until he spoke again.

"Want to hear a story?"

"Definitely." Anything to distract me from this place.

"I wasn't the one who always had to keep Brandon out of trouble," Miles said. I silently laughed at the thought of Brandon getting into trouble—mostly at bars. "My dad got two dirt bikes when we were younger—one for Brandon when he visited. We usually rode in the fields, staying out of the woods. If we did, we weren't allowed to go far or off the trail. There's this part of the creek where one end is higher than the other. I made a bet with him that I could jump it. He told me that he wasn't going to bet me—that it was a stupid idea and I wouldn't make it." I heard his faint chuckle. "I jumped anyway. He was right. It was too long of a jump. I only ended up wet and bruised, but my dirt bike didn't make it. My father was furious."

I found myself smiling as he told me a few other stories until I eventually fell asleep to the sound of his voice.

"Leave her alone." Miles' growl came through the vent above my head. His tone was fierce, unlike it had been before I fell asleep.

I picked my head up off the wall, and the sun reflected off the shackle around my ankle and into my eyes. I squinted and glanced over at the door to see evil incarnate standing on the other side.

"Good morning, Isa." Krauss' voice rattled my brain like a snake's hissing tongue. I was still drained and sore. Sleeping against the cement wall hadn't done me any favors.

With the support of the wall, I pushed myself up to stand. Krauss held his hands behind his back. He wore grey slacks, a white lab coat opened to a black, collared button-up shirt, and a grey tie.

"You can't give a girl a break, can you?" I asked.

"I did." He glanced at my arm. "But you elongated the recovery."

My hand touched the spot where the catheter had been. A bruise was in its place, along with other bruises on my arms and cuts on my thigh. Some bruises and cuts were fresh while others were already green or scabbed over. My heart pounded as Dr. Krauss walked over to Miles' cell.

"He didn't do anything." I hobbled over to the front of my cell so I could see Krauss, but I couldn't see Miles.

"I know." He glared into Miles' cell before turning his glare to me and striding my way. "Let this be a warning. Next time you do anything, even as simple as pulling out your IV line that was intended to help you heal, he will pay the price. Now, eat."

Krauss walked away as Avery came into view carrying two trays with a bowl and water bottle on each. She wore skinny jeans with combat boots and a tank top that showed off her barcode tattoo on her left forearm similar to me—a reminder that she too had once been a Ject. She knelt down, opening a small, sealed latch at the bottom of my door and slid a tray through. The latch clicked when it closed, locking so it could only be opened from the outside.

"We didn't have any brown sugar or cinnamon." A snarky grin flashed across Avery's face.

I glanced at the plastic tray holding a glob of food in a plastic bowl—must be they thought I could be dangerous with a porcelain bowl or metal tray. Despite the oatmeal's unappealing appearance, my stomach growled, beckoning me to eat.

"Here you are, Officer." Avery walked over to Miles' cell and slid the food through the latch with a flirtatious smile. I couldn't help the snort that came out of me. Was she that oblivious that Miles would never have any interest in her?

She walked over and stood in front of my cell. "I'll be back for you in a half an hour."

She flipped off the switch to my speaker and walked away. The door and the wall were not completely soundproof, but they did block most of the noise. The speaker provided clarity, and I honestly just wanted to break the darn thing—I didn't want to speak to them or hear them.

I stared at the tray before picking it up and setting it on the bed. I climbed up next to it and contemplated eating. I picked up the plastic spoon and swirled the thickened gunk, sighing. I didn't want it, but I wasn't sure if Krauss would hurt Miles.

"You should eat." Miles' voice filtered through the vent, and I wished that I could see him.

"It's not the Kovars' muffins, that's for sure," I joked.

"No. It's not." He let out a small chuckle before becoming serious. "You need to eat something, even if they drugged it. Your body needs substance—it's been a few days since you've eaten. Whatever they gave you to help, it won't suffice."

"How do you know I didn't have anything when they had me?" I asked.

"They took you when you were unconscious and brought you back in a similar state." He paused. "This is the first time they brought you food."

"They've been bringing you food?"

"Yes."

At least there's that. He needed food, and I guess I did too, but I didn't care if my body thrived right now. They needed my body—even if it was weak—but if it was beyond its current point, maybe they wouldn't be able to get what they needed.

He sighed after a few minutes had passed.

"You still haven't touched it," he said.

A small smile crept onto my lips. He knew me too well.

"I'll eat." I grabbed the spoon and took a small bite, swallowing hard. If this had an inhibitor or sedative in it, it would work soon.

I wasn't sure when they had given me the inhibitor last. I could feel the slightest spark, but it was out of reach. I couldn't even summon the strength from my beast. If I did have any extra strength, it would be healing me. I forced myself to eat half of the bowl. If I ate any more, I would throw it all back up.

Avery was back like she said she would be, and this time, she brought Damien, who had the wheelchair again. He pushed it near the door and leaned over it while keeping his hands on the handles.

"Don't touch her!" I heard a loud smack through the vent and knew Miles had hit the glass.

"Yeah, right." Avery glanced at his cell, her voice muffled. She looked up above my door and nodded.

"Harper! Stay strong!" Miles shouted just before the vent sealed shut and a clanking noise came from above. I climbed off the bed and backed away until my back was against the wall.

Here we go again.

CHAPTER EIGHT

I WOULDN'T HAVE KNOWN that a month had passed if it weren't for Miles. The days felt long yet flew by. I was out for most of it after Krauss drained my blood and collected tissue samples. I had bruises and holes all over my limbs and spine. Apparently, he was covering all aspects to see if he could find something viable enough to use.

Viable.

I wasn't sure that word had any practical reference to my body anymore. I didn't bother yanking on the shackles strapping me to the bed. After my previous stunt of pulling out my catheter, they shackled me down until the fluids ran their course. They would turn the gas on just enough to make me drowsy, and two of them would come in with gas masks and undo the shackles. The door would shut behind them, and a third person stayed on the outside to let them out. I guess they couldn't risk the door being opened from the inside and supposedly needed two people and the gas in case I magically felt my power. I stopped feeling a small spark return after the first two weeks and assumed they had me on the inhibitor around the clock.

Avery and Damien usually assisted, and besides Krauss, they were the bane of my existence. After they exited, they would leave a tray of food, a bucket filled with soapy water, a washcloth, and a clean bra and underwear. I barely touched the food but occasionally washed up and changed my lingerie. Rarely would they leave me a new gown. I felt like I was in a mental ward on steroids. It was nothing like the Vault.

Through the skylight, the sky was a mute blue, and soon, it would turn sky blue. It was morning, and I silently waited for them to notice I was awake.

I prayed they wouldn't.

As soon as Miles knew I was awake, he would talk to me, tell me stories about his life. I loved hearing his stories. His stories, along with his voice, were the only things holding me together. I wanted to say something to alert him that I was awake, but I couldn't. I should have, but I didn't want him to hear the damage in my voice.

They were breaking me.

"I would have projected to have found something by now."

I lifted my head long enough to get a look at the man the voice belonged to before I fell back onto the pillow. Dr. Krauss was outside my door. He hadn't shown up for the escort lately, so I was surprised to see him. The dissatisfaction on his face brought me joy but also made my skin crawl.

"Ultimately, I have found the part that makes you unique, but I haven't been able to extract it into a usable form. It's like running in circles on stage one." Was that a touch of anger in his usually composed voice?

"I'm not sorry to have disappointed you." My voice came out in a hoarse whisper.

"No need to be concerned. I will figure it out. Meanwhile, I need you to eat."

"I've been eating." If that's what you call forcing down a bite here and there.

"Not nearly enough to keep you healthy."

"You mean to keep my body alive"—I needed a breath in between words—"so you can keep experimenting on it."

His steps echoed through the speaker. "It will only hurt you and the officer, Isa."

"How do you know who I am?" I barely squeaked out the words and sat up as far as the chains would let me. This wasn't the first time he's mentioned my birth name, and his spiel at Macleay Park hadn't clued me in on anything.

"Your history proceeds you." He looked at me with a sinister smile. "I knew Dr. Westbrook. I also knew you—well, mostly the stories he told of you. I only met you a few times in the six years, including your father's funeral."

Six years? My father had died when I was six. I gripped the comforter.

"I was his apprentice, honored to be working alongside a genius. I was so young and naïve." He tilted his head at me. "That's all you need to know."

"Did you kill him?" I gritted my teeth and yanked on the chains as hard as I could, which was a minuscule amount.

He paused as he turned to walk away.

"I would never kill a brain with so much potential," he threw over his shoulder.

Krauss walked away. I yanked weakly on chains that didn't budge. I tried to reach the opposite chain with one hand to try to pull it with both, but I couldn't reach it. Precisely why they were made the way they were, so I couldn't touch my arms to yank out my IV line. I grunted in frustration.

"I'm so sorry, Harper." Miles' voice was filled with remorse, but he had nothing to be remorseful about.

I went to reply, but Avery and two other Hybrians showed up. Damien wasn't among them for once. I rested my head back on the pillow and quietly lay there, waiting for them to turn on the gas.

I lay unshackled on the bed, waiting for the cell to slowly form back into one solid piece. Once I was coherent enough, I stumbled over to the food. I started eating the toast and eggs, and then flushed it down with the juice that was left for me. This time, I ate all of it—not because Krauss had asked me to, but because I needed the strength to kill him.

"Hungry, are we?" I jumped and looked up to see Avery standing in front of the cell door.

"You look pathetic," she scoffed when I didn't say anything.

"Don't you normally leave and come back?" I muttered.

"I was going to see if the officer wanted a more feminine escort to his shower later." She was testing me.

I rolled my eyes and dropped the tray.

"What? No comeback?"

"I didn't hear anything that required a comeback." I shrugged, leaning against the wall.

"So you don't mind if I take your new boyfriend to the showers?"

"She's not taking me anywhere," Miles said. "She's just trying to get under your skin." He would be able to clearly hear her through the vent, but I also imagined she had his speaker on. She liked to put on a show.

"I know." A psychotic grin crossed my face, and I wasn't sure where the extra energy to put up an argument had come from, but I was going to use it.

She tossed her deep red hair over her shoulder and crossed her arms. "You don't mind then, once we're done with you, we'll make it so he won't remember you. He won't care about you. He'll forget you ever existed."

"You underestimate him."

"Do I? I think you underestimate Dr. Krauss." She took a step closer to the cell.

"You know what I think?" I used my hands on the wall for support, making my way closer to the glass wall and stopping just before it. "I think that you're jealous that I have people who actually care about me. I have friends who care about me. Who do you have? A doctor who uses you for muscle and soon as a test subject."

"You don't know what you're talking about." Her arms fell to her side.

"Don't I?" Sure, she had the respect from the other Rogues, but that was just by status. None of them acted like her friends. "Frank cast you out before knowing that you were spying—I bet that hurt."

"You better watch what you say." Her hands balled at her sides.

"What are you going to do? Turn on the gas, then beat me while I'm already unconscious? Pathetic." My voice cracked because it was dry, but there was power behind it.

"You don't know who you're messing with." Her eyes narrowed.

"A very lonely woman who has nothing better to do than stand around and attempt to harass someone you feel inferior to." I couldn't help the hysterical laugh that bubbled out of me as I spoke.

"You're wrong." Her brows pinched together.

"Not only do you hate that I have friends and you don't, but I outrank you in a fight. You had Maya do your fighting for you," I said.

"No. She did that."

"You mean you didn't subliminally arrange for her to try to kill me?" I don't know why I was trying to push her buttons. My hatred for her was rising, and I felt like nothing else could physically hurt me any more than I already was.

"I would demolish you in a fight," she hissed.

"Oh, like you did in the alley?" Last I remembered, Chloe and I got away.

"We were outmatched."

"With what? The two of us versus you, your two friends—and your tranq gun?" I rubbed my sore neck. "I don't have my power now."

I silently sighed at the vacancy in my chest. I wouldn't have thought I would have missed that part of me so much. I missed my beast.

"I'm not going to fight you right now."

"I know. You're too afraid I'd still beat you, even in this state." I studied the anger and restraint in her face. "Or is it because you can't touch me unless Dr. Krauss says so?"

She growled.

"Maya was right." My lips curved into a sneer. "I'm needed more than you. After all, there is only one of me. I bet if it was my life versus yours, Dr. Krauss would choose mine. Wouldn't he?"

She didn't answer.

"Harper, think about what you're doing," Miles warned from the other side of the wall.

I closed my eyes and rested my head against the cool concrete. "You're scared, Avery. It's okay."

Seconds later, I heard my cell door open. I opened my eyes to see Avery wedging a wooden block in between the door and the jamb so it wouldn't completely close. She faced me, eyes locking onto their prey and her lips in a snarl. She closed in on me and put her hands on my throat. I didn't care as her grip tightened.

I was finally going crazy.

I didn't fight it as I let my arms dangle. A deranged choking laugh escaped my mouth as a delusional grin crept along my lips. Something about this ending excited me. I got under Avery's skin, and a dead me would foil Krauss' plans.

I stared at her, tuning out Miles' faint voice yelling my name. Avery wouldn't end up killing me—I could see the fear she had of her leader, and surely, she knew the repercussions. Technically, she had attacked me, so no harm should come to Miles.

I could see the same thought circling in her head. Her eyes widened and she released my throat, taking a step back. I fell to the ground and coughed.

"Done already?" I sputtered out between coughs. I brought a hand to my throat and rubbed the tender spot. I glanced up at her. Shock filled her eyes. Krauss was never gentle with me by any means, but I'm sure entering my cell and attacking me without his permission wouldn't bode well for her.

"You wanted me to do that." She took another step back.

"Why'd you stop?" I slowly stood back up, beckoning her to continue.

She shook her head at me and turned around.

"You're weak," I said to her as she put a hand on the door. "Come back and finish it!" I yelled, too deranged to be shocked by my own indignation.

When she didn't turn around and started to push the door open, I let out a frustrated scream and shot my arms forward. Two bolts surged out and struck Avery in the back. Her body went stiff, shaking until she collapsed. I blinked multiple times while staring at her unconscious body as the door jammed into her rib cage.

An entire new wave of exhaustion washed over me like a bucket of water being dropped on my head. Had I really done that? I didn't feel any lingering static or power left—just the fatigue.

I gradually became aware of Miles still calling out to me and shook myself out of my own bewilderment. The door was open. And Avery was unconscious. I made my way over to the door as quickly as my drained body would let me. I patted her for keys or a weapon, but she surprisingly had neither on her. I pushed her just far enough into my cell with the little strength I had, and exited.

After the door shut, I walked unsteadily over to Miles, who was leaning against his glass door with his arms above his head. Creases lined the undersides of his eyes, and his lips were turned downward. Long scruff replaced the stubble on his face, and sweat laced over his upper body and dripped at his taut waistline just above his grey sweatpants. He looked like he had just got done working out and grown more defined, unlike my body.

Miles watched me with concern and shocked eyes that had turned the color of steel, not hazel, like they had been the last time I saw them. I propped myself against the door, feeling the desire in my legs to give out.

There was a keypad on the door, but I didn't know how to hack it.

"Try two-three-five-six." I glanced up to see Miles examining me with a guarded expression.

I punched in the code—it didn't work.

"Five-six-eight-nine." Miles didn't take his eyes off me.

I punched the new numbers into the keypad, and sure enough, it opened.

"How did you know?" I managed to ask.

"Location of their fingers when they entered the code."

I pushed myself off the door and pulled it open. My heart crippled at the sight behind him. There was no bed. There was no rug. Concrete was not a surface to sleep on for one night, let alone weeks.

"You lied." Or had he? I had asked him if he had restraints on his bed—he said he didn't. I guess he technically hadn't lied if there wasn't a bed.

Miles glanced at Avery in my cell, ignoring my statement, and pulled me to him, wrapping his arms tightly around me without causing pain. I relaxed in the comfort of his arms. Miles must have felt my feebleness because he supported me with his arms. My legs could no longer bear my weight, and I felt like I couldn't walk. The burst of power had drained me even more than I already had been.

"Let's get you out of here." He scooped me up into his arms, his muscles surging beneath me.

"Us," I murmured. Get *us* out of there.

Miles gave me a gentle kiss on the forehead and then looked down each end of the hallway, his face hardening. I only remembered coming back from the right, which was the opposite of Miles' cell. He was probably thinking the same thing as he turned left and jogged down the hallway.

"Where did they take you?" I mumbled into his chest, fighting off the sleep that danced along the rims of my eyes.

"Damien would take me somewhere I could shower." He knew I was questioning why they would open his cell door enough times so he could guess the code. There was a toilet in the cell, they gave food through the slot, and they gave me a bucket to wash up with.

We turned a corner, and it was hard for me to focus on my surroundings. It was a concrete hallway with fluorescent lights, much like the Vault, except drearier and dated. I tried to watch where we were going, but the movement was making me queasy. Instead, I focused on Miles' warm bare chest.

It felt like we had made it quite some ways before Miles stopped dead in his tracks, his arms going stiff around me. I could feel his heart rate quicken before settling back to its normal rhythm.

"It was a bad idea to try to escape."

Damien.

Multiple footsteps echoed behind us, and I knew we were trapped. Given the state I was currently in, there was no way Miles was going to fight his way through. There were too many of them, they were strong, and I'm sure they had guns.

I had failed Miles.

CHAPTER NINE

I T FELT LIKE I was in my own frozen time bubble while everything around me kept moving. Dr. Krauss, Avery, the Rogues... they had all moved around me with such speed. I never had a conversation with Avery about what had happened, at least not one I remembered. I either didn't know someone was trying to talk to me or I just didn't care. However, I do remember Dr. Krauss telling me what I did was brilliantly conniving, yet foolish, even if it wasn't planned.

He had me on an ethanol drip and would change my IV catheter every few days—*I think*. The inhibitors weren't trusted after I had hit Avery with a blue lightning blast, so they resorted to alcohol. Basically, I was drunk all the time. The floor would randomly shake, and I couldn't even tell if it was all in my head.

I didn't bother moving as I lay on the bed. I didn't think I could even if I wanted to, and it wasn't because of the restraints. Just moving was too much. The world spun whenever I shifted, and I couldn't keep anything down. They had to be supplementing me with something because I should have been dead by now from alcohol poisoning.

I'd given up.

I had reached the lowest point I'd never imagined was possible and no longer had the will to fight. They kept the vent closed after my little stunt, and I could no longer hear Miles—unless it was muffled when he yelled at them. But it's been a while since I've heard anything from his cell. I didn't even know if he was okay.

I lay there as a phantom tear ran down my cheek. There should've been one, but my eyes were dry. The first week—weeks; I wasn't sure—I cried nearly every night. Now, there were no more tears left to fall.

I heard my door open and footfalls in my cell until they stopped at my bed. They didn't need to use gas anymore. I blinked as a face appeared, blocking the light shining from the skylight. After a few more blinks, a square jawline with clean-cut lines carving out a well-trimmed short beard appeared.

Cobalt eyes as cold as ice stared down at me.

"Good morning, Isa." Krauss didn't grin, which was unusual for him. I also didn't bother correcting him on my name anymore. "We're at a standstill. Nothing seems to be working, and we can't constantly keep you"—he coughed—"on a dissociative. Even in Dr. Roulings' controlled environment, he had no luck."

Frank never shared his findings or my files with Avery, so I knew he had to have guessed based on what Avery had informed him of.

"I think maybe a visit with a friend might help," he stated and disappeared from overhead.

My head lolled to the side, and a black and silver blur came into focus. A wheelchair. I didn't bother looking to see who was behind it. Two figures approached me, and I felt the piercing cold from the shackles disappear.

My body was like a ragdoll as they moved me into the wheelchair, and I was surprised I didn't throw up. They didn't bother strapping me in—I wasn't going anywhere. And any electricity I could have summoned would be gone before I could even release it. I didn't feel anything anyway.

They pushed me out the door, and instead of going right, they went left. We were going to pass Miles' cell. That was something we never did. I pried my dry eyes open as we passed, wanting to see if he was okay.

My heart sank as fury and grief hit me, overflowing what was already there beyond my defeat. The image of the empty cell with a single shackle and toilet tormented me.

"Where is he?" My words weakly escaped my lips. I wanted so badly to get out of that wheelchair and demand answers, but a few meager words were all I could manage.

"He's fine. You'll see him soon," Krauss said. He had better not be lying, and if he was, there was nothing else keeping me alive.

We turned down a hallway with similar cells before going through a door to another hallway. We passed a window that opened to a block with three levels of prison cells—all with rusted bars. *So this is a prison.* I would have laughed at the irony if I could've mustered it.

Eventually, we arrived at a door with a window slit in it and an exit sign above it. The bright sun poured through the slit and onto the concrete ground. Someone walked in front of us and opened the door. My hands itched to shield my eyes from the blinding light but stayed lazily in my lap. I was wheeled onto a paved sidewalk that led to a completely fenced-in outdoor area. The prison yard—I assumed. A figure was sitting on the ground against a picnic table that was turned on its side.

My heart fluttered as soon as I recognized Miles' outline. The sun shined against his chest and shadowed his sweatpants. I urged my body to get up and run to him, but it didn't. His head turned my way, and he abruptly stood. The wheelchair stopped moving, and Krauss walked around and knelt in front of me. He unhooked the line from the catheter and hung it up on the pole carrying my personal alcohol bag on the back of the wheelchair.

"Maybe this will give you the motivation your body needs." Krauss started coughing, and I swear he was going to hack up a lung. Once he finished, he stood. "We can't slow down."

Krauss stepped aside, letting whoever was steering me push past him.

Miles didn't say anything when we reached him but scowled at the person behind me.

"You have an hour, and that's him being generous." It was Damien. "We'll be watching." Damien's footsteps receded. There were murmurs and then a door closed, the murmuring ceasing with it.

Miles knelt in front of me. His gaze shifted over my face as he gently caressed my cheek. I leaned into his palm and took a deep breath. He looked strong but drained. I've never seen his eyes so dark and sunken. His face was riddled with exhaustion, both physical and emotional, as sweat glistened on his brow.

"What are they doing to you?" he whispered, not expecting an answer, but in all honesty, I couldn't fully answer that myself.

"Can I join?" I asked meekly and looked over at the picnic table on its side.

He raised an eyebrow and followed my gaze. He glanced back at me and nodded. He went to pick me up, but I shook my head. I wanted to stand on my own. I used what little strength I had to hoist myself up, but my legs collapsed underneath me. I sighed in frustration as Miles caught me. He kept an arm around me and supported my weight as we shuffled over to the picnic table.

We sat down on the orange dirt with our backs against the top of the table. He wrapped an arm around me, pulling me close. Somehow, he still smelled of leather and pine. It's like the pine was infused into his skin and he was still wearing his leather jacket.

I looked out beyond the barbed wire fence. An orange haze reflected off the sand dunes that rolled into the horizon. That would explain the dusty earth scent and constant sun during the day. We were in a desert. Speaking of days...

"How long...?" I couldn't make out the rest of the question.

He was quiet for a moment before responding.

"Five months."

I opened my mouth, but nothing came out. I closed my eyes and took a deep breath. He had been sleeping on concrete and held hostage for five months.

"I'm s-so sorry," I rasped.

"I would *never* want to be anywhere else that wasn't with you." He pulled me tighter and rested his chin on my head. "Without you, I wouldn't have found happiness again." His eyes lightened, a tint of green swirling in them. "I also wouldn't have gone home to visit my grandparents, let alone stay the night. That's something I failed to realize they needed, just like I needed you—still need you."

I swallowed. I should have been hot in the desert heat, but I was cold and his warmth was inviting. I looked back out at the horizon, where orange sand met vibrant blue. The sun should have felt revitalizing like it did after the Vault, though it did nothing of the sort.

We were in a desert. Liam would never find us. Miles was stranded there.

CHAPTER TEN

I WOKE UNSHACKLED IN my cell bed with the red comforter pulled over my face. My body was soaked in sweat and stuck to the sheets. I slowly pushed the comforter back as searing light from the skylight blinded me. I squeezed my eyes shut and rolled into the pillow, instantly aware of the agonizing headache pounding my skull.

A wave of nausea flooded me, and I pulled myself to the edge of the bed. Luckily, an empty bucket was already placed there and I heaved into it. When I was done, I wiped my mouth with my arm, fully aware of how disgusting the action was but too sick to care. I thought I heard my name while throwing up, but I didn't hear it again and chalked it up to the ringing in my ears.

I lay back down and raised my arm. I still had a catheter in and it was hooked up to a bag on a pole about four feet away. I didn't feel groggy, disorientated, or like I was floating all at once—just my head pounded and the world spun. The hangover feeling was still present, but the drunkenness was gone. There was something else—something that felt wrong—I hadn't been able to detect before. I couldn't place it, but this entire place was wrong.

I slowly sat up, swung my legs over the side of the bed, and rubbed my eyes with shaky hands. I squinted at the bag and noticed it was labeled differently than what they'd been giving me. As much as I wanted to take it out, I still didn't think it would be a good idea to piss Krauss off. That, and I didn't think it was ethanol. I was feeling better than I had in a while.

A plate of toast and eggs along with multiple water bottles and a wash bucket were placed near the door. I made my way to the food and water, rolling the pole along with me. I was parched and hungry. After the first bite of the toast, I thought I was going to hurl and settled for a few sips of water.

A noise from above caused me to jump. I looked up, relieved when I realized it had come from the vent connecting to Miles' cell. They must have opened it after they let us meet in the yard. I silently cursed at myself for falling asleep during the only time in months that I've had with him.

"Miles?" I stared at the vent. I didn't know why—it's not like he was magically going to come through it.

"You're awake," he said, his voice full of concern. "How are you feeling?"

"Like I was dragged through a bed of rocks and then hit by a freight train," I answered as I trudged back over to the bed with a water bottle and the pole at tow.

"You seem more aware," he said.

"I don't think they're keeping me drunk anymore. But it does feel like I have a wicked hangover." I squeezed my eyes shut and rubbed my head. "I suppose my quick healing won't make this go away anytime soon?"

"Unfortunately, no, I don't think so," he agreed.

I imagined weeks of constantly being infused with ethanol was going to take a while to recover from. Hopefully my healing would help protect my liver.

"How long ago were we outside?" I asked.

"Two days." His voice barely shook.

"You know, a concrete floor doesn't qualify as a bed," I jested, trying to help bring him some solace.

He let out a noise that sounded like something between a grunt and laugh. "It hardly does, does it?"

Another wave of nausea hit and I bent over the bucket, throwing up the few sips of water I had before dry heaving.

"You should try to eat something," Miles said when I was done.

"How do you know I have food?" I groaned as I stood and dumped the contents from the bucket down the toilet. I looked down at my scrawny legs and then at my boney hands and arms. I was only skin and bones.

"I saw them bring it to you."

"I guess that's a reasonable answer," I said as I went over to the water bucket and wiped my mouth.

I sat by the food and attempted to eat again. I made it through half a slice before I couldn't stomach any more and went back to lying down. The room started spinning, and I could feel my heart beat against my chest.

"Can you tell me the story when you and your dad went fishing and you fell off the boat?" I asked, not wanting to think about our current situation and the agonizing withdrawal I was going through.

"Of all of them, you want that one?"

"Yes." I smiled. I loved the story he told about when he was ten and had gone fishing with his dad on his dad's boat. He had caught a fish and made the mistake of grabbing the pole from the rod holder and was pulled into the river.

As he told me the story, I felt myself drift off to the sound of his voice. The picture of a young Miles in the water turned into splashes of water made by someone else. Laughter from his father changed into two children's laughter, and a dog barked in the distance. The river narrowed and its depth shallowed.

I looked up to see a scrawny young boy with curly black hair and glasses connected by a strap around his neck. He had to have been around twelve and was flying off a rope swing toward me into the water shouting, "Look out, Izz!"

Behind him, a brown dog with a white chest barked and jumped in after us. *Taco.* I remembered where we were—the swimming hole in the Molalla River. We would take our bikes there often to swim and climb the trees.

As soon as the boy's name came to mind, images flashed before my eyes. My missing memories played back like a video reel. Dylan, my best friend from school; my mom; my stepfather Joe; Taco; and a bare minimum of my dad all came crashing down on me. It was like my memories were paint and my body was the canvas, and someone was dumping buckets of different shades of paint onto the canvas. At first, they were confusing but soon became clear as the picture began to take shape. I remembered the night of the fake fire—well, mostly. I remembered hearing a noise behind me before completely blacking out.

My eyes flew open.

I remembered my past.

CHAPTER ELEVEN

I WANTED TO SCRATCH at whatever was sticking to my temples, but the restraints wouldn't budge. I was strapped down to a metal chair. My upper left chest and lower hip throbbed in pain, and I glanced down. My gown was backward and now tied in the front. Wires led from under my gown and my head to a monitor next to me.

On the other side of the glass stood Krauss, Damien, Avery, a few others, and Miles, who was on his knees in front of Avery. She held her stun stick to his neck, and she wore a gun on her hip. Blood dripped from his nose and a bruise was starting to form under his eye.

"You said you wouldn't hurt him if I listened to you!" I scowled at Krauss.

"I don't believe that was specifically said." Dr. Krauss took a step closer to the glass.

They were going to regret ever hurting him. I was going to make sure all of them felt unimaginable pain. Static built in my chest as I fought against the restraints. It flowed through my body and stationed at my hands, waiting to be used. My beast had surfaced.

"Incredible." Krauss looked at me with amazement and admiration that freaked me out. He walked over to the desk off near the window and stared at a monitor. "Your heart is its source. It's working with your brain, which sends a signal to your heart, powering it."

He waved over a woman who appeared to be in her early thirties. Her heels clicked against the concrete as she walked, and she wore a bright white lab coat like Krauss did.

"See here. The patterns connect with these," he explained to her, pointing to the monitor.

The woman nodded in agreement and stared at the screen in awe. It was like I was a new species that they were researching—*almost spot on*. She wrote a couple things down on her clipboard and walked over to a door leading to the room I was in. Her side-swept pixie-cut hair bounced as she walked. She stopped and stood at the door and hugged the clipboard to her chest.

"Barbara is going to come in and collect some samples," Krauss said.

The door opened and Barbara strode in. Her high cheekbones were coated with blush and her lips caked with red lipstick. She walked over to me and gave me a quick look over from behind her black-rimmed glasses. She grabbed some supplies from her pocket and prepared the syringe, her face lacking any sympathy.

She wasn't afraid of me. They knew I wouldn't do anything while they had Miles. My eyes changed back to their normal shade of brown, like a candle being blown out.

"Oh, dear Isa." Krauss looked up from the monitor. "We need that spark in you as she takes the samples. Avery, some encouragement."

"No!" I yelled as Avery raised the stick to Miles' neck.

Miles gritted his teeth as he fell to the ground. He closed his eyes and bore the pain before opening them and looking at me, telling me he was okay. I admired his will and strength. I felt the static rise but not as forcefully as the first time. I focused on keeping tight in my chest and anywhere but my arms while Barbara wrapped a tourniquet around my arm.

"Slight pinch," she warned as she drew my blood. Her voice sounded innocent and sweet, but obviously it was deceitful. Afterward, she pushed the rim of my gown up, revealing multiple bruises and wounds. She rubbed my thigh and knee with gauze.

"A sharp pinch this time." Barbara had acquired a new needle whose length had to be a few inches and had a handle on the end. She stuck it in right below my knee.

I clenched my teeth and squeezed my hands closed as it slid against bone. That one hurt. She was out in less than ten seconds. Clearly, she had done this before, and I was starting to think she was the other person besides Krauss who had been taking samples from me this entire time.

"This one will sting," she said as she grabbed a small pen-looking thing and stuck it in my thigh and twisted. I don't know why she kept warning me—it's not like she had my best intentions in mind.

She removed it and my eyes widened at the chunk skin sticking to the end of it. When I was first there, I was sedated and had an inhibitor, but I still remember Krauss doing the same things. He did it every time they took me but had taken a lot more blood. Now, I had nothing to ease the pain.

"All done." Her empty emotions turned into joy as she smiled and walked away with her bounty of pieces from my body.

She left the room and walked over to a table in the back where Krauss now stood. After what felt like eternity, Krauss walked back over to the glass.

"Fortunately, we just received all the information we needed. Now we just need to prepare."

"It's time, Isa." Krauss' cold voice whispered in my ear and a chill ran down my spine.

If it wasn't for the metal restraints, my hands would be wrapped around his neck, I was no longer in the chair but was lying on a table. Barbara had given me something to knock me out while they *prepared*.

We were no longer in the same room that had the windowed cell. I glanced down—as much as I could with my head strapped—and saw the same wires coming out from under my gown, except one of the wires branched off and led to the table next to me. I gasped when I saw

Miles strapped to it. He had a catheter in his arm that connected to something beneath the table that I couldn't see, and those white things with wires stuck to his temples. The body heat from his arms and bare chest radiated against my skin. He was so close that if I extended a finger, I might be able to reach him.

Miles' eyes briefly met mine before shifting and glowering at Krauss on my other side.

"We found the missing key. A key that Dr. Roulings could never figure out nor stomach to do against your will." Krauss straightened and moved to the far ends of the tables. "Your DNA is unique, but it didn't have the marker that we needed to create more Hybrians like you. You needed to be in your alternate form to fully activate it. With this, we can fuse it with another form of DNA that will bond with the Hybrian gene. Together, we can give Hybrians superior power such as your own."

"What are you going to do with him?" My focus wouldn't leave the fact that they had Miles strapped down next to me.

Avery let out a low laugh behind Krauss right before he spoke. "He will be the lucky one to see if it works."

"You can't do this!" I fought against the restraints and reached for the static rising within me.

"I wouldn't do that if I were you." Krauss glanced at Miles. "Do you feel that annoying pressure near your heart and the throbbing near your groin?" *Yes.* "That's a cardiac catheter. We had used it to collect readings, but now it's being used to tether you to your friend. Your heart is the spark. That catheter is made of stainless steel, nylon, and polyurethane, which will transmit the electricity through those leads and to the electrodes on his head. He will receive the full force of your power. No matter where you try to send it, it will only make it to him. Think of it as a bypass."

I instantly shut down the building static, afraid that if it got any bigger it would go straight to Miles.

"Do you like to hear yourself talk?" I scowled at Dr. Krauss as his fierce cobalt eyes watched me like a snake. They reminded me of a dull version of my beast's eyes, but my beast was no monster. Krauss was a monster.

"We need you to be morphed, but not use an inch of that power," Krauss continued, ignoring my question. "When we give you the tranquilizer, your power becomes dormant. Your father didn't have the backbone to do what needed to be done," he continued. "Dr. Roulings attempted, but his intentions were rather riotous. His cause was inferior. The Alliance sees the good in this world and wants to destroy their version of bad. Lack of empathy creates inexorability, which leads to strength—strength is power."

I had no clue what he was talking about. He walked over to a monitor. Barbara appeared with another long needle and handle in a clear package. He grabbed it with a longing smile and waved it in the air.

"This will retrieve your bone marrow. Bone marrow contains stem cells that transform into blood cells, or stromal cells, which produce fat, cartilage, muscle, and bone. Your stem cells are unique and make you what you are. Your mother's body was done forming, so the serum your father made didn't last on her, but you, you were still growing. It became a part of you, and we can isolate it to create more. When it works, I'll need to do more studies to see if I can extract it from the new Hybrians." He handed the package back to Barbara.

"So you do like hearing yourself talk," I answered. Why else would he explain something that he was going to do regardless and still not let us go afterward? It's like a villain M.O.

He smiled at me, not affected at all by my comment.

"You can also be my prodigy once your mind is cleared and you see our way." He walked toward me, ignoring the sound Avery made at his comment.

"Don't touch her," Miles growled.

"I'm not going to. Barbara, darling, are you ready?" Barbara nodded with a smile.

"Coward," I spat at Krauss. "You won't do it yourself because you're worried about what I could do to you."

"I wouldn't call it cowardliness, just logical. Barbara knows the costs."

My jaw dropped. How on earth could someone be okay with putting themselves in danger for him and his delusional psychotic cause?

"Let's get her to change." Krauss nodded at Avery. "This is to ensure you stay changed and make sure you're at your maximum. We need the stem cells to be pure and activated. Pain is an exceptional influencer to bring forth the Hybrian."

I've heard fear was too.

Avery grabbed a foot-long thin metal pin from a table and handed it to Barbara.

"This is going to be painful, and we can't use any local anesthetic." Barbara walked over to my side with the pin. *Wasn't that obvious?* Local anesthesia would do the opposite of what she was trying to do.

"Barbara is an expert with the neuropathway and the brain." Dr. Krauss took a couple of steps back so he was out of reach.

"I will kill you," Miles growled, not just to Krauss, but to all of them.

Krauss nodded at Barbara to carry on.

Warm fingers brushed against my hand and I welcomed the contact. Miles grabbed my hand and squeezed. His restraints must have had a little more leeway. I glanced at him. His beautiful eyes stared back at me. I studied the swirls of grey in his hazel irises like an evening storm's clouds, the grown-out scruff that lined his sharp jawline, his black hair that feathered out from the lack of being cut, and his hard, firm lips—he was beyond handsome. I relaxed, praying that I could keep the sparks at bay. A smile spread across my face that I swore would make him think I was crazy.

In the next instant, a sharp, shooting pain pierced my abdomen. I slammed my eyes shut and screamed as Miles' hand tightened around mine. I wanted to let go in case I accidentally shocked him, but then I realized it didn't matter. It wouldn't make it to my hand anyway.

"Harper, look at me," Miles ordered softly. "Look at me!" he said again when I didn't listen. I tilted my head and opened my eyes. "Focus on me, okay?"

And that was exactly what I did. I concentrated on his forbearing eyes and thought about our time together. I thought of the first time we met in the alley, our awkward first motorcycle ride, the time he climbed a tree after me, sat on the roof at my old house, rode the horses at the farm, the night we danced by the fire, our first and second kiss we shared too long ago, and the moment he completely trusted me and opened up—the hotel in Seattle.

The pain continued to radiate through my abdomen, like someone set fire to my nerve endings. It didn't spread over my entire body, but it hurt far worse than anything I had experienced. Bile rose in my throat, but I swallowed it back down. I focused on the memories I had with Miles and then ran through my old ones. The happy ones with my mom, Joe, my dad, Taco, Dylan... all of the memories that were stolen from me.

Ultimately, my thoughts ventured back to Miles. It's like strength flowed through his hand to me, and I forced my power to stay dormant, like a piece of flint touching a rock but not striking.

"I've never seen someone with such pain tolerance," Barbara said.

I ignored her and stayed focused on Miles. He stared helplessly into my eyes, searching and wanting to help but knowing there was nothing he could do.

"I haven't had the chance to tell you that I remember." I forced a smile against the lacerating fire that shredded through my stomach.

"Remember? Your memories?" His voice was low, laced with agony.

I nodded in response.

A more intense wave of pain coursed through me. I didn't think that was possible, and my eyes slammed shut. I grunted and turned to see Barbara backing away, leaving the metal pin sticking out of my abdomen. It scraped against the table underneath me when I barely shifted.

That's nauseating. I had a large metal pinlike needle going in my front and out my back.

My powers heightened and that was when I morphed, turning my eyes blue. I had given in, but I had to control the spark inside me. I had to contain the flame and had to control the beast. I couldn't hurt Miles.

"She's in control. Proceed." Dr. Krauss' voice echoed through the room as he still maintained his distance.

Barbara walked over and touched my knee with something cool. Then a small sharp pain hit, but the fire in my stomach overshadowed everything else. I laid there, my body on fire, while she continued her demented testing.

After who knows how long, she stuck something in my shoulder and injected. She undid the strap over my head but left everything else in place and stepped back. I felt the beast start to fade away. When it did, the pain became even more debilitating. I squeezed Miles' hand and bit back a scream, trying to ignore the pain to no avail.

"She can't do anything. She doesn't need that in her!" Miles yelled.

"She has quite the reputation." Dr. Krauss said from the corner.

Barbara went over to Miles, but I couldn't concentrate through the pain to clearly focus on what she was doing.

"Lucky for the officer, your blood types are compatible. His and your blood are now cycling through each other. Until we can modify the serum, we will continue to need your blood, Isa." Krauss stood at our feet with a murky blue syringe in his hands. "Hopefully this serum won't be as particular with its host and will deliver Hybrians overnight rather than weeks to months.... or even years." He strode over to Miles.

He was going to turn him.

CHAPTER TWELVE

A S THE SERUM TRAVELED through Miles' body, his veins turned into blue webs, similar to my injections in the Vault. I focused on the pain from the pin and the anger from what they were doing to Miles. I willed my beast forward to try to use the strength without summoning the electricity. If I could break free, I could stop them. Nothing came. The inhibitor had worked. I wasn't breaking free of these shackles just like I wouldn't have been able to moments before with the beast. I was helpless, and there was nothing I could do except watch.

He shuddered. My hand still held his, and I squeezed, letting him know I was there. His breathing picked up, and I could feel his heartbeat in his palm as sweat started to drip off his forehead and down his neck.

"It's hurting him! Stop!" I demanded, but no one moved. Tears pricked my eyes as I helplessly watched.

"I'll be okay." Miles let out a grunt.

"I'm sorry... I'm so sorry..." It was all I could say. My heart wept as if it had been slashed open.

The room went dark, and seconds later, blue lights turned on. It took me a moment to realize the power went out and a backup generator must have kicked on. Three of Krauss' men entered the room carrying guns.

"Sir, the entire facility is down," a man said.

"It can't be a coincidence." Dr. Krauss frowned and turned to face Avery. "It appears we have some company. You know what to do."

The double doors opened on the opposite side of the room and my heart skipped a beat. Liam, Travis, and Maya entered the room in their beast form, armed with guns. Adam was with them and looked just as lethal. All of them were dressed in black. They looked like a SWAT unit.

"Step away from them." Liam aimed his gun at Krauss. The door opened again behind them, and an older man with grey-blond hair and blue eyes walked through.

"Dad?" I whispered, still in pain. He was much older than I remembered.

"Doctor Benjamin Westbrook. How nice to see you again, mentor." Krauss slowly backed away from Miles with his hands up.

"What have you done, Killian?" My dad's eyes were wide as he scanned me and then Miles.

"What have *you* done?" Shivers ran down my spine at the dark change in Krauss' voice—I didn't think it could get any darker. "Back from the dead like your daughter? I've searched high and low for you until I found what I needed. My intuition told me it was your darling daughter, but I wasn't certain until I saw her."

"That's enough." Liam's voice boomed.

Krauss glanced at Avery, then Damien, and nodded before he grabbed Barbara's arm and ducked for the back door.

A deafening shot was fired before hand-to-hand fighting broke out.

Seconds later, my dad appeared over me, keeping his head low. His woeful eyes stared at the pin through my stomach. "I'll untie you then we'll pull this out, okay?"

"Get him first!" I glanced at Miles, who was trembling.

"I'm getting my daughter first, then I'll get him," he said as he worked to get the shackles off.

Once both of my hands were free, he started unshackling my ankles. I grabbed the pin and pulled. Searing pain shot through my stomach as a painful cry shot through me. I thought the pain would've vanished once it was out, but it lingered like a phantom.

I started ripping off anything attached to me, ignoring the burning sensation and blood everywhere. I found the bundle of wires that flowed out of the bottom of my gown. A small tug told me it was the reason my hip burned, and my dad's eyes went wide.

"Wait! That can kill you if you don't do it carefully," he said.

"We don't have time to be careful." I yanked. Fire stung my chest, I dropped the wires and a lengthy bloodied metal catheter. It hit the floor like a dead snake as I laid back on the table, fully aware of the chaos around me. I needed a moment to compose myself and fight the black dots along the edges of my vision.

I didn't hear any more shots. Guns were good when there was space, but there wasn't much with everyone in the room, yet I still stayed low when I rolled off the table. I made my way to Miles and started unhooking his wrists. Each movement felt like tiny needles over my skin.

"Get out of here," Miles grunted as blue etched his veins across his neck, down his chest to his abs, and disappeared underneath his sweats.

"I'm not leaving you." I reached over him and pulled the line out of his arm. He winced. "Sorry."

Out of nowhere, Avery was on top of us. She kicked my dad and he fell backward. I swung one of my legs, sweeping hers out from underneath her. The move caused me to lose my balance, and I supported myself on the table.

She hoisted herself up. A sinister grin spread across her face as she took something out of her pocket and jammed it into Miles' thigh before I could even react. I dove at her, knocking her to the ground. She pushed me off and climbed on top of me. I pushed against her, but I was too weak to shove her off.

"The next one's for you." She reached in her pocket and pulled out another syringe, but it fell as someone behind her jabbed the pin through her arm. She screamed and fell off of me. I looked up, astonished to see my father.

Two bodies hit the floor beside us with a loud thud. I looked over to see Miles on top of one of Krauss' men. He must've finished getting his shackles off himself. He lifted the man's head and slam it into the concrete, knocking him out cold. Miles slumped to the ground, gasping for breath. He looked like he was about to pass out, either from the serum or the injection Avery had just given him.

I rolled off my back and crawled over to him.

"You need to get out of here," Miles said as he put a hand on my shoulder.

"Not without you." My eyes teared up as his body sunk even more. I scanned the room, looking for the others. Liam and Travis were fighting a group of Rogues, and Maya was nowhere in sight.

"I don't think I'm going to make it on this train, but I'll catch the next one," Miles said, bringing my attention back to him. He wore a gentle smile.

"Don't you dare joke now. We came together. We leave together." I put an arm under him but froze.

Avery held the pin at my dad's throat.

"Set your boyfriend down." Blood traveled down her arm.

I moved my arm out from under Miles and raised my hands.

Adam came up from behind her with a stun stick and jammed it into her back. Her hand that held the pin froze as her body shook and fell to the ground. Another Rogue charged toward Adam and my dad.

I turned to shout for help. I couldn't get Miles out of there. Before I could open my mouth, he grabbed my cheek and turned it to face him.

"If I become the monster they want me to be"—passionate fury burned in his eyes—"you know what needs to be done. You are the strongest person I know. Get. Out. Of. Here."

He collapsed to the ground and his eye lids fluttered shut.

Someone grabbed me from behind and started dragging me. I kicked and thrashed to no avail. I was yanked backward and fell to the ground as the person's arms disappeared. The room spun and I fought the nausea rising in my throat.

"We have to go. Now." Liam's voice echoed as his morphed face appeared in front of me.

"We can't leave him." I looked behind where I'd last seen Miles. Damien had him slung over his shoulder and exited the same door Krauss had left through earlier.

"I'm sorry, Harper," he said, his gaze following mine. "We are losing our ground. It's now or never."

I glanced around. We were outnumbered and the others were barely holding their own. I knew Travis enough to know when he was exhausted. If he didn't leave now, he wouldn't have a chance. None of them would. Liam's hand wrapped around my waist as he moved me toward the double doors. I numbly went with him, too shocked at everything going on.

Someone whistled, and I was so disorientated I wasn't sure if it had come from Liam. Seconds later, smoke began to fill the room just as we went through the door. Travis, Adam, and my dad were right behind us. The door shut, and Liam let go of me as Travis and Adam leaned against the doors. He picked up a small plastic chair and broke off one of the metal legs and shoved it through the handles.

"It won't hold for long. Let's move." Liam walked back over to me, putting a hand on my back to nudge me down the hallway.

I took a step but stopped. Miles wouldn't want me back in the hands of Krauss and this would make the rescue mission in vain, but it felt so wrong to leave him.

"I'm sorry, Harper. He was our mission too, but once he was through those doors, we lost him. If we don't move, the entire mission won't just be failed, it would be a disaster." Liam's eyes faded to their normal chestnut color as he put aside his beast.

I nodded. We needed to leave if any of us had hope of getting out of here and finding Miles again.

Liam kept an arm on me as we ran. It was like I was running on numb legs, and I was slowing them down. Even my father could've ran at a faster pace.

We made our way outside, and a large truck stopped just outside a fence surrounding the prison. My eyes adjusted to the bright sun, and I recognized Maya in the driver seat. We ran across the sand before ducking through an opening cut into the barbed wire. Liam helped me climb in the back seat while Travis and Adam hopped in the truck bed. Maya turned to face us and glanced at Liam who gave her a grave nod—most likely about Miles not being with us.

As soon as my dad was in the passenger seat, Maya floored it. A large explosion shook the truck as we drove off. I turned to see the retreating prison. A cloud of smoke rose from the far side.

"They won't be coming after us any time soon," Maya said.

"She took out their rides. Miles wouldn't have been near them," Liam added. He must've seen the concern in my eyes as I stared at the prison. It looked like a normal prison with cement walls, barely any windows, multiple stories, and a fence—except it was in a desert, which was probably the point.

I wasn't sure how long it was until we came upon an airplane in the middle of the desert.

"It's ours," Liam said.

I had wanted to know how they got to the prison undetected, but I didn't have the energy to talk. Nor was I in a talking mood.

I accepted Liam's help out of the car and onto the plane. He led me to a tan chair next to a small circular window as Adam headed toward the cockpit. I rested my forehead against the window, staring off into the hazy-orange desert as we took off.

After a few minutes, Liam placed a soft blanket around my shoulders. I looked up at him; he answered me with knitted brows and soft eyes, and that kindness prompted me to grab the blanket and pull it tighter around me, aware of my disheveled state. He walked away and came back with a water bottle. He handed it to me as he sat down, and I chugged half of it.

"Can I get you anything?" Liam gave me a once-over, taking in my appearance.

"Is there a bathroom?" I asked just as Frank emerged from the cockpit.

"Yes. Just past that couch." Liam pointed to a small tan leather couch in the back.

"Thanks." I glared at Frank as I stood and let the blanket fall to the chair.

I ignored the eyes on me as I walked to the bathroom. Once alone, I shut the bathroom door, leaned over the sink, and ran the water to splash my face. I hoped the cool water would help ease the queasiness in my stomach, but it did nothing of the sort.

I rubbed the barcode tattooed on my left forearm that had multiple scabs over it. Krauss left no area of my limbs untested. The barcode was like a permanent scar to me, but it felt incomparable to the physical and emotional scars from Krauss.

I looked into the mirror at the woman staring back at me. I haven't seen my reflection in five months. The only thing recognizable was my eyes, yet even those appeared dull and bloodshot. I had dark bags underneath, and the entire area seemed to have sunk inward, like they too were curling away from the horrors Krauss had done to me. My hair looked like brunette dreadlocks, as it hadn't been brushed or thoroughly washed in months. Maybe Barbara had brushed my hair at one point, but I doubted it.

I stared at myself. How was I ever going to be the same person I was before all of this? Krauss had brought me to my lowest point. He still had Miles. I might have my memories and the missing pieces to my life back, but I felt anything but whole.

CHAPTER THIRTEEN

I LEFT THE BATHROOM and took the same seat next to Liam. I wrapped the blanket around my shoulders and tucked my knees underneath me, covering my bruises and scabs. The plane's cab suddenly felt too enclosed.

My dad came over and knelt in front of me. His khakis were covered with orange remnants from the desert, and I wondered how they had gotten to the prison, but I stayed quiet.

My dad was alive.

"My little girl." My dad's eyes swelled with tears as he looked at me.

"I'm okay, Dad," I said. He leaned forward and hugged me. I stiffened, unsure of both the unease and comfort growing inside me. Each time I blew out my candles on my birthday, I had wished for him to be back. Joe had become a part of my life and was a wonderful stepfather and I loved him, but no one could replace my dad. I wanted both of them in my life.

"I thought you were dead." I sniffled as I finally hugged him back.

"I am so sorry. I never intended for you to get hurt. All I ever wanted was for you to be safe," he said and I slowly pulled away.

"How are you—what's going on?" I stumbled over my words. My dad squeezed my hand before taking the seat across from me.

"I'll be over there if you need me," Liam said. I wanted to tell him he didn't need to leave, but I couldn't get the words out quick enough.

"Alan—" My dad cleared his throat. "Dr. Roulings contacted me and told me what happened. Though, he should have gotten a hold of me sooner." His gaze flicked over to Frank, who sat on the other side of the plane.

"It is not like you are an easy person to get a hold of," Frank said.

My dad gave him a look before continuing. "I use multiple burners and often have limited to no cell reception. I move around and stay off the grid. I thought that was the best chance for you and your mom to have a normal life and stay safe." His eyes saddened at the mention of Mom. "A lot of dangerous people were after me—the worst that I was aware of was Killian. They want the original serum I created as well as the one I gave to your mom, which is what makes you special. No one was supposed to know about you or her. Killian must have found out that your mom had been ill, and if he knew from what, then he would've also discovered the disease could be inherited genetically."

"Frank told me," I said. Back at the gas station, Frank had told me my mom fell ill while she was pregnant with me. It was terminal, and she wouldn't have had survived long enough to reach full term. My dad created a second serum after destroying the first one and saved both our lives. My dad hadn't suspected that the serum had affected me until I fell ill when I was young with the same disease that my mom had. The serum had fused with my DNA and runs in my blood, creating the Hybrian that I am.

"Did he tell you what makes you... you?" he asked.

"No."

"Good, because he shouldn't have known, though I'm sure he guessed. The serum was nearly a replicate of the first one, but it needed to change the way it affected its host. I couldn't let what the first serum did happen to your mother." My dad's voice was full of hurt. The first serum had created such a rage the person had killed multiple people and couldn't morph back. "I ran out of ideas. I was going to lose you both." He dropped his head.

"It sounds like you saved both of us." I tried to give him comfort. The remorse radiating off him was thick. I was still upset with his decision to leave and not tell us, but I had no room inside me to add any more hate or anger, especially against my own dad.

He took a deep breath and continued, "I used electric eel DNA. They're more evolved than most realize and can regenerate their tail if it's cut off. Mixed with pieces of the original formula, it intensified the electrical properties of the eel and left the power of the Hybrian while strengthening the healing factors they both had. It overpowered the black panther DNA in the original serum. Except this one was supposed to be short-term and not cause the same rage as the original serum. I never wanted this life for you, and I never meant to bring pain to you or your mom." He swallowed. "Somehow Killian had either gotten a hold of or learned how to recreate the black panther Hybrian serum over the years."

Black panther DNA? That would explain the others' appearances. I shook my head. It was a lot of information, and I wasn't sure I was ready to process any of it in my current state. I pressed on but focused on my dad.

"Mom told me your fishing boat got caught in a storm and they couldn't find you among the wreckage. Alcorp faked my death—did they fake yours?"

"No, and technically it wasn't the organization that faked yours either." My dad glanced at Frank. "Dr. Roulings and I faked your death with the help of Dodge—a friend we met during our work in the military. It was the only time I came home. The world could not know about you." He emphasized the last few words with great importance and grief. "For mine, Dr. Roulings helped me, along with an old friend I went fishing with. My body lost at sea after a boat wreck during a storm was a good alibi. It's hard to find a body, and the people after me wouldn't look too much into it."

"Mr. Henry," I added, remembering the man my mom mentioned he went out fishing with when I was little. They found him floating on a life ring. He had moved to the opposite side of the States after the incident. "What about the body they found in the fire that was supposed to have been me?" I shuddered at my question.

"It was a fake. We had the autopsy forged."

Relief flooded me. I couldn't take it if my father had used someone else's body, even if they had already been dead. "And Frank? If he was helping you, why did he take me?"

My dad raised an eyebrow in question before realizing who I meant. He knew him as Alan Roulings.

"He helped look after you from a distance when I couldn't be around. When you became older and were in the range of morphing, we had to hide you. Adolescence tends to be the optimal time when the body accepts the change. Putting you into Dr. Roulings' Ject program was the best option. We had no clue how it was going to affect you—we just assumed it would. He would send me updates."

I looked at Frank. "That's why my name was changed and the others kept theirs?"

He nodded.

Isa still sounded off, but only because it felt like Harper had been given to me as a nickname and no one had used my birth name during the five years in the Vault. Krauss hadn't known it was me until he saw me in person, and Avery only knew me as Harper. Besides Frank, no one knew who I really was... except maybe...

"Dr. Cole." She had mentioned that I was like my father. "Did she know who I was? And why the name Harper?" I asked my dad.

"Yes. She knew who you were. She's one of the select few I trust. Dr. Roulings had kept it a secret. Adam hadn't known exact details, but for obvious reasons, a few others had suspected you were special. She worked with me when I started Westbrook and knew everything that Dr. Roulings and I had worked on in the military. I have a lot to tell you." My dad stared at me like I was a lost yet newly found puppy. "And as far as the name, I think that was a little bit of payback. I didn't get a say in your name in the Vault." He put a hand on my knee and gently squeezed. "Your real name, Isa, means strong-willed."

His gaze shifted to Frank.

"It is my middle name, dearie." Frank wore a huge grin.

Great. I was named after a man who I once hated—still hated. My dad made it sound like they were still friends even though they had a falling out. He trusted him, but that didn't mean I had to. Even though it seemed Frank had helped me, I was guarded. He hadn't done himself any favors to earn my trust, and I started to get angry the more I thought about the Vault.

"Why all the theatrics? Why not just tell me? Tell all the Jects in the program? You even showed me your office when you were pretending to be a Ject!" I looked from Frank to my dad. "You could have told Mom and me, and we could have gone with you. And the injections. Why give me those if this beast was already in me? Everything in the Vault was so controlled and outrageous. I could have said goodbye to Taco…"

"I had them give you an inhibitor at first, but I realized it would still come out eventually and it might even protect you," my dad answered.

"We created the inhibitor to have the same memory loss effect as the serum so it wouldn't interfere with the other Jects or if you ended up needing the true injection," Frank added. "The reason I took you to my office was to give you a break from your routine." Taking me to his office wasn't a trick to get me to trust him, as I had thought at the time, but that didn't change the anger I felt.

I remembered that the first year, the injections hadn't caused the sapphire blue color in my veins. They must've made the inhibitor look the same as the actual injections and must've switched it after that.

"So, you initially took my memories when they didn't need to be taken and then tried to make me turn quicker?" I asked.

"Yes and no." It was Frank who answered. "The serum was supposed to help bring on the change but also reduce the side effects. As for the memories, it was to help with the process down the road."

"Did your emotions feel wired and off right before you realized you were different?" my dad asked.

"Yes." I wanted to strangle Ellie out of jealous rage, among many other things. I shot a glance at Liam, who was looking out the window, but I knew he was listening. Everyone was—it was a small plane.

"We theorized the rage would have been worse and would have taken longer to fade without the injections." My dad shifted in his seat. I thought about what I would've been like if my emotions were more intense—*bad*.

"And I gave you a little kick start. As I mentioned, fear is a good motivator." Frank waved his hand. "Dr. Krauss has been attacking our strongholds. Who knows when he would have found the facility in Portland and taken you."

And his *kick start* was making me think they were going to kill Liam and then have Adam kill me.

"Why are you even here?" I asked Frank. He frowned, as if the question had hurt him.

This was all too much, and I just wanted to sit in silence.

CHAPTER FOURTEEN

I LOOKED OUT THE window as the plane started to descend. The plane tilted on its side, revealing the paved landing strip below. I stared at the snow-covered mountain next to it as the plane leveled out and landed. Across from the runway, a large metal door was built into the side of the mountain, and the door itself had to be two stories tall and five cars wide.

"Where are we?" I asked Liam as he sat down next to me. He held a thick winter coat with faux fur trim on the hood and a pair of winter boots.

Liam had told me that we had been flying for about a day and had stopped twice for fuel. I was surprised I hadn't woken, but exhaustion and the need to heal had knocked me out. I still ached and felt weak, but I wasn't as tired.

"Headquarters in Montana." He held out the coat and boots. "You're going to want to put these on."

My hand trembled as I took them from him. I gingerly donned the jacket and started putting on the boots. "Headquarters?"

"The Alliance has strongholds all around the world, but this one is the headquarters for Alcorp."

'What's the Alliance?" I remembered Krauss had mentioned it.

"The Alliance is our worldwide organization, but Alcorp is the subdivision for the U.S." There was pride in his voice. "Most strongholds stand alone, but there is one with a small facility."

"Facility? As in there are more places like the Vault?" I paled.

"A small one. The Alliance is working on finding recruits who need help in other parts of the country. Others will go through training at a stronghold without the Ject program." Liam glanced at the others, who stood as the plane came to a halt.

"We'll catch up," Liam told them as they all glanced our way.

The door opened, and all but my dad exited. He stayed for a brief moment and gave me a small smile before leaving. Sadly, I was more comfortable with Liam than my own father. Adam came out of the cockpit and gave me a small nod before leaving.

"Did he fly the entire time?" I doubt he would have landed us so smoothly if he'd been awake for that long.

"No, your father knows how to fly. He relieved him a couple of times." Liam looked back at me. "So does Dr. Roulings."

"Oh." I wondered if they had learned how to fly during their time in the military.

"We will go in whenever you're ready." He relaxed on the couch next to me.

"Thanks," I said and took a breath. "So, what should I expect on the inside?"

"A lot of gawking. You're a legend around here." He smiled.

"What?" I frowned.

"With your dad emerging, a lot of people know your identity and also what you can do. Word spreads quickly."

"Oh." I blushed.

"And a lot of familiar faces," he added. I raised an eyebrow at him. "From the Vault. Our little maneuver cost a lot of Jects to fall out of the program and were shown the videos of them giving consent. It was a fun time for Doc. Some went through the change and some decided to wait and see what would happen. A few opted to go to the other facility and continue their trials, even though it is very limited in how many Jects it holds."

I pursed my lips before letting a small smile slip through. "I guess they kept the secret from the wrong group, huh? They underestimated you."

"And you." He smiled, but it didn't hide the hurt in his eyes.

"Is there a warm shower inside?" I asked after a few moments.

"Yes. Along with food and your own bedroom."

I took a deep breath. "Alright. I guess we should go then before a bird tries to nest in my hair."

"Trust me. There are no birds out right now." He chuckled softly. "Alright, sunshine. Let's go." He stood and held out his hand. I slowly took it as he helped me up. "You should shower and rest when we get in. Afterward—whenever you're ready—I can show you around."

"I'll definitely shower, but I don't need any more sleep." I followed him to the door.

Liam grabbed a coat that was laying on a nearby chair and put it on. He flipped up my hood and opened the door. He closed it behind us as we stepped out onto the plowed runway.

The frigid wind burned against my exposed knees. It was cloudy, but no snow fell as we trekked toward the door. Liam went to wrap an arm around me, but I instinctively jumped at the contact, and he pulled away.

"Sorry," I mumbled and leaned into him, welcoming his support.

Once we were off the runway, our boots sank in the deep snow. Liam lowered his arm once we reached the door and punched in a code. It was marked with a thinly-lined circle and had a branch of leaves extending like wings on either side.

The heavy door lifted upward, and we stepped inside. A small shiver ran up my spine as the door shut behind us. I couldn't shake the uneasiness settling in my stomach. We were in a small corridor that had another door like the one we had just come through. My breathing picked up as my hands started to tremble. I was boxed in.

"What's wrong?" Liam put his hands on my shoulders.

"I feel"—my breath hitched and I swallowed—"like I'm trapped."

Liam dropped his hands and entered the code, opening the second door.

"Hey, it's okay." Liam turned back around and rubbed my arms.

I closed my eyes and clenched my hands, mastering the shaking. I took a deep breath and opened my eyes. I nodded at Liam, who nodded back and stepped aside.

I expected it to be similar to the Vault and also have a metallic odor like the prison. I was wrong. Sure, the ground was still concrete and the ceilings were vaulted, but the piping and vents were not exposed and the walls were painted in white and Egyptian blue. A large opening came into view as we started walking, and a couple people roamed off to our left. I tucked my head, not wanting to be seen or recognized.

"This way." Liam led me in the opposite direction and down a wide hallway.

I was thankful he wasn't parading me around in front of people. If he thought people would gawk at seeing me in general, I didn't want to see their reactions if they saw me in this state. Even though the coat provided cover, I still felt exposed knowing underneath I still wore a hospital gown.

The ceiling dropped down to a normal height the farther we went, and Liam led us up a set of stairs. The stairs kept going, but we stopped after the first set. He pulled out a small black fob, similar to the ones the sentinels had in the Vault, and held it out to me.

"This will get you into your room," he said as I took the key from him.

"Is there only one key?" I asked, examining it.

"No one else has a key to your room. Although I'm sure it can be reprogrammed, but no one here is out to hurt you. You can also lock it from the inside." He paused and waved to a door as we passed. "I'm twenty-one and you're twenty-four. There are ten rooms on each floor, and three floors. The first number is the level. Room ten is the first room."

We walked a little farther before stopping in front of a contemporary wooden door with a little black *24* on it. I held the fob halfway out toward the reader and hesitated.

"Don't worry—the rooms are nothing like the Vault, and you can't get locked in."

I pressed the fob against the scanner and the door clicked. I pushed it open and my jaw almost dropped at the modern boutique studio room. It had bunk beds in the corner by the windows, a couch, a small counter on the opposite side, a quaint but nicely done half bath, and two tall, slotted windows that were only six inches wide. It looked out over the side of the mountain and into the valley, and the view was astonishing despite the narrow windows.

"I should have swapped with your room. You can't see as far in the rooms on the other side." He smiled. "There's a women's shower down the hall with private stalls and a shared kitchen on the main floor."

I noticed a large duffle bag sitting on the bottom bunk and strode over to it. Next to it lay the red dove painting from Liam's room in the Vault. Inside the duffle were my clothes from my apartment, and I sighed in relief. I turned from the bag and picked up the painting.

"You didn't hang it up in your room?" I glanced at Liam.

"Eh." He shrugged. "I had it for a while. I figured someone else could use it."

I gave him a thankful smile and looked over the red dove on the white canvas. "Freedom, hope, strength," I mumbled as I laid it back down.

"The top bunk comes down and you can have a bigger bed if you'd like," Liam offered.

"This will do just fine, thank you."

"We cleared out everything when we had to move Chloe out of the apartment." He nodded at the bag.

"Is she here?" I perked up.

"No," Liam frowned. "She came here for a little bit but chose to stay with Brandon in Portland to help keep an eye on the Kovars'. She would have come on the rescue mission, but we didn't let her. She was pretty upset."

That made sense. Both the staying to protect the Kovars' and being upset about not being allowed to go. Chloe had become close with Brandon's parents just like I had when we worked at the café.

"I'll let you shower and rest. I'll be on the main floor if you need me. Just give me a ring." He nodded at a phone on the small table next to the small counter and mini fridge.

"When do we go get him?" I asked, wanting to leave this instant despite my frail state.

"We are doing everything we can," he answered. I had no doubt he was telling the truth, but being safe while Miles wasn't didn't sit well with me.

"Thanks, Liam." I moved to give him a hug but froze. He felt my hesitation, and I could see him hold back the urge to hug me himself.

Tears danced on the rims of my eyes. I had felt violated as Krauss' prisoner, and all the effort I had put into opening up since the Vault was gone.

I urged myself forward, tucking my head into Liam's shoulder. He wrapped his arms around me, and I let the waterworks flow. He was my best friend. We might have had bumps in the road, but we would always be there for each other, no matter what. I didn't need to hide myself from him.

CHAPTER FIFTEEN

I WORKED ON BRUSHING through my hair in the half bath of my new studio. After showering, I had made my way back to my room, wanting the privacy of my own space, even though no one had been in the showers. It took a lot of lathering to get clean and handfuls of conditioner to work out the knots in my hair. Despite the lack of nourishment, my hair had still grown and needed a good few inches taken off. There were scissors in one of the counter drawers and hair ties in the bathroom. I put my wet hair in a low pony and cut a few inches off, removing some of the dead hair.

After cleaning up the mess, I stared at the opened bathroom door. I hadn't been able to bring myself to close it, let alone completely close the door to the shower stall or the one to my room.

My palms were sweaty, and I wiped them on my leggings as I left the bathroom. I made my way over to the couch, trying to ignore my rising anxiety. My stomach grumbled, but I didn't feel like eating. Something black in the small closet near the apartment door caught my attention; I hadn't noticed it earlier. My heart caught when I realized what it was: the leather jacket Miles had given me. I pulled it on, reveling in the mixing of his scent with my own.

The clothes I wore were mine, and I was glad to be in something other than the gown. The apartment was equipped for me, and I wondered if it had been vacant the entire time I was gone. If half the Jects had come here from the Vault, they would have taken up over a quarter of the rooms, though I'm sure some would have shared.

Someone knocked at the door, causing me to jump. I mentally yelled at myself to relax.

"Harper?" Liam called softly. "I'm not bothering you, am I?"

I went over to the door and opened it. His gaze flitted to the rolled-up washcloth I had used as a door stop.

"Of course not." Maybe his company could ease my anxiety.

"Someone is very eager to talk to you." He pulled out his phone. "Are you up for a video chat?"

The screen showed multiple messages from Chloe, asking about me.

"Yes." I waved him in.

He stepped inside and hit the video button. Chloe answered on the first ring.

"Remember what we talked about," Liam warned her and gave me the phone. I imagined it was along the lines of not asking me a million questions.

"Harper! I'm so glad you're okay! I wish I was there. I'm coming to visit"—she looked at Liam behind me—"in a couple of days once you're rested. I know it's all so overwhelming."

"I'm glad to see you're okay, too." I had to force a smile even though I was truly glad. "I love the new hair." Her new bob-cut looked cute on her and made her look older.

"Oh!" Chloe grabbed a strand of hair. "Thank you. I needed a change."

"Well, it looks good." I realized I didn't recognize her surroundings. "So, I've heard you've been staying at Brandon's?"

"Yes." She blushed. "With the two of you missing... it was hard. I didn't want to be alone and needed somewhere to stay. We both worried about his parents, and I figured at least by working at the café, I could help keep an eye on things. I was at headquarters for a little bit and worked on training—I figured that would help. After getting my memories back and with everything going on, I decided not to restart the treatments—I can be the girl version of Adam."

"You'll need to work on your accent," I said, forcing a smile at my lame joke.

"I'll start today." Chloe grinned. "Brandon says hi also, but he's currently at work. We would have flown out right away if..." she paused. "We both would be there right now if we had our way."

"I know you guys would be." If Brandon's parents weren't possibly in danger and Liam didn't want to give me time to adjust, things would've been different. Our adventure at the cabin and journey in Portland had created a close friendship amongst the four of us. "I'm sure you enjoyed the training, and the Kovars' are lucky to have you around."

"The training wasn't the same without you." Chloe sighed. "I guess I should let you rest. Liam put my number in your phone—call me whenever you want to. I'll see you soon."

"Tell Brandon I'm sorry..." *for not bringing Miles home.* "I'll talk to you soon. Bye, Chloe." I gave her a brief smile and handed the phone back to Liam. I missed her and was happy to see she was safe. I felt bad I wasn't peppier, but I didn't feel like myself, and I'm sure she understood.

Liam waved goodbye to Chloe and hung up, shoving the phone back into his black cargo pants.

"Are my mom and Joe okay? Do they know I'm okay?" I asked, having no clue what they'd been told.

"They're safe. I got off the phone with them not too long ago. They can't wait to see you again, but I told them it might be a while. We have operatives watching them."

"Operatives?" I asked.

Liam rubbed his chin. "Think of them like FBI agents, only they work for Alcorp and the Alliance. They can be a Hybrian or trained personnel."

"So they're members?" I'd heard the word members mentioned before, but not operatives.

"Yes," Liam answered. "It's interchangeable. Anyone who devotes themselves to the Alliance and anyone that operates under the Alliance is an operative. Like Maya, Travis, Adam, and I. And you... if you want to be."

"I'll think about it." I wasn't going to give myself any titles, but I was going to fight to get Miles back. "Does my mom know about my dad?"

"No. He doesn't want to overwhelm her. Doc did talk to her, though. He gave her a light version of what happened in the Vault. He didn't mention anything about the serum, Hybrians, or your powers, just that he was trying to protect you from people that may have wanted to cause you harm for being the daughter of Benjamin Westbrook. He told her that the things they worked on in the military were top secret and for some reason, they might go after you."

"She didn't question it?" I didn't see my mom buying that.

"Oh, she did, but Doc didn't say anything else. He said that he couldn't say anything else to protect you, her, and Joe."

"I see you've been using Travis' nickname for him." Travis had called him Doc at the fishery—which seemed so long ago.

"It's actually what most of us call him." He shrugged. "I should let you rest."

"I still don't trust him." I sighed. "And I'm not going to fall asleep. I had plenty of sleep on the plane. How about that tour?"

"Only if you're up to it." He eyed me curiously.

"We'll find out."

He glanced down at my bare feet. "Want any shoes? The floors are cold."

"I think I'll pass. I'm surprised you're wearing shoes inside." Everyone I would encounter knew about the Vault and would understand.

"I actually hadn't realized how much I missed shoes—besides when fighting or training." Liam grinned.

He led me past the door we'd entered the facility through and to an area he called the main floor. It had massive floor to ceiling windows shaped in narrow slits like my room. They overlooked the valley, and I wondered if the six inches were for protection. No one was fitting through them.

"How do you build something like this?" I whispered to Liam as we walked past a few people I didn't recognize, and sure enough, they were staring.

"Good question." Liam led me over to the windows. "From what I know, Alcorp used some pre-built places for their strongholds and facilities."

"Like the Vault," I noted.

"Precisely. Some were dated Alliance buildings that were restored. The Alliance was founded long before Alcorp and revolted against menticide torture and experimenting."

"My dad wasn't behind this?" If the buildings were so old that they needed to be restored, then the Alliance had been around for a while.

"The Hybrian aspect, yes, he started that, but trying to create super soldiers, no. I'm not sure on details, though."

I sighed. "So Frank doesn't own Alcorp then either?"

"No. No one technically owns it, but he's basically the CEO or president. He is the founder, and it's named after him—Alan. They even have a board." Liam sounded so sure of this *Alcorp*.

"Isn't that Harrison guy the CEO?" I thought back to the man in the suit I had threatened after we had found the Vault empty.

"No. He's my associate," Frank said from behind us. "I hope you found your suite to be comfortable."

"Where's my dad?" I asked.

"He's in communications." Frank pointed around the bend. "If you have any questions, I'll be in my office." He gestured up toward a second-floor lofted office opposite the long, slotted windows. The office wall closest to us was entirely made up of glass.

"I'll take you to your dad." Liam started toward another bend and I followed, leaving Frank behind.

Around the bend, two rows of computers faced a large screen made up of multiple TVs. It looked like something you'd see in NASA. Adam sat at one of the desks, and behind him were my dad, Travis, and Maya.

"Harper!" A familiar voice stopped me from walking. I turned to see a man with sleek black hair walking toward us with a young bald man in tow.

"Blake? Jeremiah?" I thought I'd never see them again. If I was being honest, I haven't thought about them in the last few months.

"I told ya you weren't going to scare her away from us for good," Blake slapped Jeremiah on the shoulder.

Blake acted as if he were going to go in for a hug, but then his gaze shifted behind me. Liam probably gave him a warning not to. I would have to thank him later.

"You're the talk of the town." Blake attempted one of his goofy grins, but it didn't reach his eyes.

"So I've heard. Are you guys...?" They hadn't gone through the change the last time I had seen them, and I wondered if they had afterward.

"Yes. Both of our bodies accepted the change. Pretty cool, huh? We went to another facility and continued our trials, but after everything, it took less than a week. The rage on this one." Blake tapped Jer's chest, and he frowned in return.

"Only he would think turning into an animal is cool. Well, and Travis," Jer said, rolling his eyes.

"Careful, Blake, or she'll shock you down a few pegs," Travis said as he came over, giving me a friendly wink.

"We're very relieved to see you're alright, Harper." Jer smiled. "We won't keep pestering you. I'm sure you have a lot on your plate right now."

"Thanks for saying hi." I nodded as they turned and left.

Blake seemed a little reserved, and I had a feeling it was because of me. I'm sure *the talk* wasn't just about my powers but about what I had just gone through. I looked like I was dragged through a sewer—at least I didn't smell like one anymore.

"I didn't expect to see you up," Travis said kindly, and I noticed Blake wasn't the only one acting differently around me. Normal Travis was always full of mockery and jokes—no matter the circumstance.

"Liam's giving me a tour."

A woman with long brunette hair walked by us. The tips of her hair had looked like they'd been dipped in turquoise paint. She talked into an earpiece as she scrolled across a tablet.

"Ellie?" I recognized her, but her hair was no longer bright blond.

"Yes?" she said, turning and looking up from the tablet. Her dark blue eyes went wide when she saw me. They flitted to Liam and then back to me. "I'm sorry. I didn't mean to interrupt."

"You didn't... I just thought I recognized your voice."

"I'm glad they were able to get you out. It must have been miserable. I can't imagine."

"It was," I blurted without thinking.

She blushed. "I didn't mean to upset you. It wasn't meant like—"

"It's okay," I said. "I didn't mean to say that. I'm just thankful I was rescued."

"Me too. We all are." She smiled, the dark circles etched underneath her eyes becoming more noticeable. "Well, I have to get back to helping Rome with a system error. It was nice to see you again."

"Like Italy's Rome?"

"Yes," she said and went to walk away.

"Ellie." I took a couple steps toward her. "I'm sorry for what I did to you in the Vault. I hope there's no hard feelings between us."

"No. I'm just a little engulfed with this system failure." She gave me a nod and walked away.

"She's still upset with me," I said to no one in particular.

"She has a lot on her plate," Liam said. "She's been our main IT person."

"She was resourceful in the Vault." She had helped Liam plan the escape.

"She'll go with us on missions and be our eyes in the van also," Liam added.

"Why didn't she do that for you guys when you came for us?" I asked.

Liam frowned. "We didn't want more people than necessary to be there in case something went wrong."

"My dad and Frank?" I raised an eyebrow at him.

He shrugged. "We didn't have a say."

The three of us headed over to the others. Ellie had settled at a computer in the other row, typing away on the keyboard.

"Hey, beautiful," Maya said as we approached. Her voice was chipper, but her eyes didn't gleam. It felt like no one knew how to act around me, and I wished they would just be their normal selves—besides any touching.

"Hey," I said, trying my best to be cheerful. I glanced up at the large screen made up of multiple TVs. It showed a map of northern China and southeast Mongolia. Most of it was desert.

"The Gobi Desert," Travis said from his spot behind me.

"It's where the prison is, but someone edited the footage so it looks like nothing's there," Adam added.

"That's where Miles is?"

"It was," my dad answered.

"Was?" I glanced at him.

"They would've moved him by now." My dad's face softened.

Two computers sat in front of Adam. One had the map on it while the other had multiple profiles with names below the pictures. I recognized the majority of them. Krauss, Avery, Damien, and Barbara were among them. Hate seared inside me as I glared at the screen.

"We have to check." I looked at Liam. "You said there's more operatives—strongholds around the world. Why didn't more come to get us? If apparently what he can take from me is so important and dangerous, why didn't you guys send an army?"

Liam drew in a breath and gave me a sympathetic smile. "If we had more people, then they would have known we were coming. We needed to be inside the prison before they knew we were there. It was a rescue mission, not an assassination. The two of you were our priority, and if we went all out, there would've been casualties."

His logic made sense, but my heart didn't want to comprehend it. I looked back at the screen with the profiles and stared at Krauss. My hands balled at my sides, and I felt the surge rise in my chest. My eyes had changed, and my hatred for him rose off me like fog from dry ice. The screen flickered along with a couple of lights, but I was too focused on Krauss' picture to look up.

I will find you.

CHAPTER SIXTEEN

SIX MONTHS LATER...

THE AIR WAS STALE and damp as my body hummed with electricity. Unconscious bodies were scattered throughout the old hostel being used as one of Krauss' outposts. The Rogue at my feet struggled in his attempt to crawl away. He had already been debilitated from the electric fireball I struck him with when he had attempted to flee. I kicked him over onto his back and knelt over him.

"Where is he?" I fisted his shirt, fully aware my eyes were radiating like blue plasma orbs.

The fear in the Rogue's eyes told me he had heard of me, but now wished he had never met me. My reputation was spreading around the hidden world of the Hybrians. The electricity I emitted was now known as electric fire. The normal Hybrian eye color was orange-yellow with slight variations when morphed, and mine was blue.

The Rogue's lids started to close.

"Don't you dare pass out on me!" I shook him fiercely and delivered an extra zap through my fingertips against his collarbone, but he still lost consciousness.

"Worthless." I sighed and released him, letting his head fall to the ground.

"A bit harsh, don't ya think?" Dylan's voice echoed from the com in my ear. Dylan had a front row seat through the camera on the collar of my leather jacket.

"Call for a cleanup." I wiped the blood from my mouth where a Rogue had nailed a right hook, the only decent hit one of the Rogues had gotten on me.

I exited the old hostel and met Dylan in the grey van parked on the side of the street. No one was around to notice me leave despite the early hour, and no one would notice when members of the Alliance arrived to clean up my mess and take in the Rogues. All of them were alive despite my inclinations.

I climbed into the driver's seat, subconsciously checking the magazine in my gun and clipping it back on my hip. There were the same number of bullets as there had been before I went into the hostel—none had been needed. I pivoted in my seat to look at Dylan, who was turning off his laptop in the back of the van. The Paris stronghold had let us borrow their surveillance van, which came with its own computer, but Dylan preferred to use his.

"He called again." Dylan made his way to the front passenger seat and adjusted his black-framed glasses back into place.

"Which one?" I started driving, heading in the direction of the stronghold.

"Well, your father hasn't called since last night," Dylan said. "But he's called three times today."

I focused on the narrow road lit by the antique streetlamps lining the curb. Ever since we left—or snuck off—Liam had called multiple times a day. He still tried my phone first but would try Dylan's afterward, knowing that he would answer. It wasn't fair to Liam, but I haven't been in the right mindset to talk. There had been one thing on my mind, and that was to get Miles back from Krauss.

I parked on the side of the street in front of a small library antique shop instead of pulling into the small garage connected to the side. They didn't get many customers, and someone would probably be taking the van anyway to go help clean up. I hopped out of the van and opened the shop's door for Dylan, who was carrying his backpack with his laptop.

The bells on the door chimed, and as soon as we entered, two members of the Alliance walked past us. I tossed the keys at them. They were no doubt heading to the scene I had just created, and I imagined a few others had already arrived.

I went to the narrow stairs in the back, Dylan following. If we went down, we would have wound up in a small training gym, but we went up, to the communal bar. I poured myself a drink, ignoring the stares of the people present. The members were either scared of me or idolized me. And I hated both. At least they didn't pity me like everyone had back at headquarters. Miles never pitied me.

My reputation had grown after I took down another outpost in France and two in Asia. Krauss had more of an army than anyone had imagined. With Dylan's help, the Alliance was able to snuff out a few locations. Asia was first on my list because Miles and I had been held in the Gobi Desert, but there were no signs of him there.

Dylan sat on the barstool next to me, his curly black hair slightly disheveled. I poured him a glass from the bottle sitting on the counter in front of me, but he didn't touch his either.

"It's been six months and we haven't found a single thing on Miles." We had left the States two months ago in search of him.

"You can't do this to yourself. It's okay to have help. Thor—the God of Thunder—even gets help." He grinned.

"You're lucky I took you with me." I stared at the full glass of whiskey.

Everyone had argued against my plan of going on my own to search for Miles. Dylan had too, but he also proposed another option. He said that it would be easier with his help and to take him with me because he knew I was leaving regardless. So we took off with a bunch of supplies. He's helped me more than I can thank him for.

"It has been quite the adventure," Dylan said.

Leaving headquarter hadn't been hard. Dylan had disarmed the outside alarms, and we had taken a four-wheeler to the closest town.

From there, we started our journey tracking down any leads that could potentially lead to Miles.

Dylan's tablet dinged.

"What is it?" I asked.

"There's Rogue activity in London." Dylan glanced up at me.

"We'll leave in the morning."

"Can we take a Jet?"

"No." I removed the hair tie holding my French braid in place and shook out my hair. Although the Alliance was happy to provide a jet, I preferred not to involve others in our travel. Dylan had made a device that hacked the scanners and metal detectors so it was easier to conceal my weapons. "We'll take the train."

CHAPTER SEVENTEEN

I BRUSHED PAST THE bustling people while keeping an eye out for any sign of a Rogue nearby. My ears weren't as sharp without being morphed, but I couldn't walk around with glowing blue eyes. The Red Light District of London was surprisingly not what I had expected. It had marvelous little shops, restaurants, and bars. I had expected more profanity, but I hadn't seen any besides a few neon signs here and there.

There had been attacks there at night that matched the descriptions of Hybrians. I wasn't the only one patrolling tonight, but I went my separate way from the other operatives. The London stronghold was smaller than Paris and only had eight members. They were kind and weren't bothered that Dylan and I kept to ourselves. A smaller group meant they could form a closer bond and knew how the others operated—outsiders could easily interfere with their methods.

"I'm not picking up anything on my end," Dylan said through the com. He was hunkered down at the stronghold a couple blocks away.

"Me either." The prickling at the back of my head was going off so I knew at least one of the two Hybrians from the London stronghold were nearby. It was unfortunate that we couldn't detect Rogue Hybrians, and I had a feeling Krauss had something to do with that.

As I walked, the streets became less crowded. I was nearing the end of the district and was about to turn around when I saw a woman with her hood up leave an alley. She looked around before walking away from the crowd.

I kept my distance and opted to follow her. She stopped in front of a tall building that was partially fenced and enclosed with caution tape. I briefly turned away and lowered my green hat when she looked around her, and when I turned back, she was gone.

"Crap," I muttered to myself and ran toward the building.

"Nothing good ever comes from going in a closed construction building late at night." Dylan sighed.

"Hopefully something good comes out of it for us." I ducked under the tape and placed a hand on the door, expecting it to be locked, but it opened with ease. "Here we go."

I entered a boarded-up dusty hallway and followed it until an opening came into view. Voices drifted from around the corner as I slowly crept along the wall. The static flowed from my chest to my hands as the dusty air became grittier, a woman's voice became sharper, and the dark room lightened. Something felt different about whoever was behind the walls, but I couldn't place it.

Electric fireballs swirled in each of my hands. If they weren't Rogues, I would just be scaring some trespassers, and they would think they had imagined the blue orbs—hopefully.

I took a deep breath.

"I wouldn't move if—" I rounded the corner, but I was the one who froze, my heart stopping in its place as steel eyes that had once contained green landed on me. A cool, heartless expression crossed the face of the man that I loved and longed to see again. "Miles?"

The woman had her hood down, revealing her long black hair and vibrant green highlights as she held out a manila envelope to Miles. He swiped the envelope, shoving it in a leather jacket I hadn't seen before. He quickly reached for his gun as his eyes turned an iridescent golden-green with purple flecks.

Wow.

I dove behind a nearby forklift as bullets flew past me, my hat falling off. The electric fire I yielded extinguished, but I stayed morphed.

"Is that...?" Dylan's concerned voice rang in my ear.

"Yes." I would recognize Miles anywhere, and even Dylan could spot him through the tiny camera clipped to me.

The firing ceased and I peered around the machine. Nothing. They would've had to move quickly to make it to the only other exit. I grabbed my hat from the dusty ground and started down the opposite hallway, only to immediately freeze when I heard a clank. Off to my left, a piece of wood shifted ever so slightly, and a fresh footprint appeared in the dust next to it.

Hot static surged from my hand as a flaming blue electric ball shot in that direction and the woman with green highlights flickered into form. She was still standing, but I blasted her again, knocking her to the ground.

"Did you see that?" I exclaimed as I walked over to her body, her chest rising and falling.

"Yeah. I already called for backup." Dylan normally waited for me to tell him when to contact the Alliance, but I was completely fine with him contacting them in this scenario.

"Do you have eyes on him?" I took off down the only other way Miles could've gone, leaving the unconscious girl behind.

"No, it's like he vanished." Dylan was probably thinking the same thing I was—had he gone invisible too?

I eventually ended up outside in a crowded street behind the building. Miles was nowhere to be found. I went back inside and waited by the unconscious Rogue until the others showed. They wouldn't have believed me about what I had seen if they hadn't known my story. Plus, Dylan had a recording of it.

An operative slung the girl over his shoulders and carried her outside. I followed as he weaved through the crowd outside, pretending she was passed-out drunk. Getting a van through this mess would have been pretentious and time consuming.

We neared the old cathedral stronghold, which was immaculate despite some decay and was spacious for only eight members. The fence around kept any passersby out even though the street was eerily vacant all the time. The locals knew the church had become condemned and was bought by a private rich family who prosecuted any trespassers, and rumors circulated that some trespassers never left and were never seen again. In this case, the Alliance was the rich family.

We entered through the arched doors in the front after one of the members scanned their finger. Its pointed arched mosaic windows let light shine through from the streetlamps outside. I found Dylan sitting in a pew with his laptop out. He waved me over and I turned off my com before sitting next to him.

"Check this out." Dylan showed me a view from a camera out back near the building that was under construction. It showed Miles exiting the building, momentarily pausing before becoming a blur and disappearing out of view. "I slowed it down, and if you know where to look, you can see his blur, but I can't find him anywhere else. He's almost impossible to spot if he isn't holding still."

"So he doesn't go invisible like the girl?" I stared at the screen in shock.

"No. I think he's just really fast. Not quite Flash fast, but fast nevertheless. And the girl may become invisible, but she clearly isn't intangible." Dylan eyed the members standing next to the pew talking about what had happened while three of them took the Rogue down to a holding cell.

"I have to call Liam." Heat scratched at my chest and my palms became sweaty. This meant Krauss was able to create the serum he wanted.

We were in trouble.

CHAPTER EIGHTEEN

Liam sat next to me on the private jet while the Rogue sat bound across from us. She was out cold from the sedative and the inhibitor she was given before we left Paris.

"It's like he didn't recognize me," I said. Miles hadn't thought twice before pulling his gun and firing. If I hadn't been morphed, the bullets would've hit their mark.

"No one knows what influence Krauss has had over him." Liam stared at the Rogue as if he was half expecting her to wake up.

"Who knows what other Rogues he has experimented on or created." I swallowed.

"We'll catch him. Evil has a way of getting caught up with itself." Liam glanced at his phone. It had been buzzing nonstop since he had arrived.

"Come on, Harper. You've seen the movies and shows—the bad guys get what they deserve," Dylan piped in from the other side of the jet.

"Not always." I sighed.

"I have to agree with the computer whiz over here," Travis said from his spot next to Dylan.

Liam and Travis had flown out immediately to help transport the Rogue. It took some convincing from Liam for the Paris members to let us take her back to Alcorp's headquarters. They finally agreed we could because they didn't have the capability of defending a large attack by Krauss. Krauss could deploy Rogues to get her back and even though the cathedral had security measures set up, it was nothing compared to headquarters. Frank was also eager to see what Krauss had done—not in an excited way, but in a nervous way.

We arrived at headquarters and stood outside the entrance door as Liam punched the code into the pad. I stared at the Alliance symbol—a circle with branches of leaves extending like wings on either side of it—that was on the center of the door. The symbol was designed after the Greek Goddess Soteria of safety and preservation from harm.

A wave of fresh, warm air swirled the hair that strayed from my ponytail. The mountain lacked snow during summer, much to my relief—especially during the escape Dylan and I had made. Four-wheelers had been easier than using snowmobiles.

I took a deep breath as we entered. I haven't been back once in the two months since Dylan and I had left. We made our way to the main floor where a small crowd waited for us. Travis carried the unconscious Rogue toward HQ's holding cells, and Frank gave me a nod as he turned to follow Travis. As much as I still despised Frank, he cared about my safety—something I'd never thought I'd admit.

"Isa." Arms wrapped around me and I caught a whiff of cologne.

"Hi, Dad." I hugged him back. "I know you've been concerned, but I promise I can take care of myself—and Dylan."

"Doesn't ever stop me from worrying." He smiled, his dimples showing. I slowly pulled away from his hug, trying to hide my spike of anxiety from being touched. It didn't matter who it was, my hair stood on end and goose bumps rose at contact from anyone.

Off to my side, I saw Liam give Ellie a small smile. She nodded in return. Jer gave Dylan the man gesture of a pat on the back, and Dylan's cheeks reddened before turning to the others to say hi. They both had developed feelings for each other over the four months of my recovery there. However, Dylan would only admit to me that he had a *thing* for Jeremiah.

I had enlisted in Dylan's help to find Miles after first arriving at headquarters, knowing his skills would be useful. Frank had said he was better than any of the FBI members, or anyone in Alcorp for that matter. He had invited Dylan to stay permanently, and he happily accepted the offer.

I made my way past everyone and went straight to my room on the second floor. As much as I wanted to completely shut the door behind me, I couldn't bring myself to do it. I went over to the couch and lay down. My breathing picked up as I rubbed my sweaty hands on my black cargo pants and stared at the ceiling. Miles had been in the same room with me last night, and I had lost him—again.

Someone knocked on my door, and I forced myself to slow my breathing. Once my emotions were under control, I went over and opened the door the rest of the way.

"Want company, sunshine?" Liam asked, glancing at my hand, which firmly gripped the edge of the door.

"That might be a good idea." I loosened my grip and waved him through, leaving the door cracked.

I sat on the couch, pulling my knees to my chest.

"He's different." I couldn't get the way Miles' eyes had changed and that he had looked at me like I was a stranger.

"But alive." Liam had seen the video on the jet. The details weren't crystal clear, but with Alcorp's technology, the cameras were top quality. "A bunch of us are worried about you, Harper. I'm worried about you."

I risked a glance at Liam. He hadn't used my nickname, which meant he had set all joking aside

"I'll be okay. Dr. Cole gave me a clean bill of health before I left."

"Yes—physically." He sat down next to me, his brows creasing.

"You guys would've talked me down or tried to come. I could keep Dylan out of the immediate action, but I wouldn't have been able to do that with you or the others." I placed my hand over his. "I'm sorry for worrying you, but I won't stop until Miles is safe. Until everyone is safe from Krauss."

"You can't take on the world alone." He returned the gesture by placing his hand over mine and squeezing gently. "Whatever Krauss is doing is huge, and he can't be doing it alone."

"Which is why he needs to be stopped."

Liam and I sat together for about an hour, catching up on what I had missed there and filling him in on my trip, until he left to go see what information they had gotten from the Rogue. After he left, I decided to take a long, hot shower. I grabbed my things and made my way to the women's showers down the hall. I propped open the door with a doorstop that had suddenly appeared after I had used a towel a few times—complements of either Liam or Maya.

I went into the stall with doubled curtains, closing them behind me. My dad had replaced the privacy door with the curtains after hearing I would leave the stall door open a crack. The stall was always dry, so I assumed I was the only one who used it anyway. The hot water felt nice, but it wasn't comforting like I had hoped.

I placed my hands on the wall and let the water run down my back. Crimson red started to swirl down the drain at my feet, and one glance at my body showed needles sticking out from everywhere. Pricks of pain etched my skin, leaving no area untouched. I squeezed my eyes shut and felt the static hum around me as I tried to make the false images and pain disappear. I opened my eyes just as the light flickered above. The humming ceased as I took deep breaths and the imaginary blood disappeared.

This wasn't my first panic attack, nor would it be my last. My first one had occurred the second time I had been in the showers. The same thing had happened, except the pain and panic were more intense. I had started screaming, and all of the lights in the room flickered and the bulbs burst. Blood had been everywhere, and Krauss would appear with a wicked grin on his face and then suddenly vanish, his laugh echoing off the walls.

Liam had run in after hearing my screams. He had quickly turned off the water and grabbed my towel from the hook, covering me. Despite getting zapped, he had wrapped his arms around me and had held me tightly until my episode had passed. After my screaming had ceased, I broke down crying in his arms until my limbs felt numb.

"I should have ended it," I had mumbled into his shoulder.

"There was nothing you could have done." Liam's voice had been soft.

"At Macleay Park. Miles would be safe, I wouldn't be an obligation, and Krauss wouldn't have gotten what he needed. No one here would be in danger—you wouldn't be in danger."

Liam had stiffened before squeezing me tighter. He knew what I had meant by those words. One swift motion by my hand with the knife...

"You are never an obligation." Liam had pulled his arms away to move his hands to my face, softly forcing me to look at him. "Harper, listen to me. I want to live in a world with you in it—you are more than my best friend. We love you, you are our family, and *nothing* will ever change that. None of what is going on is your fault. Don't ever think that." He let go and wrapped his arms back around me. Liam was amazing, and I was broken. I didn't deserve him.

I focused on the present and hit the wall with my palm before running my hands over my face. I needed to pull myself together. Not just so I could get Miles back, but so I would stop hurting everyone around me. I finished showering and changed, then headed to the lounge area on the main floor where most everyone was.

Dylan had his laptop open on the end table next to him while he talked with Jer. Travis and Maya were intent on their game of Ping-Pong. The table had been brought in after their arrival as a gift from Frank. Those two loved this game. Adam and Liam weren't around, and I assumed they were talking with our new guest. As much as I wanted to interrogate her, I needed to stay away until I had a clear mind. Maybe tomorrow.

"Who's winning?" I took a seat near Travis and Maya.

"Who do you think?" Maya smirked.

"I'm just going easy on her. I figured she needed to win once in a while after losing all of her training sessions with Adam," Travis said. Adam still trained Maya, but even using her beast, she only won once in a while.

"Travis, when are you going to accept a loss?" I jested back.

"I don't lose." Travis grinned as he hit the ball and it spun off the table on Maya's side. "Point."

I couldn't help but laugh. I really did miss my friends and couldn't wait until things would be fine—if they ever would be.

Maya ended up winning, and they started a new match as Dylan headed in my direction, his brows creased.

"Hey." He knelt next to me, his auburn eyes containing a cautionary gleam. "I got a hit on a private plane entering the States. I think it belongs to Krauss. I think it might be Miles."

CHAPTER NINETEEN

T HE SLEEK NAVY-BLUE YAMAHA motorcycle roared as I headed south of Portland. The scent of pine and leather filled the helmet, making my heart squeeze. If Miles was back in the States, there was a possibility he might show up at his grandparents' house. Rose and Russell should be warned that he might be under the influence of the person that captured us. They didn't know the details about our five-month absence together, just that the person Miles was helping me hide from had captured us. I had delivered Rose the news that Miles was still missing over the phone after I had arrived at headquarters.

I turned down the long drive lined with trees with white bark and branches heavy with luscious green leaves. The beautiful white farmhouse came into view, and I parked the bike off to the side.

I had warned them I was coming this morning after Dylan informed me about Miles potentially being back in the States. I hadn't wanted them to think it was Miles on his bike. Something about riding it provided me with security and sentimentality.

I climbed off the bike and went up the stairs. Before I could knock, the red door opened.

"Harper!" Rose opened the screen door and immediately gave me a hug. I bit the inside of my cheek, telling myself not to freak out. Everyone else had known not to hug me.

"How are you doing?" I pulled away and looked at her.

"I should be asking you that, dear." The rims of her eyes were red as she scanned me, and she looked thinner than the last time I was there with Miles.

"There's no need to worry about me." I smiled, thankful that I still had my jacket and jeans on to hide my scars. "I can only stay for a little bit, but I wanted to talk to you and Russell about something."

"Come in. I made homemade chicken noodle soup." She waved me in.

Rose led me to the kitchen, where Russell greeted me with a handshake and friendly smile. They welcomed me with open arms despite the fact that Miles was still missing. They weren't angry with me nor did they blame me, even though a part of me wished they did.

"Here you go, dear." Rose set a steaming bowl in front of me and then another in front of Russell. Homemade chicken noodle soup was always comforting. Chase came over and sat on my feet, his thick merle coat radiating heat through my boots.

"Thank you." I waited for Rose to sit down before continuing. "We believe Miles is back in the States."

"That's good news!" Rose's green eyes lit up, but her brows knitted when I frowned.

"He's no longer locked up but is still under the influence of the man that took us. We suspect that the man messed with his mind." I held my breath for their response.

"What does that mean?" Rose asked as Russell briefly closed his eyes behind his glasses.

"The son of a bitch still has our grandson. That's what it means. He brainwashed him." Russell stared at his untouched bowl.

"When I saw him, he attacked me," I said gently. "He didn't hesitate."

Tears started to flow down Rose's cheek, and Russell reached out to hold her hand.

"He might come back here, but I need you guys to understand he is not himself, and to call me or the other number I gave you." They both gave a knowing nod. I had given them my father's number when we first talked because I wasn't stable—plus, he would be able to send someone out more easily than I could've. "I'm sorry I don't have any more information for you. But he is alive, and I am going to get him back."

"Dear, you need to keep yourself safe too. Our Macky wouldn't want you to get hurt. He would want you to stay as far away as possible from this man that took you." Rose wiped away the tear on her cheek with her hand not being held by Russell's.

"He shouldn't be in this position." I leaned off the table and folded my hands in my lap. "He was only trying to keep me safe."

"He took an oath to protect and serve. It's in the MacLand blood to never go back on an oath or fail to help anyone in need," Russell added and leaned over, kissing Rose on the temple. This side of him was new to me—he was normally grumpy, and my heart ached knowing the devastation it was causing them.

"We are also beyond graced that he has met you." Rose smiled. "I haven't seen him that happy in years. If anyone can bring him back, it's you. But that doesn't mean you go put yourself in harm's way, dear. Do you understand?"

I nodded, knowing she wouldn't take a no for an answer.

She narrowed her eyes, not fully convinced. "Good. Now let's eat and talk about something cheerful because this grief won't do any of us any good."

"You're here!" Chloe stood at the pool table and spotted me as soon as I entered. Mel's Pub wasn't packed, but was still busy for a Wednesday night. I walked over to Chloe and Brandon.

"I said I would be." Thankfully, I didn't have to yell over the mixed Irish and pop music.

"Glad you made it." Brandon smiled, his blond hair slightly disheveled.

Chloe awkwardly stood there, wanting to give me a hug. The first time she had seen me at headquarters, Liam had warned her about my aversion. Sadly, at that time I hadn't had it in me to give her one.

"Come here." I held my arms out and she let a grin slip as she strode toward me. When she pulled away, I didn't shudder like I had expected. "Your hair is growing out."

"A little bit. I might get it cut again." She ran a hand through her hair, which now fell just below her chin. It suited her.

"Hope you're hungry. I just ordered wings and pizza." Brandon laid his pool cue on the table. "Kat will be here shortly." I had kept Kat updated, and she happened to be there in Portland with her girlfriend until they leave for New York City in the morning. Frank had recruited her to work alongside the Alcorp FBI members and wanted more personnel covering NYC.

"I'm not that hungry. I just wanted to see you guys while I was nearby." I had filled them in on my run-in with Miles.

"You used to eat pizza like it was your job. I'm not going to let you stop now." Brandon waved a hand in the air.

"I agree with what blondie said." Chloe put her arm around Brandon's shoulders.

"Alright, shorty." Brandon bent his knees so he was Chloe's height. They laughed and made their way over to the booth.

"So you two are official." I slid into the seat across from them. Chloe had been staying with him since I was taken.

"We are." She leaned over and gave him a quick kiss on the lips.

I was thankful they were happy together and were able to joke, but I also saw the sorrow they carried—especially Brandon. He was still his natural outgoing self, but it seemed slightly forced.

After dinner, I decided to stop at Miles' place to check things out. Brandon and Chloe suggested it was a bad idea after I was his bullseye, but I had told them I wouldn't be long. It was unlikely Miles was in Portland.

Everything was untouched. A dishwasher held a few dirty plates, expired milk sat in the fridge, curtains had been drawn on the enormous windows, and his laundry basket was full. I plugged my nose and opted to dump the chunky spoiled milk down the drain. I was surprised no one had come to check on his apartment, especially Kat or Brandon.

The door was propped, but I had the safety chain in place. I would hear that break if Miles or anyone else entered. After cleaning up and tossing the garbage bag full of spoiled food near the door, I went to his bedroom and grabbed a plain t-shirt from the laundry basket. I clutched the shirt against my chest, allowing myself a few minutes to let go of any composure I had before leaving his apartment.

Normal people would think that I was crazy and psychotic, but what I had been through wasn't the typical person's day, let alone months—or even years.

CHAPTER TWENTY

I HADN'T NEEDED TO worry about Miles finding me in his apartment; a camera had picked him up at a motel in Norfolk, Virginia and I was on my way to confront him along with the others.

Dylan was able to monitor the motel lobby from its unsecure Wi-Fi camera system. Miles hadn't been seen entering it again in the last five hours. They had picked me up at a closed airport that Alcorp owns just outside of Portland as soon as Dylan had seen the alert.

I descended the jet's stairs onto the runway where a man in a suit, an SUV, and two motorcycles were waiting.

"What? Alcorp doesn't have a private hangar in Norfolk?" I snorted as I strode toward the sleek Ducati.

"Not yet," Travis stepped around an oil spot on the ground, avoiding getting his tan combat boots dirty.

Liam followed me over to the bikes after talking with the man in the suit.

"Here you are." He held out the key to the Ducati.

"Trusting me, are we?" I asked, taking it.

"I heard you had experience while overseas. That and I suppose you were given a license." He smiled, but it faded as his gaze traveled to the bike then back to me. "Yes. I am."

"I was able to find him—just not save him." I frowned. "That might be more than I can handle alone."

Liam nudged my shoulder.

"No one will outrun you on that." Travis whistled and slapped the seat of the Ducati.

"I'm riding in that, right?" Dylan nervously looked from the bikes to the SUV.

"What? You don't want to ride with Harper?" Maya shrugged off her denim jacket and tossed it over her shoulder.

"I think I once referred to her driving as atrocious," Dylan replied.

"If I recall correctly, you said it wasn't that bad." I couldn't believe that conversation was almost a year ago.

"That's in a car." Dylan reached for his tablet that attached to the back side of his lightweight backpack.

"Fair." I glanced over at the Ducati and then back at the others. "Should we head out?"

"Yes. We'll meet at the rendezvous." Liam nodded at me and went over to the other bike while the others got in the SUV.

Twenty minutes later, we all stood in the parking lot at the small doughnut shop near the motel Miles had been spotted checking into. We had each driven separate ways and parked in different spots to ensure we weren't flagged by Miles or one of Krauss' crew. Large grass bushes lined the mulch bed full of weeds that separated the parking lots of the shop and the motel. I hoped it would give us enough cover.

"Alright. Everyone knows what to do." Liam looked between each of us and then to Dylan, who was watching surveillance from the SUV with the door open. He gave us a thumbs up.

I pushed through the bushes, heading to the motel's lobby entrance. The others were going to cover all sides of the motel. My boots were barely audible against the cracked pavement. The cement under the entry canapé was crumbling, and the siding was flaking. This was the type of motel you'd stay at not to be noticed.

I grabbed the chipped handle and opened the unleveled door. Multiple bells chimed above my head as I stepped onto the worn green carpet lining the small square office. It smelled like chlorine despite no advertisement for a pool on site.

The woman sitting behind the counter didn't look up from her magazine as she scratched her head, her hand getting lost in her frizzed, light-ash-colored hair. The camera that had showed Miles checking in was blurry, but this was definitely the same lady.

"Excuse me." I put on a huge lovesick smile as she looked up. "Hi. I'm here to surprise my boyfriend."

Her gaze slowly looked over my black skinny cargo jeans, loose white crop-top, and black boots. The style was in, and the pants along with the boots were basic operative attire when in the field. I wasn't sure why I decided to match them, but I could fit so many things in the pant pockets and the boots were versatile—stylish, comfy, and runnable on any terrain.

"Uh-huh." She finally found my face.

"He has black hair, beautiful hazel eyes, tall... strong." I twirled the end of my French braid in my fingers. "He got in yesterday. I can show you a picture." I reached for my phone, pulling up a photo.

"Hard to forget a face like that." She looked back down at her magazine.

"Do you know what room he's in?"

"I do." She didn't say anything else.

"Any way you can help me out?" I asked. "Please?"

This would be easier if she just told me.

"Will that make you leave and not come back?" Her gaze flicked to me and then back down.

"Yes."

"Room thirteen."

"Thank you." I gave her a fake warm smile even though she wasn't looking at me.

I went back outside, the bells chiming as the door closed behind me. I texted the others as I made my way down the cracked sidewalk to room 13.

I reached his room. A "Do Not Disturb" sign hung on the rusted doorknob. Liam met me and I knocked on the door. Between

Liam, Maya, Adam, Travis, and Dylan's surveillance, the motel was surrounded if he decided to flee out a bathroom window.

No answer.

I knocked one more time before settling on reaching for the pins in my hair and picking the lock. My eyes turned blue and the electricity hummed in my fingertips as I pushed open the door. The full-size bed was still made, and the only thing that showed any signs that someone had been there was an empty water bottle in the trash can.

Liam entered behind me and cleared the bathroom. He told the others the place was empty, and they met us in the room. I had begun searching for clues when Travis pulled a duffel bag out from underneath the bed.

"He's still here," I whispered as Travis pulled out clothes—the only thing in there.

"If he is, why hide the bag under the bed if it just had clothes?" Liam asked as he scanned the room.

"There has to be something else." Maya lifted the mattress but nothing was underneath it.

"I've got an idea." Dylan attached his tablet to his backpack and checked the lamp shade and then under the table. He pulled out a manila envelope with duct tape hanging off the edges.

"Ha. It's like *The Firm* or *The Mechanic*. He's pulling a Jason Statham and Tom Cruise. There's a gun underneath there too."

Travis looked. "I'll be—" The sound of tape being pulled off wood cut him off. "I would have expected it to be in the nightstand or under a pillow."

"He was expecting to come back." Liam glanced at the gun in Travis's hand.

"He might not know we're here. We could set a trap?" Maya asked.

"Uh, you might want to look at this." Dylan held out the papers from inside the envelope.

Liam took them. There were three sheets with images stapled to the top corner. Each picture had a name and home address, nothing else.

"Is that a—"

"Hit list," Liam said, answering my question. Everyone gathered around.

"What is he doing in Norfolk, Virginia?" Adam looked up at Liam. "None of the addresses are here."

"Wait. Go back to the second picture." Travis leaned closer. "Him. He's after him." Travis pointed to one of the photos. "He's the Commander of the NATO Joint Force Command."

"You know that?" Maya asked.

"Social studies buff over here, and traveling is my specialty." Travis shrugged.

"The Allied Command Center is here." Dylan's face turned pale.

"I'm betting he's here alone or the other two have a meeting with him," Travis added.

CHAPTER TWENTY-ONE

THE WARM, SALTY BREEZE wisped against my neck as I stood with Liam and Dylan on the sidewalk near the NATO Allied Command Center. Travis was stationed on the street behind, and we had left Maya and Adam back at the motel with the bikes in case Miles showed up, but I doubted he would. He probably had memorized the list, and if we didn't stop him now, we'd be too late.

Liam hung up the phone and put it in his pocket.

"We're on our own. The closest operatives won't be here on time, and Doc doesn't have anybody on the inside," he said.

"You mean with all of the connections, he has no one in NATO?" I rubbed my temple. This was going to be difficult. I'd rather get dropped in a pit full of Rogues than try to sneak into a government facility.

"He has military connections, but none that can help us here."

"We could walk up to the front gates and warn them there's going to be an attack," I offered.

"And get taken into custody while Miles eventually finds them anyway?" Liam frowned.

"Well, we need—" The sight of a motorcycle across the street stopped any words from flowing out of my mouth.

I started toward the road, checking for traffic first, and crossed.

"Harper?" Liam called after me as he and Dylan followed.

My heart slowed—if that was even possible—as I ran a finger across the bike's leather seat and over the helmet. It was the same brand

Yamaha motorcycle as Miles', except in black. I picked up the black helmet, turning it upside down, and glanced around to make sure no one was watching. I let my beast out just long enough to pick up the scent of pine and leather. My heart skipped a beat.

"He's here." I glanced at Liam. "And he's probably already inside."

"Then we need to hurry." Liam turned around to cross the street.

"The cameras hadn't picked him up." Dylan pulled out his tablet. He had done a scan earlier which had come up empty. "But if he's moving as fast as he did in Paris, then they wouldn't have."

We moved toward the front of the large two-story building with multiple flags posted in the front lawn, each flag representing each allied country.

"I've got an idea." Liam eyed a group of high schoolers following their teacher down the sidewalk past us toward the Center. "Dylan, I'll need you to be my eyes inside. Harper, be my eyes out here. Travis?"

"Still here," Travis said through the coms in our ears.

"I'm going in. Keep an eye out for anything odd. Remember, he moves fast." Liam took a step toward the group, but I grabbed his arm, pulling him back.

"You look suspicious." I waved up and down at his all-black attire, then to mine. "I'm dressed more appropriately."

"She's kind of right about that." Dylan adjusted his glasses.

"Also, if anyone can get through to Miles, it's probably not you." I put a hand on his shoulder before walking backward and giving him a salute.

"Harper..." Liam grumbled as I blended in with the crowd. "Be careful."

I followed at the back edge of the group, thankful they were all too into their phones or the hype of a field trip to notice me. The poor teacher looked flustered as she ushered everyone inside the large entryway and spoke with the guard standing outside, not even glancing at me.

The teacher shut the door and walked around the big group and through the door leading inside. I noticed the metal detectors that arched over each doorway and paused. I still had my knives and gun on me. I silently cursed, wishing I had Dylan's device, but I had left it behind because we took Alcorp's jet.

If I held out my hands, I would be able to send a charge to the detector, frying it. However, the guard on the other side would notice that the light would turn off, and I needed a distraction. I was next to file through the door.

In front of me, two boys were messing with a group of girls. I sent a quick bolt around the two boys in front of me and to the group of girls in front. It hit one of them and she yelped and turned around with fury in her eyes. She glared at the boys behind her and started going off on them.

Perfect. The guard was watching the verbal quarrel, along with everyone around me. I reached both arms, touching the smooth plastic panels of the detector before going underneath. At the contact, I sensed something different with the static emitting from the electricity contained inside the scanner. It called to me, and I almost reached for it before remembering what my mission was. It could set off an alarm.

I released my own static waves through the panels. The path stayed connected to my fingertips like a taut string until I found the area emitting the electricity. I summoned a little more energy, shutting the machine down. I breathed out once I was through with no alarms and no one glancing my way. I'd be gone before the guard noticed it wasn't working, and they wouldn't suspect it was a high schooler, just a malfunction.

I rubbed my fingertips together, wondering where that amount of control and feeling had come from. I hadn't been able to feel electricity until practicing more at headquarters, but it had never felt like I could syphon it. That was something I'd have to test out when I wasn't in a government military facility.

"No sign of him, but the conference rooms are on the second floor," Dylan informed us through the coms.

"Now I just need to get up there," I mumbled. The Vault had prepared us with tactical training and awareness, but not sneaking around. Being in the field and taking down Rogues had helped me learn to blend in and to go mostly unnoticed.

"It's pretty boring out here. Next time, I vote I go undercover. I would make a great high school student," Travis said through the com, and I rolled my eyes.

I slipped around the corner, thankful the guards were still eyeing the boy who told the teacher he hadn't done anything. The one girl's face was red, causing me to believe they had history. I almost felt bad for the boy—he was telling the truth.

The hallway was large, with marble-like floors and white walls extending to the ceiling drop tiles. A camera sat on the wall, and I kept my head down. Two women in dress clothes and ID badges clipped to their blouses walked in my direction, chatting away. I pulled out my phone and pretended to be occupied typing a message. I angled my body at the woman closest to me, bumping my shoulder into hers and letting my phone go flying.

"Oh my gosh! I'm so sorry!" I faked an apologetic voice as I reached down to grab my phone. "That's what I get for trying to send an email to my boss while walking. I'll never get used to it being so busy." I faked a nervous chuckle and continued walking before they could say anything.

"Smooth. That was one-hundred-percent flustered intern style," Dylan commented. Hopefully they didn't notice my crop top—it wasn't something an intern at a government facility would wear.

I ran a finger over the smooth edges of the badge that I had snuck off the lady. I flipped it over. *Sophie Carter*. The name suited the lady.

"There'll be an empty staircase to your right." He had hacked the cameras, and this time, I wasn't wearing a camera on my jacket—those were for our solo missions. He was my eyes, and I was thankful because I had no clue where I was going.

There was a scanner next to the stairwell door and I swiped the badge. I smiled when it unlocked. I started the small trek up the tiled stairs, the stairwell smelling an awful lot like a giant car air freshener.

"Any eyes on Miles?" I asked.

"Nothing yet."

"I can't just walk into a meeting, and this badge is only going to get me so far until the lady finds it's missing." I put my hands on the door.

"Wait," Dylan warned, and I froze. "Someone's walking by."

I held by breath but the door never opened.

"All clear," Dylan said. I entered a similar hallway to the one downstairs.

"Dylan found a door with a guard standing outside of it. It's probably where the commander is. There's a small seating area at the end of the hall. Think you can blend in?" Liam asked.

"In this outfit, as Sophie Carter, sure." I looked nothing like the middle-aged woman in the photo.

"Go left and take your next right."

I followed Dylan's instructions and came to a hallway with a million doors with a seating area at the end.

"The next hall is where the guard is."

I took a deep breath and continued down the hallway.

"Did you see that?" Liam asked, but it sounded like it was directed at Dylan, who was probably next to him.

"See w—" My question was cut off when I went suddenly crashing through the door to my left. I righted myself, rubbing my shoulder and staring at the tall, strong figure closing the door and locking it behind him as the automatic lights flicked on.

"Harper! What's going on?" Liam asked in alarm. "We don't have eyes on you anymore."

"Miles." It was all I said as Miles turned to face me with glazed steel eyes, hiding any green that remained.

"Isa." Goose bumps rose along my skin as the two-syllable name rolled off his tongue, laced with hatred.

We were locked in a second-story conference room of a secure government building. Now was the time to talk him out of what he was there to do, but his brooding glare said he wasn't in a talking mood.

"What are you planning on doing here?" I asked in a calm voice.

His lips remained pressed in a hard line, and the only evidence I could see that he was about to strike was a slight twitch in his leg.

I barely saw him before he was on me, and I instantly summoned my beast. I went flying backward, landing in the side of a large oak conference table. The blow was lessened in this form, and I stood, readying myself.

Miles stared me down, his eyes now an iridescent golden-green. Purple specks glinted in his irises.

"Can we talk?" I held out my hands.

Miles struck again, blurring as he attacked. I tracked his movements and held out my hands where I best guessed he was going to be. The electricity sparked on contact, causing Miles to stagger backward.

"I guess not." I inhaled as he sprang again. I took a punch straight to the stomach and doubled over. Crap. He was fast and strong.

I deflected his next attack and elbowed him in the face. He barely flinched as his leg swept out in a blur, and I barely dodged it. His next strike came at my face, and I held up my arms to block his fist, and not even a split second later, he landed another blow to my stomach. Adam and Dodge—who trained me during the three months of my recovery at headquarters—had both taught me to never block with both arms unless absolutely necessary. That was why.

Mumbled voices rang in my ear, but I drowned them out as I kicked my foot out, striking his leg. I brought my palm to his chest, letting enough energy flow to knock down a bull, but he vanished back ten feet, barely receiving a shock.

"We don't need to do this." I panted.

"We do." His eyes narrowed.

"Talking would be easier." I summoned two fireballs and held them in my hands.

He moved and I threw, missing. The next thing I knew, I was crashing hard into the wall and crumpled to my knees.

"I'm going in." Liam's voice rang in my ear right before Miles faded. I shot out a hand while still on my knees and electric sparks danced as sharp bolts flew through the air, striking down their mark. Miles flew backward into the opposing wall.

"I don't think I'm going to be able to talk him down." I breathed out and stood, pushing the throbbing pain in my back and head aside. "Miles, are you here to kill the NATO Commander and—"

Miles stood—almost robotically—and ran at me. I was able to deflect most of his attacks while keeping the electricity dancing along my skin. Any exposed skin was a weapon and shocked him every time we made contact. The only downside—it didn't last long. I grabbed his approaching fist and delivered a riveting shock. I brought my foot to his stomach, but he stepped to the side, lessening the blow.

"You're not a killer," I wheezed out between breaths and went for his right side—his weakness that didn't feel quite like a weakness right now.

Miles' lips twitched down before he tilted his head, appearing to be listening to something. I focused in on my hearing. Multiple footsteps pounded down the hallway outside the door, and a second later, an alarm was blaring. A few footfalls stopped at the door while others kept going.

"I think the guard heard the commotion," Dylan said. "They're coming."

"I'm inside. I'll be there soon," Liam said.

"No. Find the commander," I ordered.

"He'll be fine. They'll move him to a secure location."

Voices shouted from outside the door, and any second they would open it.

Miles glanced from the door, then back at me, with a clenched jaw and ground his teeth. He blurred past me, and I heard a sharp crack at the same time the window shattered. I shielded my face from the flying shards. Once it was done raining broken glass, I ran to the window. He was gone. The door clicked.

"Harper! Get out!" Dylan yelled.

"I don't think Doc can get you out of this one. The back only has a few guards if you can make your way there," Travis said. This window faced the side, and no one was in sight. I guess there was one way out without causing a huge fight. And it was going to hurt.

I turned back toward the window, hoisting myself over the sill and over the ledge. Glass dug into my hand, but that would barely leave a mark and would heal quickly. The cement sidewalk came fast, and I landed, rolling right after my feet touched ground. I took off in a sprint toward the back, not looking up to see if the guards were at the window. I rounded the corner and spotted Travis standing at the edge of the trees. As soon as I reached him, we ran and hopped the small fence in the back.

At least NATO will be on high alert, and hopefully keep the commander safe along with the others if they were inside.

CHAPTER TWENTY-TWO

"WHY DID I HAVE to leave the bike behind?" I asked Dylan as we pulled up to the familiar sage-colored house, the sun reflecting off its white trim. Dylan and I had headed back to Portland after we were unable to track Miles once he left the command center.

"Because we agreed this would be better if we arrived together." Dylan turned off his car. "No need to give Mary a heart attack."

"Like that's going to be the thing she worries about." I snorted. I had filled her in that Miles was missing and I was working to find him—but she and Joe were about to learn a whole lot more.

I had spoken with my mom a few times over the phone, but I had yet to see her. If she had seen the state I was in after the prison, she would have had a complete meltdown—one I doubted she would never recover from. I had come a long way since then.

"I think she would specifically freak out about that *and* everything else," Dylan said. His phone dinged and he grabbed it. He pushed his glasses up the bridge of his nose as a sheepish grin turned the corner of his lips upward.

"Jer?" I asked.

"I told him what we were about to do." Dylan laughed. "He just told me *may the force be with you.*"

"I would've never pegged him as a *Star Wars* fan," I said.

"He's like a chocolate-dipped ice cream cone. Hard on the outside but soft on the inside. Kind of like..." Dylan didn't finish.

"Miles. You can say his name. And only you would compare your boyfriend to ice cream." I rolled my eyes.

"He's not my boyfriend! Not yet at least," he mumbled with a suppressed grin.

I couldn't help the nasally laugh that erupted from me. It was always good to be around Dylan. Having known him since we were kids and before the Vault gave me some stable ground.

"Ready to spill the beans... lots and lots of beans?" Dylan asked.

"By beans you mean minibombs, yes." I took off Miles' green hat and tossed it on the dash. Telling my mom was the right thing to do, but that didn't stop the concern of hurting her.

I got out of the car, and the warm August breeze was so powerful, it whipped my braid against my leather jacket. The less scars visible, the better. Before I could even put a foot on the sidewalk leading to the front door, it opened. My mom rushed out, her blond chin-length hair blowing every which way.

"Isa Grace." She reached me and pulled me into one of the tight hugs she had given me so often growing up.

"Hi, Mom." I breathed in the lavender laundry softener left behind on her mauve shirt—the same she had always used because it was calming. She pulled away after a good minute and looked at Dylan over my shoulder. "Dylan. Your mom told me you got an amazing cyber security job that involves a lot of travel."

"Yes. I, uh, did." He adjusted his glasses and looked everywhere else but at my mom.

My mom sighed and walked around me to give him a hug. "I'm just glad you guys are both home now."

"Mom. We have to talk." I had told her we were stopping by but not the purpose of our visit.

"That we certainly do." She gestured toward the front door where Joe stood.

"Hey, kiddo." Joe gave us a hug and offered to take my coat as soon as we were inside, but I politely mentioned that I would like to keep my jacket on. Everything was the same in the living room from the almond-colored sofa, pictures on the mantel above the fireplace, and the hint of desolation from the past years since I *died*—and now had gone missing.

My mom gestured for Dylan and me to sit on the couch while Joe took a chair. She began pacing as we sat in silence.

"I see you finally learned to braid your hair." My mom rubbed her hands together.

"It reminded me of home." I glanced at my watch. Ten minutes.

I stood, not able to take the bleak silence anymore as it crushed down against my chest. "Mom, I'm so sorry I haven't visited since I've been back."

If this was before my recovery, tears would have already fallen. The day I ran off with Dylan, I had shut those emotions off. Heck, I had even half flipped the switch months before that. Truth was, inside I was a detached hollow shell, vacant of any other emotions besides vengeance, and that was exactly what the Rogues I had taken down had thought of me. The emotions were there, grief, sorrow, guilt...but they were locked away in a hidden compartment.

"Fr—Dr. Alan Roulings had informed you both of a few things." I looked between my mom and Joe. "But there's obviously more and I understand you have questions. I think this would be best if we all are sitting down."

My mom froze, looking between Joe and me.

"Mary, I think you should have a seat. Isa?" Joe glanced at the couch behind me, and I sat back down next to Dylan.

My mom slowly made her way to the other chair as Dylan and I shared a glance. He swallowed and nodded for me to start.

"Remember how you were sick when you were pregnant with me?" I asked.

"Of course, but how does that have anything to do with this?"

"It's where this started." Well, besides the part of my dad working on a serum for super soldiers in the military, but we won't start with that. "You were sick, and there was no cure. Dad found one."

"Your dad helped me with specific enzymes and vita—"

"Not exactly," I said. "He altered something he had created before that aided in healing. It worked, and it cured me when I was five years old and had gotten the same illness, except Dad never gave me the serum. It was already inside me because I was inside you when you were given the serum. It changed me, and that was why Dr. Roulings took me. I had no clue."

I glanced at Joe and my mom before looking at Dylan and nodding, giving him my signal to be prepared.

"There's something I need to show you. I am going to stand, but I want you to stay sitting. And just know that I am still me—I am the same Isa you knew five, well, now six years ago." I held my hands out and slowly stood. "Are you ready?"

They both nodded, lips pursed and eyebrows pinched. They had no clue what I was about to do.

I took a deep breath and lowered my hands. The energy came on command and surged to my palm, which I had twisted upward. A blue sphere with sparks emitting in every direction hovered just above my hand with small tendrils striking into my palm—an electric fireball. My mom's mouth gaped as she stared at the electric sphere while Joe's cheeks flushed, his eyes flitting from my hand to my glowing blue eyes.

After a few more seconds, I ceased the energy.

"She's harmless." Dylan slowly stood up next to me. "Well, not harmless, clearly. But she's the same girl who loves to eat ten tacos in one sitting and down a chocolate malt milkshake in one sip."

I elbowed him. It felt like not too long ago we had snuck to Seattle against Miles' wishes and had burgers and shakes late at night—one of our favorite pastimes growing up. I was about to say something when I heard the back door open. I glanced down at my clock. Time was up.

"There's someone here who can answer your questions." I looked toward the kitchen where Frank appeared, wearing grey slacks and a blue sweater—regardless that it was summer.

"You." My mother paled at the sight of Frank, and shortly after, she was charging at him.

Frank retreated into the kitchen. "Mary—"

"No! Don't *Mary* me." She halted in front of him and jabbed a finger at his chest. *Huh*. Maybe that's where I get that from. "This is your fault! You did this! I knew it as soon as it was *you* that called. You were always checking in on Isa, and I thought it was because of your relationship with Ben. You were his best friend!"

"Mary. I think we need to take a step back, take a breather." Joe came over and rubbed my mother's arms. Despite his soothing voice, he scowled.

My mom's chest heaved as her glare softened. I should have intervened, but I kind of enjoyed Frank looking rattled. He went to open his mouth, but his lips barely twitched before my mom lunged toward the counter. She grabbed a chef's knife from the knife block on the counter and held it out toward him as Frank shot his hands up.

Okay. Now I should intervene.

"Mom." I walked over and placed a hand on her shaking arm. "He just wants to talk. As much as I hated him, he's not all that bad." *Small lie.* Most of me still hated him—or despised him.

"Thank you, dearie." Frank smiled and gave me a nod. I shot him the same look Joe had a minute ago as my mom slipped past my arm.

"Don't you dare even look at her!" My mom shouted. "Isa. Dylan. Stay away from him."

"Nothing compares to the wrath of a mother protecting her child," Dylan commented.

"You're not helping," I grumbled at him as he shrugged off my glare. "Mom, let's put the knife down."

The back door opened, and Liam came in, his dark chestnut eyes scanning the room before landing on the knife my mother held. His face remained neutral as if there wasn't a sharp weapon pointed at Frank's chest.

"I heard the commotion and wanted to make sure everyone was okay." Liam held up his hands as my mom gave him a quick once over.

"I think everyone needs to calm down so we can talk and get the entire story." Joe was back at my mom's side, one hand on her shoulder.

I used the brief distraction and put myself between the knife and Frank, knowing my mom wouldn't cut me like one of her delicious pies. I doubt she would've drawn blood on Frank either, but like Dylan said…

"Joe's right, Mom. I think you should listen to Dr. Roulings. He can explain it better than I can. Let's go back into the living room and sit, please." I used my best reassuring daughter voice.

My mom let out a sigh and lowered the knife. Joe gently took it from her and slid it back in the block. He rested his hand on the small of her back and guided her to the living room. She turned slightly so she could keep Frank in sight.

"I see where you get your fire from," Liam whispered, leaning toward me.

"You could have easily disarmed her." Frank glanced at me.

"Where's the fun in that?" I shrugged, which caused Frank to shake his head. "She needed to do it herself."

"You run a secret organization with skilled fighters; you couldn't have?" Dylan asked Frank.

"Doc's better at the science and planning, not so much the physical aspect." Liam grinned and turned to me. "I'll be outside, keeping watch."

The FBI no longer watched my house, but Frank had had a camera installed on the streetlight out front. With Krauss still out there, and even Miles, we couldn't take the chance.

I palmed my face, rubbing my eyes, and then peeked at my mom and Joe, who watched us warily from the living room. This was going to be fun.

CHAPTER TWENTY-THREE

*S*ILENCE.

That had been my mom's response once I had told her my dad was alive, and that if she had wanted to see him, he was nearby. She had a select few words with Frank when he filled her in. Certain details were left out, and I hadn't elaborated on the extent of the trauma I had gone through in the months I was Krauss' prisoner.

Now, I was in the passenger seat of the van while Liam drove with my mom in the back. Frank and Dylan had stayed with Joe back at the house. We couldn't risk my dad being seen or caught on any cameras near the house.

"We're here." Liam pulled off into a park near the river that appeared to be practically deserted. How they knew about these places, I would never know. "He's up ahead on that trail."

I stepped out of the SUV and scanned the surroundings out of habit—just like a true operative. Dusk cast an orange glow over the tall grass and reflected off the Willamette River. If the lawn hadn't been unkempt and the playground in the distance didn't look abandoned, this would have been a beautiful park. Although, to me, it was beautiful. Something that was once full of life and laughter had faded into a quiet, forsaken land but was still standing. To me, that was where the beauty lay—in the strength to keep going.

I tucked away my thoughts and opened the door for my mom. The noise from the closing of the door echoed through the deserted park and I cringed, not meaning to have shut it with such force. I apologized to my mom—she looked like a ghost had just jumped out at her. To be fair, she was about to see the husband she thought was dead. He may as well have been a ghost.

Liam waited by the SUV as I led her down the path. A bench appeared beyond a few trees in front of the SUV by the river. A dark outline of a man sat on it, the footsteps behind me halted, and I turned to see my mom staring at my dad's dark, shadowed figure, eyes wide. I reached out my hand and she glanced at me. She took it and we went the last few steps together.

My dad cocked his head to the side at our arrival and stood. He wore a sincere smile, but it couldn't hide the sorrow and guilt behind it. My hand was being squeezed like a python was curling its strong body around it, and I looked over to see my mom holding a shaking hand to her mouth as a tear ran down her cheek.

"Ben?" she choked out and swallowed, clearing the imaginary frog from her throat.

"Mary..." My dad's voice filled with anguish. I hadn't seen him this distraught since the airplane when I had been rescued from Krauss' prison. I released Mom's frozen hand as my dad reached out to take her in his arms, but she pushed him back.

"Don't." Tears began to flow down her cheeks. "How could you do this to our daughter? You were alive this entire time. We grieved over your death... and Alan... you and he..." She broke down and my heart shattered at her despair.

I had felt something similar when I had first seen him, but he had been gone since I was six. They had loved each other... and clearly, my father still did. He attempted to wrap her in his arms again, and this time, she didn't push him away. Fourteen years. She had grieved his loss for fourteen years and her daughter's loss for five.

I slowly retreated, giving them their space, and made my way back to Liam. If anything, my presence would be a catalytic reminder and now she wouldn't hold back—not that she would anyway. She was going to let him have it.

"That sounds like it's going as to be expected." Liam leaned against the SUV with his arms crossed over his chest.

"To the T." I leaned against the black SUV.

"At least she doesn't have a knife." Liam side-eyed me with a smirk.

"Not one that we saw," I said, the corner of my lips tugging up.

"She is your mother after all."

Talking helped and was the first step to recovery, but it also only went so far, and we both knew that—we had done it a million times back at headquarters. Liam had helped me heal, and even though I wasn't fully myself—if I'd ever be—I was working on it.

Liam and I stayed near my parents but had walked the park for half an hour until we decided to check on them, catching a part of their conversation.

"—both were close until you left the military. He occasionally called for updates on Harper, and I thought he felt guilty for your disagreement over work." My mom's eyes were narrowed on my dad, all tears gone. "Now, I see why, though it seems you talked more than you let on after your fallout. I wasn't naïve; I knew the work you were doing was confidential, but I never thought you'd experiment with our daughter. You did what you did to save her, and for that, I am grateful, but her life is now condemned—" The anger rising in my mom's voice ceased—all words ceased—as I approached.

My mom gave me a warm smile and turned back to my dad, letting out a sigh.

"You did what you had to in order to save us, but I was your wife. Her mother. We both deserved the truth." My mom turned away from him and grabbed my hand, steering me away. I glanced at my dad and gave him a small shrug. I had reacted similarly, though I'd had less energy to express my outrage. Time has passed, healing some wounds while the others I learned to deal with. Chances were, I would've done the same thing if I had to choose whether or not my child lived. I would have done it if it were Miles, Liam, or anyone I loved.

"Mom," I said gently. "Dad's going to ride back with us. You can take the front, or I'll ride in the back with you."

My mom halted, putting on a brave face. "I'll be more than happy to have your company in the back seat with me."

Dual meaning understood. She didn't want herself or me to sit next to him.

The ride home was uncomfortable, as my mom's glare burned holes in the back of my dad's head. We pulled in, and I got out with my mom as Frank and Dylan walked outside with Joe.

"I'm going to head out with them, Mom." I glanced at the SUV and avoided her eyes, knowing she would be hurt. "I need to continue to search for Miles."

"That's okay, Isa," she finally said after a moment. "I can't understand what you're going through, but I'm always here. As much as I don't want you leaving this house ever again, I know I can't do that to you. Please be safe, and please, please call me every day."

I raised my eyebrow at her.

"At least send me a text saying you're okay, and visit whenever you can. I'll march right up to that headquarters of theirs if I have to."

I laughed. "Mom, you wouldn't want to march there if you knew where it was—even in summer."

"I will if I have to." She put her hands on her hips and glared at the SUV where my dad and Frank were.

"I don't doubt it." I gave her a long hug, stifling the miniscule amount of anxiety at the contact. She was my mom. It was fine. "Remember, you don't know about us."

"I'm here for you, sweetheart." My mom kissed my forehead and turned back toward the house. She didn't go inside, but stood in front of the door with Joe as he wrapped his arms around her and she leaned into him. She may have loved my father once—part of her still did—but there was no doubt that she loved Joe and this wasn't going to change their relationship.

"Is your dad still alive?" Dylan asked as he made his way over to me.

"Yes." I rolled my eyes.

"What?" Dylan held up his hands. "She was going to shank Frank. Imagine what she'd do to your dad."

"I'll see you tomorrow." I waved him off and got into the SUV. Dylan was going to visit his mom tonight.

Liam started the SUV, and we were on our way. Soon after, I pulled my dad aside as Liam and Frank went inside the fishery.

"I'm sorry about Mom."

"She'll be okay. She's tough, like you." He winked, covering his hurt.

"That's not what I meant." Part of me ached for my dad. "That your relationship is over."

He sighed, knowing the truth. "We had a wonderful chapter of our lives together, and as much as I wish everything was different, it's not. She's on a new chapter—with someone she is safe with and who also loves her."

There was no doubt that Krauss still wanted my dad, just like I could still be of interest. Krauss had looked like he was given a birthday present when my dad had showed up at the prison. No one we loved was safe. At least this way, it lessened the target on my mom's back as long as it appeared she thought we were both gone. Krauss wasn't the only danger—just the immediate threat, and that sent shivers down my spine.

CHAPTER TWENTY-FOUR

Another plane, another city. I've been nonstop since leaving headquarters, but I couldn't allow myself to rest. Resting led to thinking, and I needed to be out of my own head. I wouldn't rest until Miles was safe—even if that was from himself.

"NYC operatives are meeting us here," Liam said. He walked next to me, boots clanking against the wet sidewalk. "El, let us know when they arrive."

"Copy that," Ellie said through our coms from the SUV parked down the street. Dylan had to help support his mom, who had just lost a close friend of hers the day before, so Ellie was our eyes.

"Sorry to cut your night short," I told Kat as she walked on my other side, wearing her usual FBI business attire: flat dress boots, dark-teal blouse, and black slacks. We were lucky she had already been in New York City.

"Duty calls." She shrugged.

The two days we were at the fishery, there had been no sign of Miles anywhere, but a homeless person had reported seeing a human that looked like a werewolf attacking two guys on the street in the middle of the night. The NYPD dismissed it, but it was flagged by Alcorp. The NYC operatives had been watching closely throughout the day, but there weren't any signs until our scanner picked up Rogue activity at a club less than an hour ago.

Blaring music came from inside the nightclub in front of us, but there wasn't a bouncer out front and the doors were shut. Liam was the only one who carried an inhibitor. It wasn't something easily mass-produced, and we also couldn't allow our enemy to get a hold of them and use them on us. If Miles was focused on me, Liam could use the inhibitor on him.

"Kat, can you wait for the others and surround the perimeter while we go in?" Liam asked as Maya pulled on the door. Locked.

"Yes." Kat rested a hand on her gun and walked a few paces away from the door, standing in front of a concrete wall.

The street was eerily empty and every other place in the small strip appeared to be out of business. The only thing that didn't look like it had been abandoned was the club.

I walked up to the windows, but I couldn't make anything out through the dark glass.

"There's a door at the side. Breaking that might be a better idea," Ellie said.

"Heading there now." Liam nodded at the camera on the side of the building. I followed Liam down the side alley, with Maya and Adam right behind us. The paved alley floor was full of puddles, but my boots were waterproof. My calves weren't so lucky, as dirty water splashed on them.

Liam held a hand up and I flattened myself against the wall next to the door, the others doing the same behind me. I pulled my gun and waited. Liam pulled on the door handle, but it was locked. He transformed and yanked on the door, breaking the lock.

I stepped into the doorway after he opened it, gun drawn. An empty hallway led to a black door. I strode down the dark hallway, careful to keep my boots from clanking against the cheap laminate flooring. I summoned my beast, waited for the others besides Adam to do the same, and opened the door.

An empty lounge greeted us with a few red sofas arranged sporadically around the room. The air reeked of liquor and iron, and a mini self-serve bar was pushed along the far wall with a half-empty drink.

Glass crunched under my boot, and I looked down. The floor was slick where a drink had been dropped and a straw laid a foot away from the glistening shards.

I glanced over my shoulder to give the others a warning. Travis went left and Liam went right as we started to fan out. Travis reached a sofa and paused. Fingers coated in red peaked out just behind the sofa, dark crimson in comparison. Travis shook his head at me, and my gut twisted as my muscles tensed with anger. Whoever they were, they were dead. The Rogues had either been there and left or were still there.

"The other operatives arrived and are surrounding all exits," Ellie said.

"Thanks, Ellie," Liam whispered.

Liam nodded toward the door the music was coming from. We prepared our stances as he opened the door.

A loud roar filled the room as all five of us flew backward. I crashed into a glass coffee table, shattering it into a million pieces. Cursing, I glanced at the soft sofa right next to me. *Really?* I couldn't have crashed into that?

I groaned and got to my feet, rolling out my shoulders. Liam was already in action fighting a Rogue whose hair had been intricately braided and trailed down to the back of her knees. Her mouth opened as Liam smashed the butt of his knife into her cheek. A small boom roared from her mouth, and the wall she faced fissured, traveling up a good foot.

"Help!" a soft voice yelled beyond the door as more Rogues rushed in.

I reached for my gun, but it had been flung across the room. Fighting broke out and the room lit up, blinding me as I ran toward the door. *What was that?* I shielded my eyes but forced them open as someone rushed me. Instinct kicked in, and I focused the hot energy into my right hand. I ducked, dodging the attack, and slammed an electrified fist into the side of the Rogue. They went flying, crashing into the soft cushions of the sofa. *Really?* At least they were down from the mini-electrocution, but they would be up in seconds.

I heard a scream from the other room. A glance at the others told me they were holding their own, and I sprinted through the door.

The main room of the club was a disaster. White strobe lights flashed, lighting up human bodies scattered across the dance floor and sprawled in the chairs at the bars and tables, while broken glass littered the entire black laminate flooring. Music was still playing, and the floor vibrated from the bass.

The whimpering sounds coming from the back distracted me from checking to see if anyone was alive. There was a dimly lit hallway, and another cry led me to the door of the women's bathroom.

I tensed, very aware that this could be a trap. I opened the door to darkness. I didn't dare be distracted by a hunt for the light switch—it wouldn't have mattered anyway. The light was smashed, and my morphed eyes could see fine.

"They're all dead," a broken woman's voice mumbled from the large stall in the corner.

"I'm here to help," I said, not wanting to startle her, but something seemed off. I walked over to the stall and pushed it open.

The huddled figure in the corner slowly stood...and stood... rising a good foot above me. A face rose out of the shadows, baring their wicked teeth, and my hair stuck on end—definitely a Rogue.

"Help me, please!" a voice that shouldn't have come from the man before me said. He laughed, a deep rumble.

That was unexpected.

His eyes morphed into black beads while brown and black horizontal stripes morphed down the length of his dark hair, like dye being poured from the roots to the ends. His tall and lean figure stayed the same.

Fangs pressed into his lower lip. "Not what you were expecting?"

"What are you?" I asked, unable to stop staring.

He answered with a roundhouse. I took a step back, dodging his attack easily.

"So"—I swallowed—"Krauss got everything he needed from me."

He laughed, a bone-chilling child's laugh, one you'd hear from the ghost of a serial killer in kid form.

I didn't have time to brood over his words as his fist grazed the side of my face and I spun, delivering an elbow to his collarbone. He dropped his shoulder and took a step back—if he wasn't a Hybrian, his bone would've shattered. I took the free moment and sent a roundhouse of my own to his chest, sending him back into the stall. He landed on the toilet, bending the pipes and causing water to spurt out the side.

I went to attack again as the Rogue stood.

"Please don't!" The scared helpless child's voice instantly made me freeze.

Instinct wanted me to listen to the poor child in distress, but the face it wore was a leering man who was already on his feet, rushing me. He lifted me over the sinks and shoved me against the mirror, shattering it.

I brought my shin to his groin, and he dropped me. I landed awkwardly on the counter and put my hands next to me for support. Leaning back, I shoved both feet into his chest, sending him hurtling through a different stall door. I approached and used one finger to open it. The Rogue lay on his side, staring up at me.

"Please! Don't kill me. I'm not who you think I am." The child's voice was back. "I'm trapped inside this monster."

"I'm not playing your games." I shot my hand out, sending an electric bolt into his chest and rendering him unconscious.

The way he used a child's voice sickened me, and there was no way I was falling for his claims of being possessed. This was my genetics at play. Mine included electric eel with black panther. Krauss must have combined whatever he pulled from me with his serum and some type of voice-mimicking animal gene.

Staying morphed, I ran out of the bathroom and back into the main room, where bodies still lay on the ground. The room where I had left the others was eerily quiet. I pulled a knife and rushed through the door.

My beast faltered. My heart stopped. My stomach knotted. Bile rose in my throat and tears threatened to escape.

The knife slipped from my hand, piercing the floor like it was my heart. My feet moved one after the other, like a string tugging them. All the sounds were muted as I walked over to the body my friends surrounded. Why weren't they trying to save him? Giving chest compressions? *Doing anything?*

My friend lay motionless on the ground. His chest wasn't rising, and his eyes blankly stared at the ceiling above. There wasn't a single part of him that moved.

I pushed through my friends, unsure of who was who. The edges of my vision blurred—the only clear part was the lifeless body on the floor. I went to kneel, to try to do *something*, but someone's hands wrapped around me, pulling me back.

"He's gone," a calm voice said in my ear.

"No," I whispered as the hands tightened and a warm cheek pressed against my temple. "No!" I shouted, wanting to believe in that little word that rendered the truth. *No.*

"I'm sorry, sunshine." Liam held me as I fell to my knees. I reached for Travis, but Liam's grip wouldn't allow me to move closer. "We can't touch him. We don't know where the poison is or anything about it."

I turned my head, looking at Liam. Blood dripped from his nose, and his eyes were bloodshot—a mix of physical and emotional distress. "What do you mean, poison?"

"It's one of the Rogue's abilities." Liam stared vacantly at Travis. "I couldn't get to him in time. He was already gone."

I finally allowed myself to look at the other two in the room. Tears streamed down Maya's cheeks, causing black streaks from her mascara while Adam slowly rubbed her back. I sank backward into Liam, giving up.

The front door flew open as Kat rushed in with her gun drawn, followed by Ellie. Kat halted, but her grim expression told me she had already been filled in, most likely by Ellie, who probably saw everything. I don't remember hearing anything and lifted my hand to my ear—my com was still there.

"Our coms were destroyed when that wave hit us after we opened the door," Liam answered my thought. He glanced at Ellie and his face dropped even more—if that was even possible. She had fresh tears falling down her cheeks as she froze in place, staring at Travis. I forgot how close everyone else had become with him while I was gone. It wasn't just Liam, Maya, and me who loved Travis.

And now Travis was gone.

"This is my fault." My eyes finally gave way to the tears threatening to drown them. I stood, letting Liam's arms fall away. I pushed past a couple NYC operatives who entered, and tuned everything out. I shoved open the door and stepped onto the sidewalk into dysphoric silence. Two operatives were outside—one sitting against the brick wall while the other attended to their head injury. They looked up at me, but I turned on my heel and walked the other way.

Soon my walk turned into a sprint. I didn't know where I was going, but I knew I needed to run. Run from all of it.

Travis was dead—like my nightmare. Someone I loved was dead because of me. My stem cells did this. His happy-funny personality was gone forever and would only live on in memory. If I had kept Krauss from getting his hands on me, this wouldn't have happened. There were many ways I could have destroyed the electric spark inside me—after all, my spark would die with me.

CHAPTER TWENTY-FIVE

I HAD RUN AND hadn't stopped, wanting to be alone. Now, days later, my feet sank into the soft moss ground blanketing the Black Forest of Germany. The sun was starting to rise, casting rays through the trees and thick fog. Water rushed in a stream somewhere nearby, and birds sang their morning song, but it hadn't brought me serenity like the forest had at the cabin—when I truly hadn't known how better off life was. No one had been dead. No one had truly been in trouble.

The others had gone back with Travis' body to headquarters. Dr. Cole had examined the toxin that killed Travis and learned it was from a golden poison frog. It paralyzed the victim, essentially stopping their heart in minutes. There was no helping Travis once the toxin had touched him unless an antidote had been given or if the situation had been prevented.

I had multiple missed calls, but I had only sent messages to a few people, letting them know that I was okay and needed time alone. The next day Dylan had called. They had found a potential hiding spot in Germany for Krauss. My father had mentioned Krauss was born in Germany and moved to the United States to intern with my dad when he was twenty and had continued taking courses in molecular biology and engineering. I guess his resume and letter had impressed my dad enough to take him on.

Krauss had held Miles and me in the Gobi Desert; why not have a location that was closer to home than the States? There was Rogue activity in the States, but it had been more prevalent oversees recently.

The Alliance was everywhere, so why wouldn't he be organizing worldwide? Dylan had searched the Alliance records, assuming Krauss knew the entire time about the organization, and found a location in Germany that wasn't in use nor had been talked about for over a century. Dylan had informed Liam, and he and the others would be here anytime now. My beast beacon wasn't picking anything up, and the prickly sensation it caused would alert me as soon as they arrived.

I pulled out my phone, knowing I still wouldn't have any service, and pulled up the map of southwest Germany. I had to have gone at least five miles from the spot a local dropped me off. The local questioned dropping a girl in the middle of the forest, but a hefty commission later, he left in silence.

I should be coming up on the old Alliance building, which had never been finished being built due to the Franco-Prussian war and smallpox outbreak in the 1870s. Dylan was fascinated with all the information—but all I had cared about was the location.

The minor pressure in my side told me my gun was secured in my jacket. My plan was to do recon and report back to the woods so I could inform the others of what to expect—if there was anything at all.

I heard a roar in the distance and looked up to see clouds rolling in through the dawn sky. I kept going until the trees started to thin and the outline of a building appeared. I pressed flat against a tree and peered around it. A massive building of conglomerate stones and cement showed signs of age, with moss and vines crawling up to the third row of windows.

The coast was clear and, surprisingly, I didn't spot any cameras. I sprinted, jumping over brush and fallen trees until I reached a large piece of the building that had broken off from the top corner. This place looked deserted. I brought my beast out and sighed at the faint voices coming from farther inside the building.

I rounded the corner—which I was hoping led to the back and not the front—and came across a small window with pillars on either side.

They really had gone all out for a secret building in the middle of nowhere.

I peeked through, only seeing an empty room with busted stone walls. My hand pressed onto the gritty ledge as I silently climbed over it. I crept along the broken wall and into another room. The voices grew louder as I approached, and my heartbeat rang in my ears at the recognizable rough voice.

Damien.

I stayed low, creeping along the wall. Soft water droplets landed on my head through the opening in the ceiling at the same time the rain splattered the foliage outside, creating a slapping sound. I made it into an adjoining room with an unglazed window framed by stone and a mostly intact roof. Damien was talking, or should I say scolding, someone.

Looking over the ledge, I could make out the back of Damien. He spoke with a Rogue whose natural emerald green eyes were focused on her feet. One hand clenched the edge of her athletic shorts. Her long black hair was tightly knit in silky cornrows that fell just below her shoulders.

"—now, will you do what is required of you?"

"Yes." She swallowed, turning her head to the side—in my direction. My eyes met her now bright yellow ones; they stood out against her coppery skin. I held my position, not breaking eye contact. She had seen me, so she was going to give me up whether or not I was looking. The electricity thrummed through my veins and I pulled my gun.

"Get back down there then," Damien ordered.

"Yes sir." Her gaze left mine. She turned around and strode down the steps into an area where other Rogues were training or watching. Large slits lined each side of the back of her shirt, but I didn't see any blood.

I silently sighed as she walked away, pulling back the heated energy to my core and letting my beast rest. She hadn't turned me in for some reason, but I knew that look she had given Damien. She loathed him, and I couldn't help but think she was one of the involuntary recruits.

It was time to get out of there and meet up with the others. I took a step back the way I had come but a piercing noise struck the same time the wall behind me came crumbling down, sending me to the ground. I cursed as my ears rang, and I searched through the rubble for the gun.

"I knew I felt something." A man wearing only maroon sweats and combat boots stared me down. The Rogue from the club stood next to him—the one that had blasted us with a sonic boom.

He took a step toward me and without thinking, I turned on my hip and sent two fireballs his way. His large hands reached out as if he were going to catch the electric flames. My eyes widened as they struck his hands, but instead of sending him flying, the electricity merely licked at his palms. Sweat dripped down his chiseled chest as the energy from the orbs faded in his hands, like a sponge absorbing water.

I got to my feet as the Rogue lowered his hands, glaring at me with yellow eyes. Single opaque ivory claws protruded from each of his outer wrists, extending five inches. I was in trouble.

Someone lunged for me from the side and I took a step back, ducking and throwing arm at their midsection. The assailant hunched over, and I sent a blast of electricity directly to the Rogue's back. It struck, sending sparks around his convulsing body.

He wasn't getting up any time soon.

"Not so tough when I'm not drugged, huh big guy?" I muttered at Damien's unconscious body, a small smile tugging at the edge of my lips.

"He's not here, darling." Krauss suppressed a cough with his hand before smoothing his white-collared dress shirt. It was unwrinkled and tucked into his grey slacks. Even his golden-walnut hair was smoothly feathered back. He angled himself behind the shirtless man who held his arms out at his sides, hands wound tightly into fists so his claws extended past his knuckles.

"It's a good thing I ran into you, then." I straightened, feeling the energy drip off me and into the air like gravity didn't exist. The clawed Rogue shifted, as if sensing the change in the air more than anyone else. He must have noticed the slight tilt of my head in response as the corner of his lip lifted into a sneer.

"You're quite marvelous. It's a shame it'll be easier to kill you than capture you." Krauss' eyes gleamed as his gaze roved over my body. "Your mind could have been manipulated just like the officer's. If you don't die here, he will have no problem finishing his mission to exterminate you. After all, you're his enemy now."

The static crackled in the air around me and blue hazed the edges of my vision. I threw my hands forward and two lightning bolts merged into a bright blue streak, sweeping across the space. The blue haze that fizzed around me syphoned into the bolts. It struck the clawed Rogue's hands with a large crack that shook the building, causing pebbles to rain to the floor. The Rogue had absorbed the strike again, but this time, he flew backward into Krauss.

I ran toward them but was intercepted by three other Rogues. Fists and feet sailed at me, and I effectively dodged them all. I struck the closest Rogue and sent her to the ground. Just as I turned, a fist caught the edge of my cheek, whipping my head to the side. I swung my head back, glaring at the Rogue who had struck me. He went to attack again, but I slammed my palm into his chest, delivering a high voltage of shocks.

The first Rogue had gotten back up, and I turned to face her and the third. I picked up a faint, high-pitched sound just as the three of us were blasted by something invisible and sent flying into the stone wall. Small chunks of rock fell on top of me, and the dust went through my nose and out my mouth as I coughed.

I rose to me feet, ignoring the sneeze I needed to get out. The clawed Rogue and the one that had blasted us strode toward me. I focused on the sonic Rogue, knowing she was less likely to absorb anything I sent her way. I was about to release the energy drumming against my palm when a white blur smashed into her, sending her sailing to the ground with a heap of white on top.

The white heap shifted as feathers that looked like white clouds shuttered, shaking off the dirt and revealing the person attached to the pair of wings. Bright, stark yellow eyes glanced my way and then back at the Rogue below her. Her fist came down, striking the Rogue's mouth before she could open it while her other hand held her down, talons digging into the Rogue's shoulder. She was the one who had been talking to Damien, the one with the natural emerald-green eyes.

And she was giving me an opportunity to attack.

CHAPTER TWENTY-SIX

I FACED THE CHARGING clawed Rogue, pulling out a knife. If I was going to win, it had to be without my powers. It would only drain me. Everything I had sent his way, he had absorbed. I planted my feet and waited for him to come to me. He swung a claw and I leaned back, avoiding the sharp tip as it swiped inches from my face. I slashed the knife toward his chest, barely grazing him, and brought my fist upward, smashing his nose with a sickening crunch.

I had gone to deliver the final blow when the ground shook, sending me off balance. I turned to see the girl with wings thrown backward by a sonic roar.

A sharp pain throbbed on my upper arm, and I glanced at it to see a small slash oozing blood. The clawed Rogue grinned as blood dripped from one of his claws. An annoyed grumble rose from my throat as I took a step forward but halted as stinging pain scratched at the inside of my upper arm and began to spread downward, releasing the knife in my hand.

"Venom." Krauss dared to move closer as the pain debilitated me. "Simple, actually. It's from a platypus. Something so minimal and extravagant can become lethal and painful with the Hybrian serum. I couldn't get your specific powers from your stem cells, but it helped bind another set of DNA."

Lethal. My stomach curdled.

"The venom won't kill you. It's just excruciating painful." Krauss grinned, but it was cut short by a coughing fit. His movements exposed a black string hanging around his neck that descended below his collar, hiding whatever hung on the end of it. Once the fit ended, that annoying grin came back. "Maybe we can try something with you after all. This time, with better restraints and security."

I glanced at the Rogue with long braided hair as she strode over. The Rogue with wings lay on the ground, struggling to move. My blood began to boil. She didn't deserve this or any of it.

"What would you like us to do, sir?" The Rogue with the dangerous sonic boom asked with a musical voice once she reached us.

"We'll take her and move her to a secure location." Krauss took another step closer, and I prayed he would keep coming. "Pistol shrimp. Another part of nature we shrug off but never divulge into the simplicity of—utilizing its delicately webbed biology. With your stem cells, the DNA merged effortlessly with the Hybrian serum and human DNA."

"Platypus and a pistol shrimp, huh?" I ground out through clenched teeth, the pain shredding at my arm like a saw from the inside. "You must be proud."

"My results from the creation of the dart frog seem to think so." He glanced at his hands as he rubbed his thumb across his fingers, like he was brushing off dust.

My ears rang from anger and pain. "You're the reason he's dead."

I sent a fireball at him, but it was intercepted by the clawed Rogue.

"Platypuses can detect electrical currents. And Elias here can also absorb them." Krauss glanced at the Rogue in front of him until his eyes drifted past me. "Hannah, darling. I know Damien has spoken with you about behaving."

I glanced over my shoulder to see the Rogue with wings rising to her feet, eyes burning yellow as she glowered at Krauss. The other Rogues—besides Damien—stirred on the ground and one had already stood. My power was outmatched.

I closed my eyes as all the pain and fear Krauss has inflicted surfaced. Memories of the pain imposed by the metal pin surfaced along with the days at the prison in the desert, Miles strapped to the table, the PTSD episodes that followed, the heartbreak riddled all over my mom's face, the guilt and sorrow my dad carried... the pain in my arm vanished as an outraged scream tore from me.

My hair stood on end as sparks and bolts flew, penetrating my clothes and dispersing in the air in front of me, like a fire engulfing everything in its path. The Rogue with the lyrical voice dropped to her knees and then to the ground, and so did Krauss. The clawed Rogue—Elias—gritted his teeth, but otherwise stayed standing as it dissipated.

I collapsed to a knee, out of breath. *What was that?*

I didn't have time to think about it as stones crunched underneath Elias' approaching feet. Three other Rogues that hadn't been hit with whatever I had just done were standing, readying to attack.

My body felt drained as the serrating pain began to throb again. I shoved it aside and stood. Before I could straighten out, arms wrapped around me and lifted me in the air. Large white wings left a shadow on the ground below, easily wider than my height, as the Rogue carried me through a hole in the vaulted ceiling. Panic seized me until I realized she wasn't attacking; she was getting me out of there.

The Rogue—Hannah, who I immediately declared wasn't a Rogue—flew over the forest as rain pelted her feathers and our faces. After what felt like a few miles, she glided down below the trees, tucking her wings behind her. She set me down, and I leaned into the tree at my back. She huffed as her eyes changed back to emerald and her wings snapped behind her back, disappearing in an instant. I searched her eyes for pain, but all she showed was exhaustion.

"Thank you," I said after a moment, pain still radiating from my arm.

"The pain will recede in about twelve hours." Her gaze tracked my hand, covering my bloodied upper arm. I gave her a small nod and an apologetic look at the understanding tone in her voice.

"My friends should've arrived in Germany. You should come back with me."

"Thank you, but I need to get home to my family. That way will take you to the closest town." She pointed behind me and went to turn around.

"Will you be okay?" I blurted before she could walk, fly, or whatever away.

"Yes. I'll be fine," she replied with a subtle accent I couldn't place and disappeared into the forest.

I pulled out my phone—no reception, but it was at least working. Dylan and my dad had created a thin coating for our phones and coms to protect them from the frequency of the Rogue's sonic boom. I shoved it back into my pocket and ran, trying to ignore the riveting pain in my arm along with the darkness rimming the edges of my vision, threatening me with unconsciousness. I had to warn Liam before they went to the old Alliance building.

Liam met me shortly after I got service in the Black Forest. He had already arrived in Germany with Adam, Maya, and Dylan, but I was able to catch them before they were deep into the forest. Dylan's idea of a good time was not trudging through the forest, and he was sorely disappointed when we hijacked an off-road vehicle and parked a mile away from Krauss' outpost, then waded through the forest.

We arrived quietly, but everyone already cleared out. I apologized for tipping them off. I had only meant to do some recon, which failed epically. Now they were in the wind, and even Liam wasn't able to hide his frustration toward me.

I had already filled in the others on everything I encountered at the old Alliance building, so I sat quietly on the jet. It was the first time I was with everyone since Travis, and I could feel the tension—not that it was directed at me. Things felt different without him here.

My phone rang and I checked the screen. *Chloe.*

"He's here," Chloe said breathlessly and I straightened. "He's at Brandon's."

CHAPTER TWENTY-SEVEN

"I**S YOUR BEAST BEACON** picking up anything?" Chloe asked me as my dad led us through a secret tunnel to the Vault.

"Yes. Me," Liam answered sarcastically.

I mindlessly rubbed the back of my neck. I didn't have a chip that blocked the sensory pathways that let us sense when others were nearby. The awareness, as Frank described, was almost like a signal emitted to others of their kind, alerting us when other Hybrians were close. But it didn't tell us how many or in what direction.

Krauss had put a chip in the Rogues so they weren't detectable, but that also blocked them from sensing us. Frank had learned all of this from the Rogue who could camouflage into her surroundings. She had been held at headquarters for a couple weeks before being relocated.

The air was humid and musky as the flashlight my father held lit the way into the dark cobwebbed tunnel.

"At least this time we know what we are getting into," Chloe whispered behind me.

"I wouldn't say that." Liam glanced back at us.

Miles had left Brandon's before we had arrived and said he wanted to meet in the Vault. The cameras had only picked up Miles and no one else. It would be hard to hide in or on the outside of the Vault, and I wondered if that's why Miles chose this place—to show he was alone.

"Why do I have to be the caboose?" Dylan asked from the back.

"Because you wanted to see the cool Vault and wouldn't get com signal out here." Jer's voice came through. We were about to lose all contact outside the Vault, including Jeremiah, who had stayed topside.

"Well, the second one isn't my fault—it's Frank's," Dylan said.

"Why do *you* call him Frank?" Chloe asked Dylan.

"Because he will always be Frank in my book. Once a Frank, always a Frank," Dylan answered.

I suppressed a laugh—I agreed.

"Sounds about right for—" Jer's voice cut off.

"We made it to the abyss," Dylan said eerily, the light from his tablet glowing against his face and reflecting off his glasses.

"The door's just ahead." My dad signaled Liam to pass and paused in front of me. "Are you okay?"

"Yes." I took a step but stopped myself from brushing past him, taking a deep breath. "I'm okay, Dad. Let's just focus on why we're here and not me. I'll be fine—I promise."

I gave him a forced smile and walked past him to meet up with Liam.

"That's a door?" Chloe eyed the small opening that was more so the size of a large panel.

"Yes," my dad said. "The doors are still unlocked, but Miles must have turned on the lights."

"Where is he now?" Liam asked. Miles had been sitting in one of the rooms.

"Same spot." Dylan flipped through the different cameras and stopped on one with Miles sitting on a bed, the white comforter fluffed from a pillow underneath it. He rested his arms on his thighs, leaning forward.

"He's still in my room. Great." Liam's eyes narrowed, his eyes reflecting the light from the soft glow of the tablet.

"How do you know that's your room?" Chloe raised an eyebrow. "They all look the same."

"After living in it for almost six years, you can't forget it." Liam's gaze was locked on the screen, and I felt his pain. Even though he had agreed to it, no one had expected him to be down there that long. That time was real to him, and it's a place that isn't easily forgotten or altered—no matter his consent.

My dad swallowed next to me, his face filling with hurt. The Vault wasn't something he had wanted or condoned, and he had expressed his feelings multiple times to Frank and to me. Yet he still hadn't stopped it; he had been too busy protecting me—which happened to include sending me down there.

"Is there a reason he would pick there?" Brandon asked, his sapphire eyes shifting to me.

"It's the first place I ran to when we came back." I glanced at Liam. I had broken away from the group to check and see if Liam was in his room.

My heart plummeted in my chest as the cold of the tunnel crept into my bones. Liam took a step closer, his hand grazing mine. I reached out and squeezed as the others seemed oblivious to my approaching panic attack. Their voices were mute to my ears as I focused on breathing and maintaining a neutral expression. The focus wasn't on me, and it needed to stay that way.

Liam held my hand tightly, and I spared a glance at him. The worry and hurt were prevalent in his eyes. We had gone through so much together. My heart started to slow as my hearing became more clear. He nodded—a silent question if I was okay, and I nodded back. I gently pulled my hand from his and looked at my dad, who was watching us carefully.

"We should hurry," I said to the others.

"This will lead to a room in the boys' corridor," my dad waved a hand at the door.

"I'll go first." Liam pulled his gun. "Stay sharp." He sent my dad to the back with Dylan and took off the panel and entered through the opening.

I grabbed my gun and followed.

When we got to a T, my dad told Liam which way to turn. Liam kept brushing a hand down his face, and I wondered why until something stuck to my hair. I pulled a large cobweb out and shuddered. Let's hope whatever spider made these webs didn't end up on me.

A small metal door appeared, its edges blending into the dirt wall around it. An unlit scanner similar to the ones I had seen inside the Vault was next to it.

"None of this is horrifying. Nope. Not at all," Dylan said.

Liam opened the door, and I instantly shielded my eyes from the bright fluorescent lights on the other side. He peaked in and gave the signal that the room was clear.

"So cool!" Dylan was gaping at the door we came through. The other side blended in with the painted white cement wall next to the toilet and ivory curtain. The only thing not white was the oak dresser, the same as in the other rooms.

"My room is around the corner," Liam said. "Brandon, you're with me. The rest of you stay here."

I nodded. I wanted to go with them, but Miles was programmed to kill me. We had talked about it on the jet and I had reluctantly agreed to not confront him first.

As Liam and Brandon left, my dad pulled out his gun. It was an odd sight, but I had no doubt he had his training. I had my powers, but I also kept my gun out. After running into the Rogue who could absorb my electricity, I was going to make sure I had a gun on me.

I strained to listen, but I couldn't hear anything in these forsaken rooms. After many long minutes, Liam came back.

"He wants to see you, Harper. He is cuffed and you aren't going in there alone or allowed to get close to him." Liam glanced at the others. "Stay here until we come get you."

I followed Liam to the room where Brandon waited by the door. He stowed his gun once we arrived. Miles sat on the bed with his head down and wrists cuffed. He looked up, as if instantly aware of my presence, and my breath caught. His steel eyes captured mine—no sign of green. A muscle in his jaw twitched, and Liam steadied his gun.

He didn't look thrilled to see me.

"I'm not going to do anything." Miles glanced at Brandon. "I couldn't even if I tried. I'm cuffed and you already gave me the inhibitor."

"Sorry, buddy," Brandon said.

"I honor the protocol." Miles looked back at me. "It's good to see you again, Harper."

"On different circumstances than last time—I hope." I went to take a step forward but Liam held out an arm to stop me.

"My mind's clear this time," Miles said. "After I heard about Travis's death..." His voice started to shake and he took a moment before continuing. "I know who you are—who you really are—Harper."

I swallowed. His eyes began to tear and I lowered my gun. I glanced at Brandon, who stared at Miles, the corners of his mouth turned downward. They were best friends and had dealt with trauma long before they knew about Hybrians.

"I know it doesn't mean much, but I am sorry." Miles stared at the ground.

"It wasn't you," I said. "I can be annoying, so I don't blame you for trying to kill me."

No one smiled at my joke as the tension in the air thickened.

"I'm sorry, too. For everything you went through." I couldn't even imagine the things Krauss had done to him to manipulate him like that.

"I wish I could take everything I did back." Miles dropped his head in his hands.

"We should get him out of here," Brandon said.

"There's cameras in every room and we are the only ones here. We have the upper hand." Liam lowered his gun. "We'll evaluate him here."

Before we took Miles with us, the plan was to see where his loyalties lie.

"Is that why you chose this place?" I asked. "Because Alcorp has easy access to it?"

"Yes," Miles answered.

"To show us you don't have anything to hide?" Brandon questioned and Miles nodded.

Brandon grabbed the others, and we made our way to the commons. We sat on the leather furniture surrounded by bookshelves—a good place to talk.

"Miles, I have to apologize for everything you have been through." My dad was sincere, and he didn't hide the shame in his voice. "I should have seen Killian's motives from the start, and my actions—and lack of action—put my family and our friends at risk. We do have a few questions for you if you are up to answering them."

I glanced at my dad. I had expected him to start interrogating Miles with questions about Krauss and how he now felt about him. Blaming ourselves must be part of our genetics—either that or we were always causing mayhem.

Miles nodded from his spot in the chair.

I had sat down the farthest I could from the spot where Travis had sat every day in the commons. He would have loved being back there despite hating it when he lived there.

"Do you still feel any of Killian's influence?" My dad asked.

"No." Miles took a breath and my heart ached. "Not anymore."

"And what broke you out of it?" Liam had kept his guns stowed but hadn't sat down.

"When I heard of Travis' death."

"We found the hit list Krauss gave you—no doubt there's already been death," Liam said.

"Liam!" My gaze shot to Liam. That was the interrogation I was waiting for.

"It's fine." Miles glanced at me, then back at Liam, lowering his voice to an almost growl. "Yes. But they didn't mean anything to her."

Liam's gaze flitted to me.

"I followed instructions even though I didn't know what I was doing. My body was on autopilot and I was in the back seat. I barely remember any of it, like it's a dream—one I want to completely forget." Miles didn't break eye contact with Liam.

"Do you remember what he did to you?" my dad asked.

"It's a blur. All I remember is being strapped to a table." Miles wrung his hands together.

Tears were at the brim of my eyes as I imagined the torture and pain Krauss and Barbara had inflicted on him.

"He used physical and chemical manipulation?" My dad leaned forward.

"Yes." Miles stopped wringing his hands together as if he had just realized he was doing it. "We were taught in the Navy to withstand a certain amount of torture in SERE training, but I never imagined the pull that someone could have on you. I couldn't keep anything straight after a while. Things that I thought were real weren't. The truths were lies. People weren't who I thought they were—everything was influenced."

"I'm so sorry, Miles." I could hear the truth and pain in his voice at the admission.

"I am too." Miles glanced at me.

Liam waved my dad to follow and left the room. I was slightly irritated they hadn't taken me, but I might be a little biased in this situation. After about five minutes, they reentered.

"We can't show you where we are going and will have to search you." Liam shared a look with my dad before continuing. "We will have to take out the chip in the back of your neck."

The chips weren't trackable, but who knew if they had been modified or if they were all like the invisible Rogue's.

Miles nodded. Liam pulled out a knife as Miles got down on his knees and turned around, baring the back of his neck. The process was quick, and Miles hadn't even flinched. Liam tossed the bloodied chip on the ground and smashed it. Chloe made a slight gagging noise but had been quiet the rest of the time.

"There's something else." Miles stood and turned around. "Remember the folder you must've found at the motel?"

"Yes." Liam narrowed his eyes.

"The names on that list along with others are to be killed at the NATO Charity Ball in France. Anyone who would oppose Dr. Krauss and hold power will be there."

"So, anyone who is against him, he is what? Killing off?" Brandon asked.

"Yes." It was my dad who answered. "Anyone who will get in his way to gain power."

"He's trying to make an Alliance of his own," Liam said.

Krauss was paving his path to have control in major areas of the world. He was looking to create an organization like the Alliance, but it would be a dictatorship.

CHAPTER TWENTY-EIGHT

L IAM LED MILES ONTO the jet after Brandon and Chloe. I was about to board when my dad rested a hand on my shoulder.

"Isa," he said as I turned. "When we get a chance, I'd like to spend some father-daughter time. It doesn't make up for the years that I've missed, but—"

"Yes, Dad," I said. "I would love to."

"We still have a lot to catch up on." He smiled but it fell flat shortly after as he became serious. "I want you to know that you can always trust Dodge. No matter what." Something in the way his brows turned downward told me he wanted to say more. Instead he said, "I guess the pilot should go get the jet started, huh?"

He waved me onward and I boarded. I debated asking him why he had mentioned his friend who had helped train me after the prison and helped me recover. I debated on asking him to teach me a few things on piloting and to question him, but our voices could still be heard. Miles was there, and it would have to wait for another time.

"Can I sit here?" I pointed to the chair next to Miles, ignoring Liam's frown.

"I don't mind." Miles glanced at Liam in the chair across from him.

"I got him," I said as I sat down, insinuating that Liam could leave but he didn't move. "You cuffed him to the seat and he has the inhibitor."

"I'll be with the others." Liam left and sat with Chloe and Brandon. They jet started to move, and we sat in silence the entire ascent.

"Did you ever talk to Hannah, the Rogue with white wings?" I asked, breaking the silence and probing my curiosity with something small.

Miles glanced at me before answering, "No. I haven't."

"Oh." I wasn't sure what else to say.

"I did meet Elias." Miles leaned forward, the chain to his cuff rattling.

Oh.

"The platypus Rogue," I said, remembering what Krauss had said about him.

"He wouldn't appreciate that name."

"That's too bad." I chewed at the inside of my cheek.

Miles stared out the window. "He was made specifically for you."

"What do you mean?"

"He was meant to take you down if I couldn't." Miles paused. "Dr. Krauss wants to add the gene that absorbs electrical currents to every new Hybrian he creates."

"Has he been able to?"

"Not that I'm aware of." He shook his head. "I don't think he can add more than one additional animal DNA to the serum."

After about twenty minutes, Miles had fallen asleep—or at least had his eyes closed. He wasn't going anywhere or able to do anything, so I took the moment to see if Liam had anything about the NATO ball. He was in the cockpit with my dad. After we left the Vault, Liam had immediately informed Frank.

"Any news on shutting down the ball?" I asked when I reached them. I stayed in the doorway because there wasn't much room in the small space.

"Unfortunately, no." My dad flipped a switch and turned in his chair. "We think Killian has people on the inside running it. We made contact with one ambassador; however, they didn't care for our accusations and said it was a perfectly safe event that will not be interrupted by false leads." Miles had given us a couple of other names that had been on his hit list.

"We hadn't even mentioned Hybrians and they failed to take us seriously." Liam crossed his arms as he leaned against the back of the co-pilot chair. "I wonder if someone tipped them off about false leads to stop the ball."

"Hopefully Alan will influence them before the day comes," my dad said.

"We'll have to leave in a couple of days in order to make it—if they don't cancel it," Liam added. "Maya and Adam will be back, and Jeremiah and Blake will join us if it comes to that. The Paris operatives will be watching the outside."

"Miles just shared something with me," I said after a brief pause. "He said Krauss is trying to use part of the DNA from the Rogue that could absorb my powers for all of the Hybrians he creates."

"He's creating Rogues with a defense specifically for your power?" Liam raised an eyebrow.

"Apparently." I glanced behind me to where Miles was. "Miles said he doesn't think he can add a third DNA."

"That would be hard to achieve—if impossible." My dad frowned.

"Let's hope it doesn't come to that," Liam added.

The rest of the flight to Montana was quiet. Liam had blindfolded Miles when we were within twenty minutes of headquarters. I gently slid my arm through his and led him off the plane. The hair on my arms stood at our contact, and it was like a force inside propelled me closer to him as we walked toward the large doors embedded into the mountainside. Once we were on the main floor in headquarters, I took off his blindfold. Thankfully there wasn't an entourage to meet us, only Frank.

"Hello, Officer MacLand." Frank's hands were courteously tucked behind his back and he wore one of his normal sweaters despite it being August. "We are delighted to have you back. Due to the circumstances, we will have to put you in holding. We hope you understand."

"Can I talk to you?" I asked Frank. "In your office?"

"Of course." Frank waved me to lead the way.

"Along with both of you." I looked between Liam and my dad. "Brandon and Chloe can watch Miles."

They nodded and I headed up to Frank's office. Once the door was shut, I spun around to face the three of them.

"He doesn't need to be locked up—he's had enough of that."

"We don't know if we can trust him," Liam said.

"I'm not saying that we have to trust him. What I'm saying is that he has been through enough. If—only if—he is okay with staying with me, he can. He went through everything because I had to go and try to play hero. I tried to save Kat. Instead, I gave Krauss exactly what he wanted, plus Miles."

"It's not a—" my dad began to say.

"Please just hear me out," I said. "We need to know whose side he's on and before the ball, right? He had to have met many Rogues and could point out the ones we don't recognize. But we have to know what he's thinking. Keeping him in a cell won't do that. We can test the waters and see how he does overnight. Someone's always watching the cameras, and we can give him another inhibitor. I'll stay awake the entire night." It's not like I had slept well since the prison anyways. "In the morning, he can go with Brandon, or whoever, and I'll get some rest then. There's no way he'll be able to do anything. Please give me some time with him—alone."

There was a moment of silence as the three of them stared at me.

"Only if there's cameras in your room." My dad's voice was firm.

"What?" Liam looked at my dad.

Yeah—what? I also looked at my dad.

"I don't trust him, but I trust my daughter," my dad said. I gave him a thankful nod but he didn't nod back. He wasn't thrilled.

"I agree," Frank said. "We don't have long until the ball. If there's something else going on—another reason he told us about it—I want to know before sending anyone there."

"This is insane." Liam ran a hand through his hair.

"Liam." I waited until he looked at me to continue. "Think of it as a mission. Think of me as a part of the team and not just a friend you want to protect for once, please."

He clenched his jaw but didn't say anything.

"We will treat this as a mission and are not to let our guard down." Frank looked at Liam. "Go with Ellie and install two body cameras in Harper's room. Make sure every angle is covered—besides the bathroom."

Liam took a second before nodding and taking off. I guess I'd settle for cameras in my room as long as they were immediately removed when this was over.

Later that night, Liam guarded the locker room while Miles showered and after dinner, Miles and I went back to my room. He shrugged his jacket off, and my hand smothered the gasp on my lips as bile rose in my throat. His arms had multiple thick scars, as if someone had cut the same spot repeatedly.

He tossed it on the couch and grabbed the pillow I had been holding out for him.

"I don't think anyone's slept up there in a while. Sorry you get the top." I actually wasn't sorry. I had to be alert, and I'd be able to monitor things better if he slept right above me.

"The top bunk's just fine." Miles tossed the pillow on the top.

He turned to face me and froze. I didn't think he had realized how close I was behind him. The heat radiated between us through the thin fabric of my baggy shirt and shorts and branded my bare skin. His T-shirt, sweats, and wet hair from his shower looked too unguarded, but his body was stiff. I could feel his breath against my cheek.

At least he could breathe.

I cleared my throat.

"Did you need anything else?" I managed to ask.

His eyes narrowed and his gaze scanned my face, searching for something, but I had no clue what.

"Just water." He brushed by me, careful not to make contact.

My feet were glued in the same spot as I watched him. He grabbed a water from the mini fridge and downed it in seconds, tossing the bottle when finished.

"Do you know why I can move so quickly?" He walked back to the bunk beds.

Because of me. I shook my head, unable to speak.

"I can mimic the flutter of the hummingbird's wings. My muscles move at an alarming rate. It's like breathing—it happens without thinking, but it can be controlled if desired." His eyes never left mine, watching my reaction. "At first, it was uncontrollable."

He slowly raised his right arm in the air until it was just above his shoulder. Trembling took over his fingers and made its way up his arm. His gaze shot to me, and he quickly lowered his arm back to his side.

"It didn't heal you," I whispered. My stem cells were potentially thought to be a long shot cure to everything—like it had cured both my mom and me from a deadly illness.

"I didn't want it to."

There was a brief falter in his expression before he masked it.

"Miles… if I could go back in time…" My voice shook just like his arm had. I swallowed and tried again. "If I had stayed put in the Vault, none if this would've happened. You'd be at Mel's Pub with Brandon, playing pool. Your entire life has changed because of one night."

He stared at me with calculating eyes, his face morphing into something that looked an awful lot like disbelief.

"I'm just part hummingbird now and you've, well, always have been part eel." A smile tugged at the corner of his lips, almost into one of *his* smiles that normally gave me butterflies.

I bit my own lip, holding back a grin—it felt wrong to smile. His eyes traveled to my mouth, and his smile vanished. He promptly headed toward the bed and climbed up.

"Good night, Harper," he said as he faced the wall.

My hand twitched at my side. These mixed signals were throwing me through a loop, but Miles had been thrown through the ringer, and then some.

I flipped the light switch and headed toward my bed, only to pause. Miles had shut the door after he followed me in, and it took restraint not to open it. Now that I was going to bed—not that I'd sleep anyway—the restraint was slipping. I turned around and quietly moved across the laminate wood flooring to the door.

I opened the door a crack and wedged the doorstop underneath. I turned back toward the bunk bed and made it to the rug before glancing up at Miles. He had rolled over and was watching me.

"I don't like to be locked in," I said, answering his curious gaze.

I hastily made my way to the lower bunk, wanting out of the scrutiny of being watched. For some reason, the feeling had unsettled me.

CHAPTER TWENTY-NINE

"W HY COULDN'T WE STAY at the Paris stronghold again?" Dylan moaned in protest.

"You know why. It's not even close. This hotel is right across the street from the ball." I stared at the makeup bag in my hands, surveying my options as I stood in front of the mirror.

The last two days at headquarters had been uneventful and quiet for those that weren't contacting government officials and getting things planned. The ball hadn't been canceled and we had arrived at the hotel not too long ago.

"Well, at least they had a free bar," Dylan said.

"You don't even drink." I stared at him through the mirror.

"Not anymore, but that doesn't mean the occasional drink is bad. Plus, I have to wear this suit and my computer is the only one going to see it." He smoothed the front of his jacket and straightened his bow tie.

"Jer gets to see it." I turned around and smirked as he laughed.

Someone knocked at the door, interrupting our conversation.

"Where is she?" Maya asked, and in a few seconds, she was in my peripheral. "We need to get you in your dress."

Multiple footsteps followed, and the tiny room became claustrophobic as Miles, Brandon, Chloe, and my dad entered.

"Maya." I set the makeup down and turned to admire my beautiful friend. Her red dress hugged her curves just right and billowed in satin waves at her ankles. "You look stunning."

"I know." She flipped her sleek black hair off her shoulder. "Now, come. We need to get you in your dress."

"Yep. Totally jealous that I'm not going in." Chloe eyed Maya in hers.

"We'll have to celebrate when this is done, and maybe, just maybe, I'll dress up and we can go out." I winked at Chloe.

"It has to be extravagant like this ball." Her eyes narrowed in a friendly challenge.

"Hopefully this isn't extravagant," I mumbled. It better be a dull, boring charity ball full of drunken laughter and no death.

"Isa," my dad said gently, "we don't know everyone who's on Krauss' side." He spared a glance in Miles' direction.

I nodded in agreement.

"Hopefully I'll get to see my little girl all dressed up when this is done." He gave me one of those proud dad smiles—a toothy, bright-eyed grin.

"It'll be kind of like a prom daughter-dad moment except *Mission Impossible* style." I smiled.

"It kind of would be, wouldn't it?" My dad chuckled.

There was a moment of hesitation before my brain decided to move my body and I wrapped my arms around my dad. He took me into a big bear hug. I stood there for a few moments before pulling away and kissing his cheek. His eyes looked like they wanted to melt at the daughterly gesture—after all, he was hurting too and no one had offered him support like they had offered me.

"I'll see you soon, Dad." I turned, following Maya out the door.

Less than an hour and a half later, we were heading toward the building, where formal versions of bouncers stood taking names at the top of a beautiful set of marble stairs. The dark violet A-line dress on me flared mid-waist with a mix of satin and chiffon, the bottom trailing behind me as I climbed the steps. The long slit made it easier to walk up the stairs; however, the heels hadn't helped. Long snug sleeves ran the lengths of my arms, covering the barcode tattoo, just like Maya's dress covered hers.

My curls helped cover the plunging dress in the back, but the way the sides of my hair were pinned did nothing to cover the sharp V-neck front. I should have known not to let Maya and Chloe pick out my dress. The outside was luring and beautiful. A knife was hidden in a holster on my inner thigh, Damien's switchblade was holstered just above it, and a tiny syringe that carried an inhibitor was tucked under my sleeve on my wrist, only noticeable if someone deliberately looked for it. There was a gun strapped to my other thigh.

My pace slowed as we reached the top of the steps, and I prayed I wouldn't twist an ankle.

"May I?" Miles held out an arm, his face expressionless.

"Thank you." My heart rate picked up as I wrapped my arm around his. It was the first time we had touched since he was back.

I tried to focus on Adam and Maya directly in front of us, but I couldn't keep my eyes forward. Miles' black suit and tie did nothing to hide the hard edge of his features—if anything, it accentuated them.

At the top of the steps, Liam gave the doorman our names as a bouncer waved a wand over us. I held in a relieved sigh when he waved us on. Dylan's devices had worked and hacked the machine so it didn't flag anything. We walked past the marble pillars and through the opened vaulted doors with gold etching the outline. The invitation list included the wealthy from around the world—so I shouldn't have been shocked.

Krauss probably suspected that we were going to be there, and we had to assume he knew. Frank had been able to get our fake names on the list, and there was only a handful of us on the inside, but the entire place was surrounded. It made things a bit more complicated when the ambassadors wouldn't heed our warning. They were stubborn.

"Let the games begin." Dylan's voice came through our coms.

"There better be no games," I said.

"Eyes sharp," Liam whispered with a smile as he gave an overly dressed couple a polite nod. "Miles, let us know if you recognize anyone."

Liam still didn't trust Miles, but he could be a huge help in recognizing any Rogues. Miles had the inhibitor and wouldn't be able to morph, and he wasn't to leave my side.

Tables were scattered about a large banquet hall with white linen tablecloths and round centerpieces with flags sticking out of them like a pin cushion. Each flag represented the countries in NATO, and it was perplexing how they could fit each one on there.

"I'm going to walk around. Find your targets and keep your eyes on them." Liam scanned the crowd. "Dylan, how's it looking?"

"Quiet—besides the partiers that are already drunk outside," Dylan said.

"Good." Liam glanced at me, his eyes inquiring if I was okay if he left. I nodded.

"It looks like our targets are conversing." Maya grabbed Adam's arm and dragged him in the direction of four people who were congregated together.

Despite the background noise, the awkward silence didn't go unnoticed between Miles and me. I fidgeted with the cuff of my sleeve and scanned the crowd for my two targets—the ambassadors for Italy and France.

"Care to get a fake drink with me?" Miles held out his arm.

"We have to blend in, right?" I looped my arm through his and let him lead me toward the stationary bar.

"You look beautiful." Miles leaned toward me, his voice caressing my cheek and sending goose bumps down my spine—good ones.

"You don't look too bad yourself." I grinned through the lie. Each time I looked at him, my breath caught. He looked stunning.

"I'll take that as a compliment."

"It definitely is."

We waited at the bar while the bartender waited on a couple. I scanned the crowd, not spotting my targets.

"Two glasses of your Chateau Margaux, please," Miles said when the bartender came over, fluently pronouncing the name of a wine I couldn't even spell.

The bartender poured two glasses and set them on the counter before walking away, and Miles left a tip in the jar.

"You know French wine?" I asked as we grabbed our glasses and turned around. My taste buds hated me at the thought of letting this very expensive wine go to waste, but I didn't dare have a sip. I needed my beast.

"Some, but not all." Miles glanced at the glass that I held in front of my nose, getting a good whiff. "That's a six-hundred-dollar bottle of wine."

I jerked, almost spilling the wine down my front. I knew it was expensive but not that expensive.

A tall, slender man with dark hair and glasses caught my attention as he weaved through the crowd in front of us..

"Mr. Romano," Miles said, seeing who I was looking at.

"You remember him?" I glanced at Miles.

"I remember all of my targets." He frowned..

Miles and I headed back to our table, trying to blend in.

"Jeremiah. Blake. Keep a sharp eye on the drinks and food leaving the kitchen," Liam said through the coms. "Who knows if that's how they'll attack."

"Aye, aye, captain!" Blake replied.

"I have eyes on the floor while Blake's in the kitchen," Jeremiah added.

"Everyone find their targets?" Liam asked.

"Yes," both Maya and Adam answered at the same time.

"Just one of mine." From where I was, I couldn't find my other target, nor could I spot Liam. "We're going to move and see if I can find the other."

I motioned for Miles to follow. If we stood near the edge of the room, we would have a wider view, and these heels gave me a little bit of help.

"They might not have checked in," Miles said, a hand hovering over the small of my back. He wasn't touching my exposed skin there, but I could feel the warmth.

"Curse them for using paper to check the guests in. I can't tell who checked in," Dylan grumbled.

"Same with the lack of working cameras inside," Liam added. Dylan had warned us ahead of time that he was blind in the main room but had eyes on the outside and some hallways. Body cameras were a part of the plan, until they hadn't been packed. Blake swore he had loaded them on the jet, but the case was nowhere to be found.

"At least we have the street cameras." Dylan's cheerfulness died a bit. "I haven't seen one of your targets arrive, Harper. Everyone else's have."

"You don't think they could've gotten to her beforehand?" I whispered as we made our way toward the edge.

"There's always the possibility," Liam answered. "She also could've not arrived yet or not have been picked up by the cameras outside."

"We'll find her." Miles put a reassuring hand on my shoulder as we reached the wall.

The contact was welcome, and I glanced from his hand to his face. The welcome feeling of his touch vanished, replaced with unease that settled deep in my stomach. His steel eyes glossed over as he stared at his hand, like he was somewhere else completely. This was becoming more common, and that unsettled me.

"Miles?" I shifted, causing his gaze to jolt to my face.

"Sorry." He removed his hand and coughed into it. "Who are we looking for?"

"Just keep eyes on Mr. Romano. I'll look for the other ambassador." I don't know why I didn't tell him my other target, but my gut told me not to. My dad and Liam's intentions had been rational when they decided not to inform him. He was still recovering and needed to prove that we could trust him.

I swirled the expensive wine in the glass, creating a smooth red whirlpool and ignoring the tension between Miles and me. After a moment, I looked up and began to scan the crowd, coming up empty once again.

"That's one of Krauss' men." Miles nodded toward off toward the bar.

"A Rogue?" I asked.

"Yes."

The man looked around and then his gaze locked onto me, like he had sense he was being watched. His face paled and he turned into the crowd, heading in the opposite direction. I squeezed through groups of people, trying to keep eyes on him.

"We spotted a Rogue," I said so the others could hear me. "He's headed toward the back of the room."

When I reached the back of the room, I lost sight of him.

"Do you see where he went?" I asked.

"No." Miles scanned the crowd.

"Crap" I set down the wine on a nearby table, no longer wanting the prop, and started walking. I came to a halt when I noticed someone movement down a hallway. I pushed through some people just in time to see the Rogue go through a door.

"He's leaving the party. I'm going to check it out." I took off with Miles right behind me.

"I'll meet up with you," Liam said. "Maya, Adam, are your targets still together?"

"Yes," Adam answered.

"Maya, watch my targets while Adam watches yours."

"Third door on the right in the back hallway," I said to Liam.

The door the Rogue had exited led to a stairwell. Inside, there was no telling which way he had gone so I took a guess and went down. The next door led to another hallway, this one much less spectacular.

The Rogue was nowhere in sight. We made our way down the hallway, careful not to make any noise. After passing a couple doors, I thought I heard a noise. I held up a hand for Miles behind me to stop moving. In a flash, the Rogue came bursting through a door and ran into Miles. They crashed into the door on the opposite side. Miles' arm must have hit the handle, and they went flying into the closet.

I morphed and ran after them.

"Traitor!" The Rogue yelled as they crashed into metal shelves.

I grabbed the back of his suit and pulled him off Miles. I sent a lightning bolt crashing into the Rogue.

I screamed as pain ripped through my chest. Something touched my ear, and I turned to see Miles holding my com in one hand and a bloody knife in the other. He tossed the com on the ground and crushed it.

I pulled my gun, aiming it straight at Miles, who stared at me with indifference. My arm shook as I glanced down at the blood gushing from my chest—right next to my heart. The only reason I was still standing was because I still had my beast, but it would fade soon.

"It was a set up," I whispered as I fell to my knees, letting the gun drop next to me.

"You're a schizophrenic, Harper." Miles glanced at the ground next to me. "Your dad never cured you. The serum just made it worse. And even when you know the truth, you pathologically lie. You played me, just like you're playing the others." He shook his head. "You've killed dozens."

"Is that..." my chest was heavy. "What Krauss made you believe?"

"No. That's what *you* hid from me." His chest rose and fell as his lips tightened. "You made me fall for you, but it was all a lie."

"That's not true. Somewhere inside you, you know that." I coughed, blood spewing out.

"You're wrong. You're leading everyone to their death." Tears began to swell in his eyes as he rubbed the back of his neck.

"You're not a monster. Don't let them make you believe that." I couldn't sit up any longer and let my body fall to the ground.

"It looks like I'm getting off the train," I whispered with a small smile. "Please forgive yourself."

My head lolled to the side. I was tired. My beast was tired.

"Harper?" What seemed like minutes later, Miles' blurry figure knelt down next to me. "No..." His hands felt colder than normal as they held my cheeks, forcing me to look up at him. "Stay with me. Okay?"

His hands dropped to my chest and blurred figures approached behind him.

"Oh, sh—" Someone's words never completely made their way to me. Multiple voices spoke, but only a few actually stuck.

"Hang in there, Harper." Liam took Miles' spot as he backed away. "Dylan, where's the nearest hospital and the closest ambulance?" Liam nodded at what I assumed was whatever Dylan was saying.

My body was numb, and I wasn't sure if anyone was applying pressure to my wound or not.

"The Rogue did this?"

"No," Miles said. His voice was hoarse, and with that one word I knew that if I hadn't killed Miles—like he had asked me to do if he changed—my death would. "I did that to her."

Silence.

I thought unconsciousness would have had taken over by now, but I could still feel the weight in my chest, like I was drowning. My body was cold. Numb. Breathing was becoming a chore, but I could still make who looked like Miles leaving and someone running after him. And then it ended.

The pain was gone.

CHAPTER THIRTY

My unconscious thoughts ventured to my happy memories—playing with Taco, hanging out with Dylan, eating my mom's pie as Joe's face lit up at everything she said, riding on my dad's shoulders through the park, the moment Liam and I became friends, watching Maya and Travis battle in Ping-Pong while sitting next to Liam in the Vault, the cabin with Chloe and Brandon, and every single breathtaking moment with Miles.

Peace—or close to it.

It was like I was almost there, but something more stubborn than my mother and me combined held me on the invisible edge from the blinding light.

Darkness.

"He's here," a firm voice said.

Darkness still consumed my vision, but voices made their way to me as if I were in a bubble. My back was against something, but that was the only thing I could feel.

"Did you alert the others?" A chair skidded against the ground.

"Yes," the unknown voice said.

Faint footsteps grew farther away, as if someone was leaving.

"Stay with her, please." This voice I knew.

Liam! I tried to yell, but only a gurgling noise came out.

"Harper?" A hand rested on my arm. "It's okay." The voice belonged to Blake.

I went to speak again—to say anything—but still only gargling rose from my throat.

"Let me get Cole."

Who's here? I had wanted to ask. *Where'd Liam go? Why isn't my dad here?* He would be there, which I assumed had to be headquarters, if Dr. Cole was there.

My questions died, vanishing inward as if the bubble I was in popped.

I could hear a steady, rhythmic beeping sound to my left. My eyes felt crusted shut, but I pried them open. Bright naked bulbs caused me to instantly squint, but after adjusting, I was able to make out a room in the medical wing of headquarters. It was small, windowless, and had a couple chairs in what little space that wasn't occupied by medical equipment. In those chairs sat two familiar people.

Dylan was typing away on his laptop while Chloe was looking at her phone. Her soft brown eyes looked up.

"Harper!" She shoved her phone in her jeans pocket and stood. "You're awake!"

"I knew it." Dylan stood, setting his laptop down on the chair. "I knew she'd be awake before Dr. Cole or Doc suspected."

"What happened after..." I left the question open. I had so many questions, but I wasn't sure if I was ready for the answers. "Is Miles okay?"

"He's okay," Dylan said, but his lack of joking was concerning. They both looked at me like I was a wounded lost puppy.

"What is it?" I tried to sit up, but the pain in my chest was too great.

"I'm going to get Liam. He'll want to know you are awake." Chloe squeezed my hand before exiting.

I looked at Dylan, narrowing my eyes. I needed answers.

"You've been out for a few days." He came over and sat on the end of the hospital bed. "We took you to the closest hospital when we were in France, and they performed surgery. As soon as you were stable, we took you to headquarters. Krauss could easily target you in the hospital. But seeing how Miles," Dylan's Adam's apple bulged. "Now it makes sense why we didn't have our body cameras or coms."

Blake probably hadn't forgotten to load the case with our cameras and coms—Miles had sabotaged it.

"Where are the others?" I asked.

"They're trying to track down the leads Miles gave us. I've been trying to narrow Krauss' location down."

"My dad? Is he helping them too?" My throat clenched. Something felt wrong that he wasn't there, and Dylan's look confirmed it.

"He's gone, Harper. I'm so sorry." He frowned as he set a hand on my leg.

Touch was comfort for some, and maybe it was for me from the right people. Dylan normally was one of the few, after getting past the first few months of the prison, but right now, I could barely feel anything.

"How?" I choked out as a single tear rolled down my cheek.

I thought he was gone once before, but this time was different. I was older and had just gotten him back. Things weren't normal or full between us, but I had thought I had time to mend the hole and get to know him, and him to know me—this me.

"I guess he figured out Miles wasn't himself and tried to stop him," Dylan said wearily. "He came back with us, but now Captain Shaw has him at the Portland precinct morgue. We're not really equipped for that."

My dad had died protecting me—for real this time. And it was at Miles' hands.

"Harper." Liam walked into the small room with Dr. Cole behind him.

Liam glanced at my cheek before looking at Dylan, who nodded. He strode over to the side of the bed and placed a hand over mine.

"I wish you never had to hear those words, sunshine." Liam's words were spoken from experience. His entire family had been killed in a car accident—not just his dad, but his mom and sister too.

"I'll be okay." I cleared my throat, ignoring the heat trailing the rims of my eyes. "What happened at the banquet? Are the ambassadors okay?"

"The ambassadors are alive." Liam squeezed my hand and stood. "When Miles left, he took out the Rogues there. He knew where each one was posted and the entire plan."

"What do you mean, *took out*?" I asked.

"Like, he took them out." Dylan stood and walked to the end of the bed, crossing his arms. "They won't ever be a problem."

"He disappeared after that," Liam rubbed the back of his neck. "Until he showed up here."

"That's who arrived when you had to leave," I said to Liam, and his eyebrows furrowed in question. "Blake had told you that he was here and you left. I wasn't sure who he was."

"You remember that?" It was Dr. Cole who spoke this time, her long, grey-streaked auburn hair pulled back into a low ponytail.

"Yeah, but that's the only thing I really remember." I looked from Dr. Cole to Liam. "We blind folded Miles when he arrived and left, scanned him, and never had him out of sight. How did he know how to find headquarters?"

"I'm not sure," Liam said. "But headquarters is now compromised."

I coughed and Liam helped me take a sip of water.

"Thank you, and thank you for getting me out of there," I said after swallowing.

"Anytime." Liam smiled gently.

Dr. Cole set her clipboard down at my feet and ran through a short exam. She changed my bandage, and the wound had healed a significant amount. When she was done, she grabbed the clipboard and started writing everything down.

"So, where's Miles? Is he... himself?" I fiddled with the sheet. They had said he was there—and I was sure he was locked up—but what state was he in?

"He's in holding." Liam ran a hand through his hair. "He came here to warn us while you were out... and wanted us to lock him up."

"So he has full control?" I asked.

"It seems like it, but we don't have a definitive way to tell." Dr. Cole's eyes moved from me to the clipboard in her hand.

"We can't trust him right now, sunshine. Not after everything he did." He frowned.

"Can I see him at least?"

"Even I don't think that's a good idea right now," Chloe said, as she entered the room. "He's a little messed up from the whole ordeal. I think he needs time—alone."

Chloe's eyes glistened, and she blinked away tears. She was telling the truth—which meant he was internally punishing himself.

"You should also rest and stay in bed," Dr. Cole said.

"I have my healing back. Can I at least go to communications to help find Krauss?" I started rubbing my chest but pulled my hand away when the pain throbbed my entire upper ribs and sent me into a coughing fit.

Dr. Cole thrust her clipboard into Liam's hands and ran over, gently patting my back. "I think some rest is warranted."

"Okay," I rasped out once the coughing fit ceased.

"Good. Now, everyone, let her rest." Dr. Cole waved the others to follow as she exited.

Chloe and Dylan gave me sympathetic smiles and followed her.

"I'll talk to you soon," Liam said, starting to turn around, but I caught his hand.

"Thank you." When he turned, I held on to his hand a moment longer before letting go. "You're a great leader, and you're going to be the person Alcorp needs."

"What?" He raised an eyebrow.

"Don't what me, buttercup." I grinned. "We both know Frank's going to need help, and he's been grooming you."

"Yeah. I don't know about that." Liam shook his head.

"We both know it's true. And a true leader isn't conceited, so obviously you won't admit it." A small cough escaped my throat. "And I think Ellie has been very helpful too."

"She has," Liam said. I attempted to hold in the smirk but was failing. "It's not like that."

"Sure. You keep telling yourself that, buttercup." I sucked in my lips, still failing to hide a grin at the ever-so-slight redness in his cheeks. "You're blushing."

"No, I'm not." Liam rubbed his forehead. "Alright, sunshine. Get some sleep."

Liam shook his head at me and turned around.

CHAPTER THIRTY-ONE

I OPENED THE STEEL door to the holding cells.

"Knock when you're done," Liam said. "I'll be right outside the door."

"Thank you." I glanced at the wide corridor.

Each cell was empty except the last one.

"You shouldn't be here," Miles said, his hair shielding his eyes.

He was on the floor against the wall with his head down and one arm propped on his knee while the other lazily rested on his sprawled leg. His jeans were clean and so was his black shirt. His brown cowboy boots sat in the corner like he had made himself at home after the last few days.

"I think this is exactly where I'm supposed to be." I stared at him as he looked up. His eyes were no longer glossed over.

Miles stood and walked over to the glass. He rested his left arm on the glass, just above his head, and glared at me.

"Your father should be alive." His voice was hard as his eyes dropped to my chest, right where he had stabbed me. "And you shouldn't have been on your deathbed."

I swallowed. "Your intimidation tactics to get me to leave won't work. I see that you're hurting, Miles. Everything you did—it wasn't your fault."

A few moments passed as we stared at each other, Miles' gaze roaming over my face. He slammed his fist against the wall and rubbed a hand down his face. He turned so his back was against the glass—facing away from me—and slid down to the floor.

I released a sigh and did the same so our backs were together, the clear barrier unwanted on my end. I should be angry with Miles. I should hate him. But I didn't. I hated Krauss, and there was no one I loathed more. None of this would've happened if Krauss had never tortured Miles and invaded his mind.

If I had never escaped Krauss' control, this would've been me. I would have killed my own father. Liam and my father had helped me with this part—the blame. I had a better understanding that I couldn't blame myself and carry the world on my shoulders, and this was where Miles was—except the blood had been literally on his hands even if he wasn't in control.

"You're not alone," I whispered. "I'll never let you be alone."

"Maybe that's how it's supposed be." His voice was barely above a whisper.

"Together, Miles. That was a promise."

Silence.

"There's something I need to know." I rubbed at my chest.

"If he suffered," Miles said.

I nodded even though he couldn't see me. This would hurt, but I needed to know how he died and hear it from Miles.

"Yes." I swallowed.

"After you and Maya left, Brandon and Chloe headed out into the hallway. Once they were out of the room, he pulled a gun on me. He told me he knew I was still under Krauss' influence. I told him I wasn't there for him, just you and eventually Dr. Roulings." He took a deep breath.

"He said he couldn't let me hurt you," he continued. "He was about to shoot. I lunged. He got a shot off, but it had a suppressor so no one heard it. Even though I felt very in control, it was as if something else inhabited my urges and instead of simply rendering him unconscious,

I tossed him to the side." There was a brief pause. "He hit his head on the corner of the desk. It was quick."

The cells across from me blurred as tears fell.

"Why didn't he say anything to us?" I managed to ask, my voice hoarse.

"I think he had his doubts about me."

"But he always doubted Krauss," I whispered.

"Yes," Miles said.

My head was spinning.

"What is it like?" I asked.

"Is what like?" His voice held no emotion, like he was lost.

"Your thoughts. Every false memory Krauss put into your mind and the real ones. What's it like?"

"Jumbled." He sighed. "But I know what's real now. The other parts are like a dream, but I can tell that's what they are now. I had an assignment, and with the emotion that came after I...."

Stabbed you. His mission was to kill me, and he almost succeeded. But he didn't.

"It's okay," I said.

"I killed your dad," he said after a few minutes, like I wasn't understanding that. "I almost killed you! It's not okay. You should be far away from me."

I turned around so I could see him. His hands clutched the sides of his head as he leaned forward. I stood and hovered a finger over the red button next to Miles' cell.

"Harper. Don't." Miles turned his head so he could see me but didn't get up.

"I'm coming in." I pressed the button and the door opened.

I stepped inside and closed the door behind me. He watched me through the strands of his hair as I made my way over to the cot, sitting across from him.

"You can't trust me, Harper," Miles gritted through his teeth.

"Stab me once, shame on you. Stab me twice, well, then maybe I should be dead." I let a loose smile play on my lips but it slipped at his glare. "You missed."

He raised an eyebrow and I released a sigh.

"You could have hit my heart—that was your target. You are obviously more than capable of hitting your mark." I made my way over to him. "You came back here to warn us and to be locked up. You took out the rest of the Rogues at the ball. You didn't kill me."

I knelt so we were eye level.

"You are in control. Not Krauss. You. Things may be messed up in your head and are confusing, but in time, you will see that you overcame Krauss and everything during that time frame was done by his hands and not yours." I placed a hand on his cheek. "You once told me I was the strongest person you knew—but you're the strongest person that I know. You're not a monster."

Miles' chest rose and fell as he stared at me. I took my hand away and his eyes closed.

"Together," I said gently.

I stepped out of the cell, hiding the imaginary stone crushing my chest. Miles was in a dark abyss, dug deep into the ground—a similar place I had been six months ago. The not-so-feeling fictional place your mind goes after experiencing trauma.

This wasn't over. Krauss was still out there, and I wasn't going to rest until he was gone. My fingernails dug into my palms as I climbed the stairs.

CHAPTER THIRTY-TWO

THE MOONLIGHT STREAMING THROUGH the narrow windows lit my room enough to where I could see the small indent in the bunk bed bar above me. It looked like someone had sat up too fast. I rubbed the smooth imperfection after staring at it for hours.

Sighing, I sat up—careful not to whack my head—and crawled out of bed. I changed into leggings and a t-shirt, leaving my shoes off. No shoes in the Vault had strengthened and improved our proprioception, something I had always questioned until leaving. I felt less restrained without shoes.

I left through my already-cracked door and made my way to communications. We were doing even more rigorous monitoring of headquarters since Miles had arrived six days ago.

"—had the opportunity yet to discover how beautiful life can be in another version," I heard Liam say as I rounded the corner.

"I think the artist was depicting not just her soul, but her daughter's also. They were both trapped, but found beauty in their bond. And the cracks there represent them breaking through," Ellie said as she stared at the large screens on the wall.

The screens displayed a large blue and black painting of an outline of a mother and daughter. An invisible barrier made with different shades encased them, and large black cracks lined one side of them, colorful flowers sprouting on the other side.

Liam and Ellie glanced at me as I approached.

"What do you think, Harper?" Ellie asked.

"Oh. Umm." I stared at the painting. Beyond the mother and daughter were dark smudges of some sort of abstract. "I'm not really good at interpreting art."

"That's the beauty, I guess. It can be interpreted as many things." Ellie gently smiled and tucked a strand of hair behind her ear.

"Couldn't sleep?" Liam leaned forward, pulling out the chair next to him.

"No." I took a seat. "I'm not even sure what time it is."

"Two." Ellie yawned as she changed the screens back to the outside cameras that the computer in front of her already displayed. "Dylan and Jeremiah are relieving us at three."

"Well, you guys are more than welcome to retire. I can keep an eye on things," I offered. There was no way I was falling asleep.

"I think the extra company will actually do us good." Liam glanced at Ellie, who nodded.

"Have you seen Miles tonight?" I asked Liam.

"No, but after watch he needs another inhibitor."

Miles has been receiving inhibitors, but less frequently than when he first arrived.

"Who—" I was cut off by a short beep from the monitors, causing all of us to straighten.

"It's coming from the south side, but I don't see anything." Ellie pulled up the camera on the computer. "It's just the valley and side of the mountain."

"Pull up the front camera," Liam said.

"Nothing." Ellie squinted at the camera, which was shaded green and black from night vision.

"There!" I pointed to one of the views in the corner of the screen where a flash of white swept through, too quick to be picked up by the monitor.

Ellie enlarged that view, but there was nothing but a dark valley. Consecutive beeps were followed by multiple reddening borders, but I didn't see anything. The square around the front view turned red as another alarm beeped. She pulled it up and sent it to the large monitors on the wall.

"How?" I whispered.

"You know her?" Liam asked, staring at the girl with stark yellow eyes that were focused right at the camera above the main entrance, her large white wings stretching out, then folding behind her back.

"Yes." I stared in disbelief. "She's the one that helped me escape in Germany."

She wouldn't have known about this place—she had escaped Krauss. There was so much hate she had toward the Rogues. There was no way she would have gone back. Unless...unless he had found her.

I shot out of the chair, standing straight up as I watched her tight lips move, slowly mouthing *I'm sorry.*

"They're here," I said right before the entire building shook and alarms started blaring throughout headquarters. The computer mouse fell to the ground in front of me as another wave of shaking hit.

Ellie pulled up the camera to the outside entrance to the garage. Crumbled rock littered the floor, and some of the dust settled, revealing a few Rogues—the Rogue with long braids down to her knees was in front. She was the one with the sonic boom and in her hand, she held a small remote.

Ellie changed the view to the inside of the garage. The Rogue tossed the remote aside.

"They blew it up," I mumbled to no one in particular. Those walls were solid enough that her powers alone wouldn't take them down, but in a combined effort, apparently it was possible.

"If anyone was asleep, they're awake now." Liam pressed a red button built into the desk next to the keyboard, the one that alerted other Alcorp strongholds that headquarters was compromised and if the alarms weren't already blaring and lights already flashing red, it would have kicked those on too. "Ellie, get Dylan and see if you guys can track their movements. Harper, head to the electrical room. We can't let them shut us down."

Ellie grabbed her tablet off the desk and ran toward the studios.

"Where are you going?" I asked as Liam turned.

"To stall them until we can get help," he said.

"I'm coming with you." There was no way I was leaving him to take on three Rogues—with at least one who had abilities.

"There are vents on the other side." He stopped and faced me. "We have to assume they are compromised."

He took off in a sprint.

"That's still—" I started to yell but stopped as he rounded the corner.

Crap.

Liam was right.

I growled and pivoted. I sprinted toward the control panel closet on the other side of the building. I paused as I passed the stairwell to the holding cells but shook my head and kept going. Miles would be safe where he was.

I made it to the closet and reached for my phone to call Dylan but came up short. Of course. I had left it next to my bed. Miles would kill me—figuratively—if he knew I had disregarded one of the first lessons he had taught me. I unlocked the control room, holding my arm with the tattoo out underneath the scanner. Morphing, I used my heightened hearing once inside to listen to anything beyond the door.

Besides the bajillion control panels inside the large closet, a tablet was built into the wall. With a passcode, you could access the other cameras. I entered the password and found the garage camera. It was empty, but the hallway camera outside wasn't. Liam was tossing the Rogue with braids into the wall. Another Rogue charged toward his back, but he lashed out with a hand, slashing his claws across their chest and sending them back with a solid kick.

Movement toward the corner of the screen caught my eye and my heart nearly jumped out of my throat. The Rogue who had killed

Travis was behind Liam. I scanned the tablet but didn't see a button for the speaker. I touched every single button, leaving slick fingerprints across the screen. There wasn't anything I could do and Toad—as Dylan had named the poisonous Rogue with black hair and bleached tips—was closing in on Liam. There was no way I would get there in time. One more step and Liam would be dead.

A scream tore from my throat as I punched the wall next to the tablet, crumbling part of the concrete. Electric sparks flew from my hand, landing on the control panel next to it. The current in the air was charged, like there was an invisible static funnel, and that funnel led to me. Hot energy filled every single exposed pore on my skin, syphoning all the electricity in the room. The room lit up, blinding me, and then went black. Iridescent blue radiated from my skin.

Dread wrapped its nasty claws around my gut as I stared at the black tablet. I tapped the screen, but it wouldn't turn on.

Oh, no.

I had just done the exact thing Liam had wanted me to prevent.

CHAPTER THIRTY-THREE

I GRABBED FOR THE doorknob, blue sparks emitting on contact. My body was on fire. It was like I could hear the buzzing through each nerve as my heart pounded against my chest, which still throbbed slightly where I had been stabbed. After making sure the hallway was clear, I bolted down the hallway toward Liam, the hallway now lit by emergency lights.

I turned the corner, almost colliding with Blake.

"Wow." He took a step back. "Harper, your skin."

I glanced down. The glow on my skin was still there but was fading. "Liam's in trouble."

And hopefully still alive.

I ran and he followed. We reached communications, and I stopped running when I saw Ellie, Dylan, and Jer headed our way.

"Did they destroy the control panel?" Ellie asked.

"Not exactly." I glanced down at my skin. It was no longer glowing. "Did you run into anyone else?"

"We found Maya with Adam and went to help Liam. When we got there the other Rogues ran," she said.

"Liam's okay?" A weight lifted from my chest.

"Yes," she answered. "The Rogues are still back that way, and the three of them went to track them down."

"Liam sent us to the weapons room," Dylan added. "We're going to get inhibitors and see what we can get back up and running."

I glanced at their t-shirts and then my tank-top. "If you can, cover any exposed skin."

"Good idea. I don't feel like death by frog is a good way to go." Dylan shuddered and Jeremiah elbowed him.

"Have you seen Chloe or Brandon?" They should've been somewhere. Neither of them would hide if they knew one of us was in danger.

"No, but we can see if we find them," Ellie said. "They might be with Dr. Cole."

"We better move," Jeremiah said.

"We are you going?" Dylan asked me.

"To help the others." I glanced at Blake. "Stay with them."

He nodded and I took off in one direction as they took off in the other. It would be good for them to have two people who know how to fight.

I reached the main floor just I time to see Avery leaving the hallway to Frank's office. She saw me and ran in the opposite direction, holding out her gun behind her. She took a couple shots, and I as I ducked, I sent a lightning bolt sailing toward her. It reached her enough to knock her down, but it wouldn't keep her down for long.

I headed in her direction but halted when the blood streaked glass above caught my attention. I hadn't seen any blood on Avery which meant that one of us could be hurt.

I headed down the hallway instead of toward Avery. It was hard to leave her, but someone needed help. I opened the door to Frank's office. A small blood trail led from the window to his desk. I summoned a fireball and rounded the desk.

I let the fireball extinguish. Frank was reaching for the phone on his desk, blood soaking through his grey vest.

"Frank." I knelt next to him. "Don't move. You're making it worse. Plus, that won't work. There's no power, in case you haven't noticed."

"It's on its own connection." He grunted as he lowered his arm back down. "You need to stop Avery."

"That's obvious, but what's also obvious is that you've been shot." I put pressure on his wound.

"It's in a spot that'll be fine. Stopping Avery is more important."

"Why?" I glanced at him. His brows creased.

"She took information from my computer. It has the locations and information on both Alcorp and the Alliance. If they can gain access to the data, not only does that give Dr. Krauss the advantage, but it puts every single member in danger."

"How easy is it to access?" Goosebumps rose on my neck at the severity of the situation.

"Not easy." He reached for the phone again. "But with the right mind, they can open it."

I grabbed the phone and lowered it down to him.

"Like if they have one of us?" My eyes widened. "Like Dylan?"

"Yes." He put a hand on the phone as I set it in his lap. "You need to go after her."

I stood but froze. Damien stood in the doorway, holding a gun.

He fired and I dropped to the floor, preparing to throw a fireball. The fireball was just about to leave me palms when a blurred figure appeared behind him and he went rigid. I straightened, still prepared to launch the electric flames.

Damien fell to the ground, a knife—*his knife*—stuck out from his back where his heart was. Miles stood above him, staring at Damien's lifeless body.

"Miles?" I held onto the fireball. His morphed glowing eyes flicked up to me, not glossed over but full of conflict. His inhibitor has worn off.

I cautiously took a few steps closer.

"How did you get that knife?" It was Damien's and it's been in my possession since I got to headquarters, but more importantly, how had he gotten out? There was a back-up power supply in holding. The cells wouldn't have unlocked, regardless.

"Your room." He looked up at me and then to the fireball in my hand. I let it fade. "I went to make sure you were alright. You weren't there, but that was."

There was silence for a moment as he stared at Damien.

"You did say you were going to return it to him." I glanced at the knife. It was evident he had the skill to pierce someone's heart. "Miles?"

His gaze traveled to my eyes.

"How did you get out of your cell?"

"I was paid a visit. He was sent to kill me, but he's now locked inside my cell."

"Harper," Frank said, and I turned to look at him as he held the phone to his ear. "Go."

I nodded and grabbed the gun from Damien's hand. After one long glance at Miles, I jogged past him.

"Where are you going?" Miles caused me to jump. I hadn't expected him to be right next to me.

I exited the hallway to find the main floor empty. Avery was no longer laying there.

"To find Avery." I didn't say anything else as I ran.

My best guess was that she headed to the garage to leave. The hallways were eerily empty as we made our way to the garage. A four-wheeler started up and I cursed, entering the garage. Avery was already out the door.

I fired a shot, but it didn't hit its mark. I grabbed a key from the wall and ran to one of the four-wheelers. The four-wheeler hummed to life and the energy emitting from inside it called to me. I wanted to reach a hand out, but now wasn't the time to see what my power craved. Instead, I hit the gas, not looking to see where Miles was, but somehow I knew he was right behind me. He wouldn't need a four-wheeler to move fast.

The four-wheeler soared across the mountain dirt and its rocky terrain. Tall pines casted shadows from the moonlight as Avery weaved in and out of the trees. Once I was close enough, I sent a fireball, striking the back of the four-wheeler. It flipped into the air, sending her skidding across the ground and into a tree.

I brought the four-wheeler to a halt and jumped off.

"Where's the flash drive?" I held a fireball between my two hands, aware she still had a gun on her.

"You'll never be free from it." She glanced at Miles as he walked up next to me, his hands in his pockets. "His voice may be the only one that can trigger you, but that doesn't mean some of us don't have recordings of it."

"Like Damien?" I asked.

"Yes." She coughed and glared at me. "You think you have him back but he won't be yours forever."

"Damien's dead," I said, ignoring her trying to pin me against Miles.

"I don't think so." Her eyes narrowed.

"I killed him." Miles hadn't moved but his eyes morphed and Avery's face paled.

Fatigue from holding the fireball was starting to set in but something pushed more energy into it. It was like the burst of electricity from the control panel had given me extra strength. I still hadn't fully recovered from almost dying.

Avery pulled her gun, but her movements were slow. I went to release the fireball but reined it back in. Miles had already reached her. The gun was tossed from her hand and Miles' hands wrapped around her neck. She kicked and flailed but she wasn't strong enough.

"Miles." I ran over to his side. If he didn't stop, he would kill her. A part of me wanted to let him, but he wasn't a killer. Neither was I.

"Miles! Let go." I put a hand on his arm and his gaze flitted to me. How many could he kill and not come back from? "This isn't you."

He glanced at Avery, who was no longer fighting. His eyes changed back to hazel and he let go. Avery lay against the tree, alive, but unconscious.

"I'm sorry." His hands started to shake as he stared at them like they were foreign.

"Look at me," I said, bringing my hands to his cheeks, gently turning him to face me. "You are in control. We'll get through this."

I've never seen him look so broken as he stared at me. He wrapped his arms around me, pulling me in. I hugged him back as we sat there in silence. This was the first time he had actually sincerely touched me since being back.

"You are my strength," he whispered in my ear.

CHAPTER THIRTY-FOUR

"A NYTHING?" I ASKED, STARING at the screen as Ellie typed away.

"Not yet," Ellie said. "Nothing from Maya and Adam yet either."

They had gone to the closest town to see if they could find anything.

"They won't get far with him." Liam rubbed out his shoulder as he watched the screens.

While Miles and I were getting the flash drive from Avery, Toad had found Dylan. He had taken him hostage and no one dared to fight back. One touch and Dylan was dead.

"We have to play it smart," Liam continued. "If we tail them now, they have Dylan at their mercy. We'll find out where they are headed and coordinate a rescue mission."

"Before they leave the states," I added and he nodded.

"I'm going to go check on Brandon," Chloe said as she turned and left.

Brandon was down in holding with Miles, who had willingly put himself back down there. Avery and the other Rogue were also locked away until the decision was made on where to keep them now that headquarters was compromised.

Everyone else gathered in communications except Dr. Cole and Frank—she was treating his wound. The power had easily been restored. I guess I hadn't fried it too badly.

Liam's phone rang and he answered it.

"Yes. Here she is," Liam said after a pause and then held out the phone to me. I took it, wondering who it was.

"Hello?" I asked.

"Hey, kid." Dodge's familiar voice sounded far away, as if I were on speaker. "I'm sorry to hear what happened. Once I'm done here, I'll head back to headquarters unless we find Krauss' location."

"Yeah, I'm sure Africa is ready to get rid of you." I kept my voice casual, but my face was a different story. Dodge has seen my lows, but he was also a close friend of my dad's, and this would be the first time seeing him since my dad's death.

"Aren't they saying the same thing there with you?" he chuckled.

"Not to my face."

"That's because they're too afraid." After a moment, he continued. "How's the Doc?"

"Good. He wanted to get right to business, but Dr. Cole wouldn't let him."

"Typical." Dodge paused. "Have you seen your mom?"

"No." My gut clenched at the thought of sharing the news of Dad's death.

"There's something I need you to do when you go home. I need you to walk out of hearing range."

Without asking why, I shrugged at the others—most of them could hear the conversation—and walked far enough away until I knew they couldn't listen in with their heightened hearing.

"Done," I said as I walked around the corner.

"Remember that picture of your dad with your drawing on your dresser?"

"Yeah?" I asked, wondering how he knew that was there.

"I need you to get the photo and keep it safe."

"Why?"

"I just need you to trust me," he answered. "And don't get it wet. Alright, kid. We'll talk later." Dodge hung up before I could ask anything else.

I pulled the phone away, confused. What was so important about that photo, and why had he not wanted anyone else to hear our conversation? I put the questions aside and headed back to the group. Our main focus was Dylan.

"Everything okay?" Liam asked as I walked over to him, holding out his phone.

"Yeah," I answered, squirming under my skin. "At least I think so."

Liam stared at me, then gave me the *we will talk later* look.

I sat down in a chair, replaying the video of Hannah at the front door, rewinding back to the beginning each time she mouthed that she was sorry. Hannah had overloaded our system as a distraction so they had enough time to put a hole in the side of headquarters.

"There's no clues anywhere!" I grunted in frustration.

A clue.

I sat straight up.

"Are you alright?" Liam asked.

"Uh, yeah. I just thought of something. Hey, Ellie, can you pull up the video of Hannah on the large screen?"

"The Rogue with wings?" she asked.

"Yes."

I had never played it all the way through—only until Hannah mouthed sorry. On the screen, after she mouthed sorry and the alarms started going off, she reached into her pocket and pulled out a small round object. She pointedly glanced down at it, then back at the camera, and tossed it off to the side.

"Well, balls," Blake said.

I got up out of my chair and headed toward the front. I stepped outside into the cool summer night—early morning at this point. The dirt crunched under my bare feet as I searched in the direction she had tossed the object. It was still dark, and even though I could see well, I morphed so I could see even better.

There.

A red object was tucked in the tall grass. I picked up the object, turning it around in my hand. *A wooden apple?*

The Huskies Best Teacher was carved into one side and on the other was *Mrs. Harrison*. The red paint was chipped, areas in the wood were dented, and the green on the single leaf was almost completely gone. This wooden apple had seen some better days.

I stood, holding it out to the others, who had followed me. Liam took it and examined it.

"What do you think it means?" Chloe asked, standing on her tiptoes to see over Blake, who had taken up most of the space.

"A clue," I answered.

A nearby window let the sun in, lighting up the hideous orange lockers of the small abandoned Montana school. *The Huskies.* I kicked an old soda can and it bounced against a locker, the ting echoing down the empty hallway. Liam, Adam, Maya, Jer, Miles and I had searched the entire building and hadn't found another living being.

Ellie had searched for teachers with the last name Harrison in the towns nearby. It had led us to this closed-down school. The roof was made of asbestos, but instead of redoing the roof, they had built a new school on the other side of the two-traffic light town about fifteen years ago.

Maya and Adam had met us there from the town over. They had stayed outside, surveying the area until we arrived, but they hadn't seen any movement, and that was because there wasn't any. There had been signs that someone had been staying there recently. Large empty syringes were found in the kitchen of the cafeteria, along with other medical equipment. Clean blankets were made into makeshift beds in a few of the classrooms and the basement had been more disturbing. A single pair of extra reinforced shackles was latched onto a metal pole, and I couldn't help but wonder if this was where they had been keeping Hannah.

It could have been from some real messed-up squatters, but everything was too clean. Plus, the large kitchen sink contained burning embers, everything in it destroyed. It had to be Krauss or even potentially Barbara, along with some Rogues. How long had they been this close? Even though we thought we had never revealed where we had taken Miles, Krauss was resourceful, and it looked like he had found us.

"I called it in," Liam said as he walked down the hall back toward the rest of us. "They can't be far. Ellie's running facial recognition with the nearby cameras." That was the one good thing that had come from the break-in.

"We'll split in pairs. Adam, Maya, go east. Harper, Miles go west. We'll take the south." Liam glanced between Miles and me, still not trusting him but trusting me after convincing him we could use his help if we run into the Rogues with powers. We didn't know if he was fully on our side, but he certainly wasn't on Krauss' after taking out some of his crew—especially Damien. "Be careful."

A few hours later, Miles and I were parking our motorcycles in the secured storage garage tucked away at the base of the mountain. We had found nothing, and the others had already headed back up.

"We're going to get him back," Miles said as he swung his leg off the motorcycle and placed his helmet on the seat. He had composed himself since the incident with Avery.

I mimicked him with my helmet, grinding my teeth at the thought of Krauss holding anyone hostage—especially those I cared about.

"Hey." Miles closed the distance between us as the breeze from outside swirled through the garage, sending a loose strand from my ponytail into my face. He took the strand between his fingers and gently tucked it behind my ear. "We will. They're more likely to just let him go than to listen to him talk anyways."

I suppressed a laugh, nodding. When I looked back up to see that stupid charming smile of his, any comment I had escaped my mind. His alluring lips were in close range, and I leaned forward, waiting to see if he would pull away and wanting to chase that pull I felt between us. I didn't want him to rush into anything—

He crashed his lips into mine.

My fingers twined in his hair. His hands landed on my hips, his fingers firmly grasping me and pressing my body closer to his. I stepped forward and continued until his back pressed against the wall. Our kisses were hard and warranted.

In a quick sweeping motion, he switched me around so my back now pressed into the cold metal siding, and my insides completely melted. I welcomed every single inch of him that pressed against me. His hand caressed my cheek and his kisses became deeper and softer. He was in control in now.

The pocket of my cargo pants buzzed—or more so, my phone did—and I didn't bother reaching for it. Miles brought his other hand to the side of my face and broke the kiss.

"You should get that," he said breathlessly.

"It's fine," I panted and grabbed his shirt, pulling him back to me. I got one kiss in before he pulled away, stepping back so we were now five feet apart.

"Now's not the time to let the phone go to voicemail." Miles crossed his arm. "I'm also pretty sure that might have been intentional." He glanced at the camera in the far corner of the garage.

My cheeks were hot as I flushed.

"When this is over, I'm going somewhere where there are no cameras in a hundred-mile radius." I pulled out my phone, putting it on speaker. "Hello?"

"First of all, sorry for the interruption. We needed to see where you guys were at," Chloe said, her grin evident in her voice. "We're picking up a weird signal that's on our frequency. It's not too far up the mountain, but whatever it is, they're headed this way. Seeing how the others are almost here, you're the closest."

"Send us the coordinates." Miles' face hardened. He held out the helmet that had been resting on the seat—some things never change.

Our phones dinged at the same time, and I glanced down to see a group message from Chloe with the coordinates. I climbed on behind him and wrapped my arms tightly around his waist. I had learned my lesson to hold on the very first time we met.

The four-wheeler hummed as we exited the garage and began our climb up the mountain, snaking through the trees and brush. The deep evergreen pines and dark trunks were something from a magazine.

Miles slowed as we closed in on the coordinates.

"I should get off and loop around. That way, whoever it is doesn't hear us coming if they haven't already," I said.

"I would be on them before you would finish the loop. You drive—I'll go around?" Miles stopped the four-wheeler and glanced over his shoulder at me.

"You're actually asking?" I couldn't help the question—he didn't ask much when it came to things like this. But that was before everything that had happened.

He turned, bringing one leg over so he was straddling the seat while facing me.

"You're the one making sure I'm on my best behavior and that I follow orders, so, yes. I am asking you."

"Yes." I swallowed. The proximity to each other reminded me of the position we had been in at the garage just ten minutes ago, and he was even closer then. "You're quicker, so it makes sense."

"Not always quicker than lightning." The corner of his lip twitched and then he was gone.

My heart thudded against my chest, and I tried to slow it down. I grabbed my phone, pulling up the map. I memorized the location and shoved it back in my pocket. Sliding forward, I took the handles and began driving in that direction.

A minute later, I slowed down and killed the engine. Morphing and closing my eyes, I used my heightened hearing.

Birds.

Leaves rustling in the wind.

A nearby stream.

A twig snapping.

My eyes shot open. The snap was too heavy for a small animal. I shoved the keys in my pocket and hopped off the four-wheeler. Careful where I placed each step, I noiselessly made my way toward my target, something that had been briefly taught in the Vault, but Dodge had touched more on it. I heard the sound again and quickened my steps to a bush in front of me, the sea-green leaves providing cover.

"Are you alone?"

I heard Miles ask and peeked over the bushes.

"Didn't anyone ever teach you not to sneak up on someone alone in the woods?" Dylan stood there, alarmed. "Although you were taught to sneak up on people."

Miles stood across from him, morphed and looking like he could kill in an instant as he scanned the forest—probably one of the reasons Krauss had chosen him. I suppose that would be a good reason for Dylan to be visibly shaking and holding both hands along with a radio in the air.

"Dylan!" I came out from my hiding spot. "You're okay."

Dylan spun around and I hugged him, forgetting about my fear of touch.

"Yeah, I'm okay. I ran as soon as I could," Dylan said, hugging me back. "The one with owl-like wings created a distraction—whether or not it was meant for me to run, I did."

"So you are alone?" Miles asked again.

"Yes." Dylan pulled away to look at him.

"And no tail?"

"None that I know of." Dylan shrugged. "I mean, they already know where headquarters is, so I think they would've grabbed me if they knew where I was. I was trying to get a message out without them hearing a word." He glanced at the radio in his hand before tossing it against a tree and smashing it. "Hannah put up a fight when they were trying to get us out of there. While they were distracted, I ran. But I'm not sure why they didn't come after me."

"We must've been closing in," I said, doing a quick scan of my own. "Let's get out of here."

CHAPTER THIRTY-FIVE

"**C**AN YOU COME IN with me?" I asked Miles.

A few deep breaths hadn't calmed the dread and anxiety about getting off the motorcycle, walking to the front door of my childhood home, and telling my mom that Dad is truly dead. My own eyes had confirmed it at the precinct before we arrived at my house.

"Always." Miles got off his bike and set his helmet on the seat.

I got off mine and stared at the front door like a lost deer, my hands shaking at my sides. My mom had literally just found out my dad had been alive. Whether or not she had been angry at him, she still cared about him. She loved him, and he loved her.

Miles grabbed my hand, ceasing all shaking. I glanced at Miles' and gave him a warm smile. Taking a deep breath, I urged my feet forward and walked with Miles to the door. I rang the doorbell, neither of us letting go of each other's hand. The storm door opened and Miles reached for the glass door.

"Isa!" Joe's eyes widened with joy, and his smile brightened even more when he saw Miles. "It's good to see you're back, Miles."

Joe studied our faces, his own falling.

"She's home?" My mom shouted from somewhere inside the house and approaching footsteps were heard right as she popped up behind Joe. "Isa, you're home!" She let out a gasp. "Miles is here, too?"

Joe stepped aside to let my mom through but placed a hand on her shoulder, shaking his head. My mom glanced at Joe and then to us, her expression sobering.

"What's wrong?" my mom asked.

"Can we come inside?" I maintained a calm voice and hoped it would stay that way.

"Oh, yes." My mom waved us in. "Certainly."

I let go of Miles' hand and walked through the threshold. Avoiding a hug, I made our way to the couch and waited for my mom to sit. If she hugged me now, there was a good chance I would break down in tears. The image of my deceased father was still fresh in my mind. I had to be strong for her—and myself.

"I have some bad news." I swallowed and Miles found my hand again, giving me courage to keep going. "Dad didn't make our most recent trip."

"What do you mean?" My mom's forehead creased, and Joe's face paled as he started rubbing soothing circles on her back—he understood.

"He's gone, Mom. He is really gone this time."

She shook her head. "No. He was just here?"

"I'm so sorry, Mom. This time it's real. I saw his body." My voice cracked the slightest. I kept my shoulders straight and swore internally at my eyes to stay dry, but they were threatening to well over.

My mom looked away, her jaw clenched as she reined in the same emotions. She took a deep breath and glanced back up, her brown eyes moist. "How did it happen?"

I froze. I was awful. I glanced at Miles and was at a loss of words. I should have known she would've asked *how* he was killed. I had been so focused on being able to get the words out that he was dead that I hadn't thought about the questions.

"It was me." Miles cleared his throat when my inability to speak, let alone move, was inescapable. "I—"

"It wasn't really him," I added, looking at my mom, then back at him. "Miles... I. I'm sorry."

"It's part of the demons I need to face," he whispered to me.

"He was under Krauss' control." I looked back at my mom and Joe.

"What do you mean?" Joe asked this time.

"I had tricked Isa and the others to think that I was myself. I had been under the influence that Isa was not who she said she was and was going to kill thousands. When Dr. Westbrook realized I was not myself, he did the right thing and tried to stop me." Miles looked between my mom and Joe. He remained collected, the only evidence of his pain was through his tight grip he had on my hand.

"He was being manipulated," I said. "The man that had captured both of us had Miles for six months longer than he had me. He had injected him with this serum, changed him, and brainwashed him. It wasn't his fault. It was this man that Dad had been worried about from the beginning. Krauss killed him, not Miles."

"Krauss?" My mom asked. "I know that name."

"He was Dad's intern for years."

My mom's face turned blood red. "This is the man that's been after both you and your father this entire time? He never told me a name."

"Yes." I bit my lip. "Well, he wasn't sure I was alive until right before I was taken."

My mom rubbed her hands on her forehead. "Do we know where he is?"

"No, but we're searching."

"So, is he like you?" Joe asked, glancing at Miles.

"Yes," I answered. "But he's different. He's quick—like really quick."

Both sets of eyes traveled to Miles as if trying to evaluate how quick. I knew what they were thinking—if Dad even had a chance. Joe assessed Miles even further, and I wondered if he was contemplating if he was still a threat.

"He's himself now." I pulled on Miles' hand, bringing his arm closer to me.

"I'm so sorry," Miles said. "I won't rest until your daughter is safe, and then I will be leaving."

I shot him a look, and he glanced at me with his mask still up. *We're talking about this later.* That's what he would have read if he could read my mind.

My mom stood, placing a hand over her mouth. All of us stayed sitting, waiting for her response.

"I don't want you anywhere near this Krauss guy," she said.

I stood, letting go of Miles' hand. "I can protect myself. We went over this, Mom."

"I won't leave her side until she is safe." Miles stood next to me, and I wanted to elbow him at his words, making it seem like he was eventually leaving... *me.*

"What if you are what she is in danger from?" Joe asked, also standing.

"Then I trust that she will do the right thing this time." He glanced at me as my spine straightened—he knew I wouldn't take his life over mine. "I also trust that she will get me out of it."

"What are you talking about?" My mom's eyes narrowed on us.

"That I love your daughter, and she has been slowly saving me without even knowing it." Miles' eyes flitted to me again, a small sliver of green glinting in the grey pools of his irises.

The only thing I could feel was my heart thumping against my chest, and the only thing I could hear was the distant foggy ringing in my ears. A smile wanted to emerge on my lips, but they stayed flat at the seriousness and somber topic of this conversation. He said that he loved me. Out loud—to my mom and stepfather. However, the anguish and torment in his voice meant there was a long road ahead and that the pain we both carried was a huge weight.

Miles waited outside while I retrieved the photo Dodge had asked me to get. He thought I was saying goodbye in private—which I also was. I hadn't heard from Dodge since, but I figured he would be on his way back soon. He was always true to his word.

A knock came from the open door to my old bedroom, and I looked up from the picture.

"You always loved that photo," my mom said as she entered. There were a few wet spots on her shirt, most likely from crying, but her face showed no signs of a meltdown.

"I remember." I smiled and glanced back down.

"I hate that you have to go, but I understand why you need to. As a mother, my job is to protect you, and I have done a terrible job at it." She stood next to me and I turned to face her, letting the picture hang at my side. "I know I can't force you to stay, just as I know you won't stop fighting until this is over. You never give up, and you are so strong—and stubborn. I loved all of those things about your father."

My mom placed both hands on my shoulders and continued, "You go get them, but don't lose yourself in the process. The thing I loved about your father the most was his morality—even if he got lost at times. You inherited that. We talked a lot that night, and though I was angry at him, everything he did, he did with integrity. Your father believed in you—still does."

She pulled me in for a long hug, and the energy swirled in sad wisps through my chest. The bedroom light flickered as a tear snuck through my barrier and I clenched my teeth, trying to shove down the pain. I wondered if my mom's eyes were closed because she didn't comment on the flickering light when she pulled away.

"Be safe." She planted a kiss on my forehead. "I know it's an awful time, but happy belated birthday, Isa. This world needed you more than I ever knew I needed you." She squeezed my shoulders and quietly left the room.

My birthday had come without me even knowing, but the date hadn't mattered. I stared back down at the photo and flipped it over. The back popped off with a little bit of force, but the picture slid out with ease. The back of the photo was plain white and I didn't see any markings. That was odd. Dodge had mentioned not to get it wet, and I wondered if whatever was on there was hidden cryptically. Dodge wanted it kept a secret. The urge to tell Dylan rose—he would know how to uncover anything hidden on it.

I slid the photo into the inside pocket of my jacket, where it would stay safe and dry until I was back at headquarters.

"Home sweet home," I said to Miles as he paused in the entry to his small Portland apartment. "It's different because you feel different, but it will grow with you," I continued when he didn't move.

Our trip to see his grandparents had gone better than expected—well, than what Miles had expected. I knew it would be fine. Rose had been very welcoming and relieved to see Miles. I think Miles was worried that he would do something wild, but he had said a piece of the weight lifted off his chest after the visit.

"It feels different." He stepped down the small entry hallway leading into the living room. "But nothing here has changed except me."

"That's the funny thing about home—it's only home because of the people that make it home." I recalled the first time I had gone home with no memory. It had felt mostly right, and that was because of my mom and Joe. "And you're still you. You just had a little bit more adventure since the last time you've stepped foot in here."

He snorted. "Adventure is one way to describe it."

"Adventures can be both fun and, well, not so fun." I slid my bag from my shoulder and plopped it on the floor against the wall as Miles made his way toward the attached kitchen. He hadn't wanted to stay at his grandparents'. I think it reassured him that he was isolated from them.

When I didn't hear anything, I turned to look at him. He hadn't packed a bag, but clutched a paper bag full of Cheng's takeout as he stared at me.

"What?" I asked, beginning to sweat under his gaze.

"I like *our* adventures," he barely whispered as a solemn smile tugged his lips.

"I do too."

We stared at each other and heat pricked up the back of my neck. It was as if I could feel his tension—and attraction—mixing with my own. I suddenly felt uncomfortable at not knowing what was going on.

"The orange chicken is getting cold," I said, glancing at the bag.

He set it on the counter. "I guess there's only one way to fix that."

I nodded and strode toward the kitchen.

"Yeah, and re-heating isn't an option," I tossed over my shoulder as I grabbed silverware.

"Not unless you want chicken that tastes like rubber." He let out a low laugh, and I turned to see him relaxed, all tension released from his shoulders.

The hold in my stomach released.

"Thank you," he said.

"For what?"

He waved a hand around the kitchen. "The dishes are clean and it doesn't smell like spoiled milk."

"How do you know it was me?" I asked.

His only response was a smile.

CHAPTER THIRTY-SIX

ADAM HAD PICKED MILES and me up in Portland and took us back to headquarters. I dropped my bag off in my room and also hid the photo of my dad. I headed to communications and wasn't surprised to see Adam and Maya weren't there—they liked to do their own thing. A pink box sat in between the computers, and I could smell its fruity, sugary contents from across the room.

"How did you guys get doughnuts?" I asked Dylan, Blake, and Chloe, who were shoving their faces with the sugary fried dough.

"From town," Dylan said around a mouthful.

"They're the best doughnuts I've ever had." Blake's shirt was covered in powdered sugar.

"Ditto." Chloe nodded as she took another bite.

"How did you even get them?" I looked at Liam, who only shrugged.

"We went down this morning," Jer answered.

"When they had me, they were going to throw away a box of doughnuts with one left so I offered to finish the last one. That would've been a waste." Dylan sighed in disapproval, as if a doughnut being tossed in the garbage was the worst thing to happen when you've been kidnapped. "I was telling them about how good it was, and voila! Doughnuts."

"You mean you went back to the town they held you hostage in while they still want you, for doughnuts?" My voice rose at the idiocracy behind his logic.

"That sounds familiar."

I whirled to see Miles behind me, the corner of his lip tugged upward. Brandon stood next to him, shaking his head.

"Orange chicken is not doughnuts, okay?" I glared at him, but he only raised his eyebrow.

"If it was a malt chocolate shake or tacos, you would've done it." Dylan gave me a pointed look.

"I have to agree with them on this one." Liam spun in his chair to face us. "But Dylan didn't go. Jeremy and Blake went, but they scanned the old school first to see if we missed anything."

"The doughnuts were just a detour." Dylan smiled.

"They're super-duper good." Chloe glanced at Brandon. "Want one?"

"I'm good," he said.

"Are you sure you? I thought cops loved doughnuts."

Chloe's comment earned a snort from Dylan.

"Liam," Ellie said. "I think I found something. Scratch that—I know I found something."

I started making my way over to her computer but stopped when Liam held out a hand.

"I'm sorry, but I don't think we should share this with him." Liam glanced at Miles. "No offense."

"None taken," Miles said, taking a step back.

The room went quiet. I understood if it was sensitive information and tried to shove down my annoyance and anger at the situation. It wasn't Miles' fault Krauss had trigger words that messed with his mind.

"Hey Mac, how about we go get some real food and then drinks for everyone?" Brandon stood.

"Good idea. I'll take a ham sandwich." Blake leaned back into his chair, examining what was left of his doughnut.

Chloe reached over and smacked Blake in the chest, powdered crumbs flying off his shirt.

"You're going to help them," she said.

"Ouch." Blake rubbed the spot she had hit with his free hand. "When did you get bossy, and when did you get so strong?" He wiggled his eyebrows and flashed his teeth in a goofy smile that was probably meant to look attractive.

"She always has been." Brandon glared at Blake.

"I was born with all these muscles," Chloe said.

"Fine." Blake got to his feet. "I guess I'll go, but I'm only going of my own accord."

Ellie waited before they were gone to talk.

"Do you know how they had stayed in an Alliance stronghold? What if they were hiding somewhere close to his home similar to—"

"You know where he grew up?" Liam asked, cutting in.

"Oh, sorry." Ellie said. "I just learned that five minutes ago."

"How did you—you know what—never mind." Liam nodded for her to continue.

"So, remember how they stayed in an asbestos-filled school? Well, what about a town in Germany that was closed due to asbestos? If you do a quick search, you won't find any known asbestos mines in Germany, but that's because someone doesn't want you to know. I dug a little deeper and found an abandoned town named Tothen. It's a very small town, but it killed hundreds that had lived there. It wasn't closed until the early 1990s. No one expects someone to set up in a toxic location."

She clicked on a file, and a black and white image popped up. About ten boys and girls around the age of twelve and wearing matching uniforms were lined up in two rows.

I scanned the names but didn't see a Killian Krauss, and it was hard to recognize any of the boys as Krauss because of the poor photo quality and his youth.

"This is him." Ellie pointed to a boy in the middle. I found the corresponding name below to be Kaisen Günzburg. "His current last name is his mother's maiden name, and I'm not sure of his first name."

"My prodigy." Dylan slapped Ellie on the back.

"Not by a longshot. This was luck," she said.

"That's not luck." Liam glanced at her. "I'll let Frank know. It looks like we're headed to Tothen."

CHAPTER THIRTY-SEVEN

*G*UN AT WAIST—SECURE.

"You're still staying on the plane."

I glanced up to see Liam scolding Frank, who was gingerly tugging on his pea coat over his wounded shoulder, and then I went back to securing my weapons.

Knife strapped to my ankle—secure.

"There's not much I can do from here. The town is still miles away," Frank said.

I felt my power vibrating along my nerves and running hot along my veins.

"And since when do you give me orders, Mr. Walker?"

I lowered my foot from the chair I was leaning against and looked at Frank. I hadn't heard him use Liam's last name before, and it threw me for a loop.

"Since you were shot and since you put me in charge of this mission." Liam raised an eyebrow. "Those were our terms if you came along. You know the risks better than anyone else."

"I am well aware. Your ability to keep a clear mind and not make this personal are two of the reasons why I put you in charge." Frank put a hand on his shoulder, pausing, and then headed to the back of the jet.

"Isn't there a thing called the Alliance?" Dylan asked as he stowed his tablet between his back and backpack. "Where's our backup? We're in Germany."

"Krauss has his Rogues making a mess everywhere, so every stronghold throughout the world is occupied. They may not have the flash drive with all of the information, but making a mess in every major city causes a lot of turmoil." Liam put his com in his ear and rolled his neck.

I shrugged off my jacket and laid it on a chair. It wasn't needed and we wouldn't run into anyone who would be alarmed by my weapons.

"He might not know we are coming, but he's always prepared," Miles said. "If he can occupy the other strongholds, then there's less resistance to whatever he's planning."

"That's why we'll need you to come with us." I reached into my pocket and grabbed two wireless earplugs and an old phone with music on it. "I know you thought you'd be staying behind, but we need you." I held them out to Miles. "These were the best we could find, but it will help drown out Krauss if you're up to it?"

"It's loaded with Queen, so you'll be set to kick some butt." Dylan grinned like a six-year-old giving their teacher a gift that they thought was the best thing ever. "The headphones alone block out a lot of noise. I also coated them like our coms to protect them from Pistol's frequency." Dylan had given her that name after learning that Krauss used pistol shrimp DNA.

Miles could move fast enough that he could put them on and press play in a second before any words were ever spoken.

Miles glanced from me to the headphones and phone in my hand then back to me, his lips flat. He splayed his hand over top of mine, his eyes demanding my attention.

"Only if you promise to bring me back."

"I promise." I nodded, forgetting that we weren't alone as static from my hand intertwined with the heat from his. He slowly retrieved the items from my hand.

"I'm not taking any weapons. If things go south, put an end to it." He strode by the others and heaved open the jet door, its hydraulic hinges hissing. He gave me one last glance before exiting.

"Why is he scary even when he's not triggered?" Dylan whispered, staring at the door. I scoffed and rolled my eyes at him.

"You're scared of him and not the fact that we're about to go into an abandoned town full of asbestos, and Rogues and Krauss are probably also there?" Maya laughed.

"He's more scared of the walk to get there," I said and Jeremiah chuckled.

"Ah. It's like you remember who I am." Dylan grinned.

I smiled as I headed outside. Having my memories back was nice.

Once my feet hit the damp pavement, I cracked my neck and stretched my arms. Nine hours was a long flight, and the unpleasant anticipation had kept me up. I was sure the others hadn't slept either.

The air was thick with fog covering the pine trees in the distance, and the mountains glowed a dull orange hue from the rising sun. The only tingle alerting my nerves was from the jet behind me and a small static disturbance down in the parking lot.

Miles stared at the boarded-up windows and cracked cement of the permanently closed stores of the strip mall. The mall was just outside Tothen's borders, and the closing of the town had caused many of the small businesses nearby to go bankrupt. Its long parking lot provided an easy landing strip despite its grass-grown cracks weaving throughout.

I scuffed my feet a couple times on the ground, alerting my presence to Miles. I reached out a finger and sent a small amount of electricity to his side. He didn't jump but glanced at me, his eyebrow raised. Good. He hadn't been expecting that.

"Just zapping whatever negative thoughts that were going through your head out of there." I went to gently knock on his head, but he caught my wrist before I even reached him. His eyes glowed a soft iridescent hue of green and purple.

"It worked." He leaned in closer. "But you have to do the same." He tapped the side of my temple with two fingers, then traced my French braid, bringing it forward to rest on my shoulder.

"I think that's something we both have to work on." I bit my lip, grinning.

He chuckled, his eyes morphing back to hazel and turned, tugging me with him back to the others.

"Everyone's coms work?" Liam asked when we reached the group.

"Sure do. We gotcha all on the big screen," Blake said through the coms.

"We are all set on our end," Ellie added.

Everyone else checked their coms, and we were all set.

"Let's go. Remember, watch each other's back. We don't know if they have anyone on the perimeter. Take them out when you can." Liam's eyes met mine. He knew what needed to be done. So did I, but I still struggled with the thought.

"Keep your eyes up. Who knows what we will run into—living or not," Miles said. We couldn't use an EMP—electromagnetic pulse—for any hidden cameras that'll let them know of our arrival. That's where I came in, but only Miles, Liam, and Dylan knew that. I didn't want others to rely on me being able to sense any electrical energy nearby in case I missed it. It wasn't always there unless I focused real hard.

I pivoted, facing in the direction of Tothen—Krauss' home town. Call it a stereotypical gut feeling, but I knew Ellie was right. Krauss was a couple miles away and not expecting us.

"It ends today." My fists clenched and my teeth ground together as I started the trek. This was it.

By the time we found the edge of the decaying abandoned town, my boots were muddy, thorns stuck to my pants, and my bare arms were scratched—but those wounds would heal in no time.

"Jeremiah, stay on the border with Dylan and stay hidden," Liam ordered. "Alert us if you see anything."

The rest of us moved forward. The farther we went into the town, the deeper my heart sank and thick, stale air clung to my lungs. Videos and images of abandoned towns tugged your heartstrings, but in person it was more visceral. Houses closely lined on the street had shattered windows—some replaced with wood; tall grass and weeds grew out of sidewalks and areas that hadn't been tended to in years; kids' tricycles and miscellaneous toys were scattered about. The images of a child's beloved stuffed teddy bear torn and dirty? Yeah. That exists.

This placed screamed of abandonment, death, and years of suffering.

"I'm getting a small signal. It looks like it's quite a few blocks from you. The building looks bigger... it's... it's a hospital?" Dylan said over the coms.

"Why there?" Maya asked.

"It's got all the tools you need to experiment on innocent people," Chloe said through the coms.

"Öffentliche Krankenhäuser Tothen," I whispered.

"What?" Liam asked, either about what that meant or at my butchering of the words.

"That's where his mom died from mesothelioma." I looked at Liam. I had studied the files Ellie had sent, staring at names I couldn't pronounce, deciphering foreign images, and attempting to translate German articles for most of the nine hours of the flight. "It was a small public hospital, but its rooms were filled and they had way too many patients. Being one of the only buildings free of asbestos due to minor renovations, people flocked there to get out of their homes at the earliest signs of any illness. Many suffocated—literally—in their hospital beds, which were called their deathbeds."

"Uhmm." Blake cleared his throat. "I just wanted to say, thank you for trusting me in keeping headquarters safe during this mission. It's high priority."

"Yeah. The urge for me to enter the center of an asbestos-filled town is so strong," Dylan said sarcastically, his voice slightly breaking with static.

"The amount of time we are here will not harm us," Liam said calmly.

"While we do know the current serum does not cure any chronic illness"—Frank spoke over the coms—"we suspect that it will help defend from future disease and illness. Liam is right that the short time there will not cause any issues. You would have to live there for a while. Adam and Dylan will be fine too."

I closed my eyes, drowning out all quarreling and conversation, and focused on the air brushing against my skin. The more I focused, the more in tune I became with the amount of static the air carried—which was more than I would have imagined. It's like I could trace the frequency in the air to its source. A small surge pricked my skin, causing the hair on my arm to stick up, and my eyes flew open as bile rose in my throat. Something dark infiltrated it, and I didn't like it.

Without a word, I headed toward the small invisible trail, no doubt leading me to the hospital. I didn't wait for Dylan to send over directions as the others were still bickering over the asbestos—mostly Blake, saying it was of the most honor to stay back. I felt a presence at my side, instantly knowing it was Miles. Glancing sideways at him, I followed his gaze to my arms, where my hair still stood on end. His gaze moved to assess the direction we were heading, then back to me, a small crease between his brows.

"What is it?" he asked.

I shook my head. "I don't know."

"It's bad." His eyes were still on me. "You can sense it."

I stopped walking and turned to face him.

"How do you know that?" I studied him just like he studied me. He could read me like an open book, but this was more. It felt like more.

"I can feel it." He took a hand and brushed my arm, my raised hair falling and the negative energy dissipating.

"You can feel it too?" It dawned on me that his serum was mixed with my blood—could every new Rogue be able to sense electricity on some small scale?

"No." Miles' traced his hand up my arm. "I can feel you."

CHAPTER THIRTY-EIGHT

I F ANYONE HAD HEARD the conversation Miles and I had about him feeling what I could, no one said a thing. I had barely squeaked out a how before the others had caught up. Our team split up once we reached the surprisingly large hospital. They must have planned to expand the town, and my heart sank at the thought.

The rough, cool cement pressed into my palms as I peered around the half wall of the dock at the back of the hospital. It was clear. Something called to me from inside. Whatever it was, was making my stomach twist the closer I got. I swallowed, glancing at Miles beside me.

Time to move.

I jogged across the wet pavement with Miles behind me as we assessed our surroundings. I hadn't seen a camera, which was odd. Miles lifted the dock door with ease, and I slid under with him right behind me. He closed the door and my eyes adjusted to the dark surroundings. I brought out my beast, heightening my senses.

We stayed low, moving around boxes and making our way to the double doors at the end of the room. I peered through the window, seeing nothing but an empty wide hallway. The cold handle bit into my hand as I turned it—here we go.

The white flooring and walls were blinding because of the fluorescent lights, much like the Vault had been. This was the only building in the town that I had seen or felt any electricity from so far. My heart remained steady in my chest as we made our way down the hall. Having Miles next to me was like my own anti-anxiety pill, and I was going to be addicted to his presence at this rate.

I could sense that Miles wanted to go ahead. He could have this entire place searched before I could cover half the ground floor, but we had promised to stay together.

An invisible force slammed into my gut, causing my heart to leap. I halted, forcing bile back down my throat. My hair stood on end. I went to look at Miles, but the sound of a distant motor caused me to face the doors behind us instead. Miles held out a hand to stay put, then blurred before my eyes.

I tracked him to the double doors at the end of the hallway where he ducked, peering through the window. The dark windows brightened as light seeped into the room.

"We have two cargo vans at the back entrance," he whispered loud enough so that only the coms would pick him up. Before I knew it, he was back at my side. "We need to move."

We started down the hall but I paused, turning and facing the door that made my stomach churn. A yellow sign with a black circle encasing three upside-down triangles and words in German hung above it. The fallout shelter sign. Without thinking, I reached for the door and went inside. A small light revealed a top landing that led to a dimly lit stairwell, descending into the dark.

I gulped, swallowing the dense air lifting from below. My senses were starting to go haywire—my ears picked up a slight ring like tinnitus, my skin crawled, and my eyes burned. Whatever was down there was bad. I shared a look with Miles, his eyes flashing before returning normal. He felt it too.

After a deep breath, I descended the steps. We made it to the bottom and slowly exited the stairwell. An industrial elevator sat to the left—the kind with the pull-up metal grate door that you don't dare enter.

"...you shortly," a voice said from around the corner.

Jogging to the corner, I spared a glance and so did Miles. A large man was facing the opposite way toward a large metal door as he pressed the buttons in the keypad next to it. From this distance, he would make it through before I could reach him and could potentially alert the others if I failed to sneak up on him.

My hand felt hot as I summoned an electric fireball. Miles' clamped his hand around my arm. He shook his head in warning, and the light pressure from his hand lifted as his eyes changed and he practically disappeared. Less than a second later, he had the man in a choke hold. He struggled as his eyes glowed yellow.

I ran over and caught the door before it closed. Miles dragged the now unconscious Rogue through the door, propping him up against the wall. There wasn't a keypad on this side, so I assumed the door was only meant to keep people out. Removing my hand, I let the door close and turned to face the large room.

If death had a feeling, it would be the sensation that was crawling all over my skin. Large metal cases sat in rows that reached just below my waist. A small green light was lit near the latch. Each one beckoned to me, but its energy was dark. Lethal.

"We got an issue." Adam's voice broke in and out. I was surprised anything made it through with the thick walls.

"By issue, he means person." Maya's voice was just as crackly, but interpretable.

"The winged Rogue from the cameras at headquarters is here. She's locked up," Adam said. I made my way over to Miles, who was examining a case.

"She's not a threat," I said, still whispering, as if someone could hear me through these walls.

"Yeah, sure. She played decoy very well," Maya said.

A brief silence passed.

"Harper, why?" Maya asked, completely losing me.

"Me why, what?" I questioned.

"I don't think Harper's coms are making it through to anyone else but us in close range, Maya." It was Liam's voice this time. "Harper, where are you guys?"

"We're—" The words stopped dead on my tongue as I stared at the case Miles had carefully opened. His eyes found mine, stricken with horror I've never seen. "We have a bigger problem."

"What's going on?" Liam asked, his voice quiet.

"Nukes. There's about ten of them," Miles stated, his hand pressing his ear probably in an attempt to stabilize the connection. Whatever Krauss had planned was bigger than any one of us had imagined.

He gently closed the lid as Liam repeated what we had found to the others.

"We need to get you out of this room." Miles stood, making his way over to me.

"We can't let them take these bombs." I planted my feet. There was a good chance these were the cargo that the vans were there for.

"And the amount of static electricity radiating off you is enough to light one of these up and cause a chain reaction."

"Yep." I nodded and turned toward the door. "Time to go."

The sound of metal clanking, followed by voices, caused me to freeze with my hand on the door. Shortly after, muffled pounding came from outside the windowless door.

"Dan, are you sleeping on the job again?" The voice rang from the knocked out Rogue's radio.

The unconscious Rogue stirred, and my hand twitched at my side. Zapping him would be so easy, but a fiery radiation death didn't sound like fun. I slammed my fist into the side of the man's face, rendering him from waking up anytime soon again. Miles raised an eyebrow and I shrugged him off.

"Come on, Dan. Don't make us radio Elias for the code."

"What's your location, Harper?" Liam asked through the coms.

"Fallout shelter in the basement. Four doors down on the west side," Miles whispered. "At least three Rogues are outside the door."

"We can't let them radio them." My voice was barely audible as I glanced at the Rogue's radio. "Can you pretend to be this Dan and say you went to get a drink?"

"They might be suspicious and call it in anyways."

I sighed. Miles was right.

"Looks like we're doing this old-school." I closed my eyes, summoning all electricity to my heart and tucking my beast far away, just like I had when Krauss had tortured me. Once my beast was stowed away, I cracked my knuckles and opened my eyes.

'What?" I asked Miles, who stared at me with one of those crooked grins.

"Nothing." His gaze went to my knuckles and back up before facing the door, eyes morphing, glowing at the challenge beyond the door. "I don't have to go old-school."

A retort was on my tongue—or so I thought. I was apparently tongue-tied. I waved him off and faced the door. Let's go.

I opened the door and Miles flashed through. He pushed back the closest two Rogues and I went for the third, wiping the shocked expression off his face with a kick to the face He quickly regained his control, eyes turning amber and obviously irate. Clearly, Krauss didn't want his special Rogues close to the bombs. They hadn't hit us with any odd abilities.

Miles finished taking out the second Rogue and faced us, eyeing the Rogue storming my way.

"He's mine," I growled as the Rogue stepped inside my pocket—his mistake. I dodged underneath his arm, twisting my body and swinging myself behind him. I punched the middle of his back and rammed my foot into the back of his knee. I aimed for his kidney and slammed my fist into his back right side, a dirty and painful shot. The Rogue fell to the ground, eyes fluttering shut.

"You've learned new tricks," Miles said.

"Compliments of Dodge." I stood.

I examined the Rogue's outfit. His cargo pants were thick, but the material wasn't as dense as the chest area of his shirt. The material overall was more lightweight than a bulletproof vest—agility was important—but sturdy. I pulled my knife, testing the sleeve. The sharp blade dragged across the black polyester-like material, not leaving a trace. I tested the point with more pressure and it gave way, tearing the material.

The Rogues had stab resistant clothes and potentially bulletproof vests. This would make things more challenging.

CHAPTER THIRTY-NINE

"L OOKS LIKE YOU GUYS have it handled," Liam said as he rounded the corner in the basement.

Liam assessed the unconscious Rogues, then his eyes fell on the door behind us, his body going rigid, eyes dilating, and his chest rising and falling in deep breaths.

"You can feel it too?" I asked him, stepping over the Rogue at my feet.

"Yes."

"Through me or in general?" I watched him step closer to the door. Liam paused, glancing at me.

"What do you mean?" He continued toward the door.

"Oh, umm." I blushed, glancing at Miles. "Nothing."

Liam pressed both palms to the door, his jaw firmly set and his eyes burning amber.

"Not through me," I mumbled to myself. If he had felt it through me like Miles said he could, he wouldn't be looking at the door like he wanted to burn it down and set the room on fire.

Miles watched him with curiosity, and so did I. It was like he had a similar reaction as I had.

"Liam," I gently said, not getting closer to the door, "we can't let them take these nukes, but I also need to get away from them."

Liam slowly turned to face me, understanding crossing his expression.

"You two need to get far away from here." Liam tilted his head toward the ground. "Adam, Maya—if you can hear me, get to the basement."

"Fighting next to it might not be the best option. You've met some of the other Rogues," Miles said, no doubt referring to Pistol.

"There's two entrances and the elevator isn't in the same hallway as the stairwell door. There's no way we can cover both." Liam glanced at the corner.

I stared at the door leading to the bombs, a sick feeling crawling up my spine. A small keyhole was drilled into the handle and that's when it dawned on me.

"What if we just have to obtain three people," I said. "We don't have to guard the nukes."

"What do you mean?" Liam asked.

"It sounds like three people know the code, and I'm betting only one has the backup key to that door." I pointed toward the handle. "Krauss wears a black string around his neck. I've only seen it once, but if it's something important, you keep it on you, right?" I thought of the picture of my dad, which I had kept on me until I had a safe place to stow it. "We get Elias, and if we get Krauss, we get the key. The only problem is the Rogue behind the door. Now that it's shut, we can't get in, but he can get out."

All three of our heads swiveled toward the door.

"I can solve that," Miles said as he strode toward the door. He pressed the buttons on the keypad and the door unlocked.

"Okay...that definitely helps," I said, taking a step backward.

"How did you know the code?" Liam's eyes narrowed as Miles dragged the unconscious Rogue out of the room.

"I saw him enter it." Miles straightened once he had the body completely out and let the door close.

"He's good at that." I had seen him do something similar in the prison.

Liam headed to the door, eyeing Miles, and smashed the keypad with his fist.

"It's only the key that we need now," Liam said, turning to face us. "Let's get out of here." Liam nodded toward the exit, and we headed in that direction. Miles stopped by the elevator and raised the door, its metal chains rattling on the way up.

"You hate elevators," I stated. "And now you want to take this one?"

Miles entered the elevator, eyeing the control panel.

"While we're smashing things..." He punched through the panel and grabbed a bunch of wires, pulling them out. Liam gave him a curt nod, and we thankfully headed toward the stairs.

The hallway was clear, and Liam used the opportunity to fill in the others. We had filled him in on the Rogues clothes as well.

"Dylan—do you copy?" Liam asked.

"Yes," Dylan responded.

"Maya, Adam, and I are going to find Krauss. He's our priority. Let us know if you see any sign of him. I'm sending Harper and Miles your way. What's your location?" Liam looked at us as we waited for a response.

"The public library. It's two blocks north of the hospital," Dylan said after several moments.

"What happened to staying on the border?" Liam shook his head. "Stay there. As soon as they reach you, get to the edge of town and keep a low profile. Ellie, how is it on your end?"

Silence.

"Ellie?" Liam asked again. "Doc? Does anyone else copy?"

"I haven't heard from them in a while," Adam answered.

"I lost visual of your cameras and lost connection with the others," Dylan said.

Liam swore under his breath.

"Continue with the plan. Find Krauss." Liam glanced at me. "Destroy the helicopter on the east side of the hospital on your way out."

"A helicopter?" I asked, not remembering seeing one. Then again, we had come in from the south.

"Yes. Along with other vehicles there. Further reasoning that Krauss is here. I doubt there would be that many vehicles and a helicopter." Liam sighed.

"What about the cargo vans?" I challenged. "Without transportation, they can't transport the nukes."

"You won't have time." Liam nodded toward the door down the hallway. "Take that and escape through an exam room window on the east side."

"I would have time," Miles disputed.

Liam glared at him. "Stay with Harper."

A muscle twitched in the side of Miles' jaw, but he stayed silent. He didn't like taking orders—he never had.

I snapped my fingers in front of their testosterone-filled staring contest.

"We get it. You don't fully trust him, but he is here." I glanced between the two of them, taking a deep breath. "We'll stick together, but we need to leave right now."

Liam assessed me.

"Be careful," he said and started to turn down the hall, but I reached for him.

"You too. No one dies today." At least no one on our side.

Liam reached out, pulling me into a hug. "Alright, sunshine. Just remember your own words."

He released me and jogged down the hallway, disappearing around a corner. I pressed the button on my com, turning it off, and pointed toward Miles', indicating to do the same. Miles reached up and turned his off.

"Good." I started toward the way we entered—toward the cargo vans. "Let's go destroy some more things."

"You told him we would get to the helicopter and leave," Miles said, voice low.

"No." I frowned, not liking going behind Liam's back despite not lying. "I said that we'll stick together."

"You're going down a dangerous path, Harper Westbrook." His voice was edged with traces of a small smile.

The outside air was still thick and dense, even with the sun in the sky. Two cargo vans were in the same spot where Miles had last seen them. I made my way across the ramp, rounding the vans slowly in case someone was inside. Crouching, I made my way to the driver's side of one van while Miles made his way to the second. I checked the side mirror to see the seat empty, and peered through the window to see the passenger seat was also.

"Empty," Miles called to me.

"Same." I walked over to the front and placed my hands on the still-warm hood. They had to have traveled far for it to still be warm, and I could feel the energy stored underneath.

"Lift the hood." Miles came up behind me.

"I have a better idea." We should be far enough away and the nukes were tucked in that bunker, so I should be safe to use my power.

The heat spread into my palms and the trail of energy from the battery below beckoned to me. They were almost drained, so this should be easy. I began drawing the energy out of the battery—similar to how I had accidently done it in the control room at headquarters. Closing my eyes, I felt the power travel from my palms and fingertips down my arm to my heart like a charge. I grinned at the jolt of energy slowly feeding me.

After all of the battery's energy emptied into me with ease, I opened my eyes and shot two bolts into the hood from my palms, frying anything else. I removed my hands, smoke trailing from underneath the edges of the hood. Black soot littered the white paint where my palms had been—that was new.

I started toward the other one, but Miles put an arm out in front of me and shook his head.

"I got this one." His eyes lingered on me a moment longer before taking off toward the other van. I didn't like the indifference in his eyes.

Miles yanked open the hood, breaking the latch and then ripping out cords. The battery still had life and its energy drew me in. The hood got closer as my feet moved on their own. I swallowed. The craving for such little power that laid underneath the hood was strong.

"Harper." Miles' deep voice knocked me out of my trance and I stopped moving forward.

I glanced at him. He didn't say anything, but his expression told me he knew how I was feeling, and I didn't like it. I was taking stupid risks by using my power. Something in this air made me feel more power hungry compared to normal, and I bet it had something to do with the nukes.

Biting my lip and taking a deep breath, I took off toward the helicopter on the east side of the hospital, knowing Miles would be right behind me—or in front of me. He blurred past me, taking the front as we ran. The woods lining the back and side of the hospital were eerily quiet and no birds were in sight.

The other side was clear and in its parking lot was a convoy of SUVs, a car, and one large helicopter. I stayed back as Miles ran over to it, climbing in and leaning underneath the dashboard. It was a shame it had to be destroyed.

"Wait!" I ran after Miles. "Is there a way not to destroy it?"

Miles sat up, staring at me. A slow smile tugged the corners of his lips up.

A couple minutes later, Miles had taken something from inside the helicopter and stashed it in his pocket. We turned our coms back on and started in the direction of the library. Miles swept me off my feet and started running.

We made it to the library in minutes, and I had to admit, the entire carrying me while running supernaturally fast was cheesy, but it hits differently in real life compared to the movies.

"I'm with Maya and Adam," Liam said over the coms. "Hannah is with us."

"We are outside the library, about to go in." I stared at the beautiful brick building.

I nodded at Miles and entered.

"Dylan? Jeremiah?" I whispered, not liking the interior of the library which was covered in shadows and cob-webs.

The old indigo blue carpet with forest green specks was covered in a layer of dust like each book on the tall wooden shelves.

"Why aren't they answering?" I asked Miles, who was in the row next to me.

The ground started shaking and the shelves shook, or I thought they did. My hair stood on end as I centered myself and scanned around me. Nothing had been moved, and the dust stayed settled. Seconds later, an invisible charged wave rushed through the library.

The energy radiating on my skin dissipated and the spark deep in my chest went quiet. My heart picked up in a slight panic, but after a few beats, the spark ignited and got stronger with each beat—like a car battery being recharged. I tapped my silent earpiece but nothing happened.

"They know we're here," I whispered. They had just released an EMP, rendering our coms useless. They were only protected from Pistol's frequency.

The source felt close, like it had come from inside the library. Miles held a finger to his mouth as he stared off into the far side of the library.

"Harper?" Dylan's voice came from the area Miles was staring at.

"Dylan?" I squinted in the dark and slowly started in that direction but couldn't see anything beyond bookshelves stocked with unfortunate books left to decay.

"I'm happy you're here," Dylan said. "Were you able to find Krauss?"

I froze and held out a hand to Miles. He looked at me, and I shook my head. "No." I kept my voice calm. "We never found him, but we found the Rogue we were looking for."

The puzzle pieces started to fit. Dylan hadn't been able to hear us, nor us him when we were down in the shelter. He had quick responses when we had come up top, and he would've had some sort of nerdy comment on this entire thing. He also would've known what happened to his visual on our cameras and our connection to Frank and headquarters.

Miles disappeared in the shadows next to me as I stepped out from an aisle and into view.

"Is Jer here?" I proceeded with caution.

"Yes," a voice answered. It sounded like Jer, but I knew it wasn't him. I wasn't going to be tricked again.

"I'm glad you guys are okay." I could feel the tendrils of current left in the air, leading to its source.

I smiled, reaching toward one just above my head. My finger sparked on contact and lightning flashed through the room, trailing the current to its origin and flooding the room with white light. A scream came from the far corner but didn't last long. Something thudded against the floor, and I jogged over. I didn't recognize the Rogue on the ground which meant—

"Don't move," said a new voice as a tall figure emerged from behind a bookshelf, holding Dylan hostage. His beady black eyes were piercing, and the black and brown horizontal stripes coloring his tied-back hair weren't easily forgotten. He was the one from the bathroom at the nightclub. The Lyrebird Rogue—or that is what Frank had thought him to be after I had explained what had happened.

Dried blood trickled from his nose and the beginning of a bruise on his temple suggested he had been in a fight recently. A knife glinted in the dark against Dylan's throat, and Dylan mumbled something, but his words were incoherent through the duct tape smothering his mouth. Movement out of the corner caught my attention, but I didn't as much flinch in that direction—I could feel that it was Miles.

"Fool me once, joke's on me. Fool me twice, that was ignorant of me. Fool me three times, well, there won't be a third time." I scowled.

"I'd say you're ignorant enough to do it again," the Lyrebird Rogue said.

I grinned at his insult like it was a dare. "What does that make you then?"

"I guess that would make me pretty smart." The knife loosened in his hand, barely moving away from Dylan's neck, but it was enough.

Miles struck, disarming the Rogue in a blur and slamming it through his boot and into the Rogue's foot. I pulled Dylan away as Miles rendered the Rogue unconscious with a swift hit to the side of the head. He fell with a sickening crack in his ankle, the knife not releasing his foot.

"Oh, man." Dylan paled as he looked down at his ankles. "I'm glad to see you guys, but I am also glad I'm not him."

"It's nice to finally hear the real Dylan's voice," I said, but even his voice sounded off. "Where's Jer?"

Dylan frowned as he wiped his cheek, smearing some dirt that had been there.

"They dumped him in the river after they shot him. He was still breathing when they tossed him in. Apparently, they only wanted me." He stared at the ground as tears traveled down his cheek. "I couldn't help him."

I put a hand on his shoulder.

"Jer is resilient." No one else dies. He had to be okay. Hybrians can handle a gunshot as long as it didn't penetrate a vital organ, right? I survived and was stabbed in my lung.

"Hope." Dylan nodded. "It's what kept the rebellion in Star Wars going, and we're kind of facing the Galactic Empire. He's alive—I know it."

"There's my best friend." I squeezed his shoulder and turned to Miles, who was examining the unconscious Rogue I had essentially fried. "We can't just hide in the woods. They know we're here, and it's only the three of them now."

Hannah was with them and a part of me was hopeful that she would help. I rolled my eyes—hope. Dylan had forced me to watch the first six Star Wars episodes.

"This was a short-range EMP." Miles twirled a small burnt grey box in his hand. "I don't think it was meant to get the hospital, just us so we couldn't get the chance to warn the others."

Miles and I stared at each other, sharing the same expression, and that was all we needed to know we were on the same page.

We weren't leaving them behind.

CHAPTER FORTY

T HE INTACT CONCRETE WALLS and surprisingly mostly unbroken windows of the hospital rose taller as we approached the five-story building's front entrance. We didn't have time to waste trying to sneak in, so the front would have to do.

Shattering glass off to my left broke my stride toward the door. A loud humming sound echoed through the air as a body flew out a fourth-story window, long black hair waving in the air.

Maya fell.

"No!" I yelled, taking off in that direction as she plummeted to the concrete sidewalk I wouldn't reach her in time. She could survive the fall if she was still morphed—and as long as she didn't land on her neck—but she could be seriously injured. There were too many variables.

A breeze brushed past me as Miles ran to get to her and I froze, watching and praying he would make it in time. He caught her in his arms, bending his knees to soften the blow. I released the breath I was holding as someone's hand landed on my back. I flinched, about to elbow the person when I saw Dylan wheezing next to me with his other hand on his knee.

"You guys run fast," he huffed.

"You ran like twenty feet." I shook my head.

"Yeah, and I thought my heart was going to leap out of my chest from Maya's cinematic fall." He lowered his hand from my back to his chest.

I rolled my eyes and ran toward Miles and Maya, who was standing on her own two feet now.

"I've got to get back up there." Maya stared at the window she flew out off.

"Who else is up there?" I asked.

"They separated us," Maya spat as she ran toward the front entrance. "Krauss was heading up the stairs to the fifth floor when we were ambushed. Pistol sent me flying out the window."

The sound of an engine spinning and the hum from a running battery called to me. I tilted my head to the west, listening until I was able to make out what exactly I was hearing. Four cargo vans came around the corner of the deserted buildings, heading toward the hospital.

"Krauss was a distraction." I scowled and turned to Dylan. "Is there a way to hack a nuke so it doesn't go off?"

"No. I mean, not unless it's a missile and you can lead it somewhere." Dylan shrugged. "Regardless, they destroyed my tablet so I can't get into anything."

"See if you can create a distraction. Something small that won't set off the nukes." I eyed him, and he nodded back at me and faced the approaching vans.

"Maya. Do your coms work?" I asked her and she nodded. "Warn them Krauss was the distraction. They're moving the bombs now."

My feet pushed hard into the ground as I sprinted toward the vans. I wasn't as close to the nukes as I had been in the back. So I shot a bolt, striking the front of the van. It veered off to the side and ramped up the curb into the hospital sign, smoke floating from the front. We couldn't let them move those bombs.

"Get down!" Miles shouted and wrapped his arms around me just as a bullet struck near my feet, denting the pavement. I glanced up to see a long barrel of a gun poking out of a fifth-floor window of the hospital. A sniper? Seriously?

Miles pulled me back in a flash to the safety of the cement entrance awning. The three vans rounded the side of the hospital, disappearing to the back. You have to be kidding me.

"They're prepared, and they have a plan. We don't." Miles looked at me, brows wrinkled and muscles strained.

"I tend to do well flying by the seat of my pants," I joked to ease his worry, but I couldn't ease the seriousness out of my tone. "Plus, our plan is hope."

"Hope's not a very good plan." He frowned.

"It destroyed a galactic empire."

"It started the destruction of a galactic empire. It didn't destroy it." Miles glanced at me, hiding a grin.

"I would have never guessed you to be a Star Wars fan." My eyes widened in amusement as I started toward the back.

"I'm not. I'm just saying hope isn't a good option."

"What about Hope's good friend Faith?"

Miles clamped his mouth shut when I slapped him in the chest as we ran. We rounded the side of the building but came up short. The vans we had rendered useless were moved so the others could take their spots, and the loading bay door was open.

The dark energy caused my skin to crawl. I stowed my powers deep down in my chest and pulled a knife, too worried about sending a stray bullet toward the nuke. I groaned as Elias and Toad strode toward us, but the absence of Krauss meant less of a chance that I would have to talk Miles down if triggered—there was no way I could use my power there.

I glanced at Miles, who was fully morphed and his eyes distractingly beautiful.

"Take this," I said, giving him the gun at my waist. "Just don't shoot a bomb."

"It might not go through to their chest." Miles glared at our approaching enemies.

"Aim for their arms," I said. If a sharp knife could tear the sleeves with increased force, a bullet could tear a hole. "The legs too."

Miles raised his left hand and aimed. Elias grinned and started in a sprint as if prepared to dodge a bullet. The zing of a bullet whizzed near me, but it hadn't come from Miles.

Miles slung an arm around me, providing cover as he aimed the gun toward the hospital. A short scream echoed through the air as a Rogue fell out the fifth-story window, missing an untended plant bed and striking the cement sidewalk next to it. Liam planted both of his hands on the frame of the window where the Rogue had just fallen through. He assessed the van below and disappeared into the black void behind him.

I braced myself as Elias and Toad closed in, losing our chance for Miles to make them a much easier target. Elias swung, aiming his venomous claw at my face like he had a vendetta against me. After all, he was created to stop me.

I grabbed a hold of his approaching claw and used his continued momentum to drive his neck into the butt of my knife. He sputtered and I sent a kick to his chest, sending him backward. I slammed my fist into his stomach, not giving him a chance to catch his breath.

Next to me, Miles fended off Toad, careful not to come in contact with the Rogue's venomous skin. Miles had known the Rogue's face didn't secret the toxin.

A shadow plummeted toward my face and I ducked, barely dodging Elias' fist. Elias rammed his foot into my thigh, sending me staggering backward. It burned like I had been kicked by a horse. Elias was much stronger and quicker than I was without my beast. I lashed out with the knife but it struck his chest, not doing any damage.

Elias charged and I went low, slicing his Achilles' tendon. He fell into Toad, and Miles shot at Toad's chest. Elias and Toad fell to the ground in a giant heap. Elias' eyes widened as Toad coughed and glanced at the gash in his sleeve—instead of his chest—panic written all over his face. That confirmed vests were bulletproof, but that also showed just how sharp Elias' claws were.

Miles and I left them in their toxic heap and took off toward the van.

"Get the bomb back to the cellar!" I yelled to Miles as we sprinted. "If we can secure the bombs in that cellar and destroy the key, it'll buy us some time until we gain control of the location."

Miles and I needed to separate, and he would be the fastest at locking that bad boy back up. I really wished our coms weren't down so we could've talked to Frank. I didn't care what distractions Krauss was causing around the world; the bombs were the priority.

Miles ran ahead and glanced into the van, his face turning an awful shade of white.

"What is it?" I asked when I reached his side, already knowing the answer as my skin crawled, the dark pit in my stomach reemerging. "Oh."

They had already loaded three nukes inside.

"I can't carry more than one. It's too much of a risk," Miles said.

"It's a good thing you're fast." I turned to face him. "You have your headphones?"

He patted his pocket, his lips flattening.

"Come back to me," I said.

"You do the same." He held out the gun. "Take this."

I nodded and took the gun. He grabbed a case, disappearing inside the hospital. I turned toward the van and then back toward the dock door. If I let any of my power near the nukes, I had no clue what would happen. I contemplated picking one up and carrying it to the basement, but I wouldn't be able to sneak by any Rogues with it in my hands, whereas Miles could.

A loud crash came from inside, and I went to go check it out but froze. I had to guard the nukes. Why had there been so many? Instead, I closed the back door and ran to the driver's side window. Keys dangled in the ignition. Idiots. If Miles wasn't back soon, I could dump the van somewhere in town until we could manage things at the hospital.

Footsteps approached and I turned, prepared to fire the gun I had automatically drawn.

"Oh, thank goodness." The metal handle bit at my fingertips as I lowered my weapon at the sight of Maya and Adam. "What happened?"

"Rogues stopped Miles, but he sent us out here to help you. Liam arrived as we left," Adam said.

"Our guns are gone, but we still have these." Maya's nails sharpened into dangerous claws in an instant.

"Hannah?" Last I heard she was with them.

"A Rogue said something to her and she took off." Maya's face reddened.

A scream ripped through the air, and I turned to see Toad rolling on the pavement, the venom from Elias burning his arm. Elias lay next to him, clutching his ankle.

"I have a way you can help," I said. "Take my gun."

CHAPTER FORTY-ONE

A MINUTE LATER AND after making sure the other vans were empty, Adam and Maya drove the van with the two nukes away. A Rogue I hadn't recognized exited a side door of the hospital and glared at me with her yellow eyes and her lip in a snarl. She started after me.

"Why do you all hate me so much?" I steadied the knife clutched in my hand. The nukes were gone, but the energy inside my core still beckoned to be unleashed.

Toad's scream behind me died out, and I assumed he had passed out.

She swung a clawed hand and I deflected it.

"Why are you doing this?" I asked between spars. "There's enough nukes in there to kill thousands."

She didn't say anything and continued swinging.

"You don't have a reason, do you?" I was hoping I could get through to her.

"Not everyone's life is perfect," she grunted as I blocked her arm with mine.

"You don't have to be a part of this. It's not too late to choose."

"I chose life. I choose power." She pulled a knife from her pocket and raised her arm. Big mistake. She left herself wide open.

I grabbed her wrist and hit her in the gut. As she hunched over, I yanked her arm down and stabbed the knife through her hand. She yelled as her hand dropped her knife. I finished with a roundhouse kick to her face, and she fell to the ground. I reached for my gun when

I heard someone running across the pavement but lowered it when I saw Dodge heading this way.

"Nice take down, kiddo," he said.

"How'd you know to come here?"

"Frank informed me, and I arrived in Germany and hitched a ride in an Audi R8. I found Roulings." Dodge scanned the area. "Did you know he had a Rogue tied up to a door handle?"

"You hitched a ride?" I doubted that. "And how did he manage that?"

"No idea, but he shocked the sucker and hit him with a tranquilizer." Dodge shook his head. "But he was firing up the jet to drive it here."

"Umm... what?" There's no driving a plane.

"He's always been an odd one. So, fill me in."

I filled Dodge in on the details as we made our way to the loading dock. When I mentioned Jeremiah, he told me that he was fine. Dodge had driven to the town instead of walking through the woods. He found Jer walking back toward the town, drenched and bleeding. Dodge took him to the jet even though he didn't want to go back.

The room was now empty, and I crept along the concrete floor until I reached the double doors with windows leading to the hallway. Beyond the window, a few bodies lay unconscious, and my worry softened as I examined each face and body, not recognizing any of them.

"Stay quiet," Dodge whispered, his hands firmly grasping his gun. "Stay behind me."

Words of protest were at the tip of my tongue, but I knew an argument about his orders was futile, much like it had been with Miles. The difference was that where Miles was brooding, Dodge was easy to talk to, but if he gave you orders, you listened.

I reached for the door to open it for Dodge but pulled away as a Rogue rounded the corner at the end of the hallway. Her nostrils flared as she rolled her shoulders like she had been slammed into something hard, anger radiating from her. She eyed the door to the basement. We had to get to her before she got there—who knew how Miles and Liam were faring.

The Rogue opened the door leading to the basement and Dodge gave me the go-ahead. I pushed on the door, opening it just enough for us to slip through. Dodge took large, long strides, quickly reaching the basement door before it closed. My training had allowed me to learn to move quickly without my beast, but he was supernaturally fast for a human—like he had just come out of the womb with natural stealth and strength.

A loud bang resonated through the air, causing my heart to leap out of my chest and a flood of adrenaline to rise. The hospital shook, but the direction of the explosion provided some relief. It wasn't from below us, and if it had been a nuke, we wouldn't be alive. I smiled to myself—I had asked Dylan to create a distraction.

My smile fell short when the Rogue turned our way from the platform below. Good distraction, but bad timing. The Rogue's eyes flashed yellow as she snarled and bolted up the stairs toward us. Instead of firing, Dodge ran at her. He slid on the ground, missing the claws she thrashed toward his face. He slammed into her ankles, causing her to fall on top of him. His arms caught her, suspending her far enough above him that he could tuck his legs underneath.

With one giant push with his feet against her chest, he sent her through the air and into the wall at the landing below. Her body fell to the ground with a slap against the concrete. I ran toward the railing and jumped, using my hip to slide down the smooth metal. The Rogue attempted to push up on her elbows, giving me the perfect opening. I landed on the platform, and in two strides, I reached her and delivered a kick to her face. She flipped to her back and didn't get back up.

"It's nice to see your training in real time." Dodge ran down the steps behind me.

"Don't flatter yourself. I did have training for five years before you," I grinned.

"And who trained that person?" He raised an eyebrow at me as he passed me and headed down the stairs.

You. I didn't say it out loud—he knew the answer. Adam was a skilled fighter because of Dodge. While Dodge was resourceful and knowledgeable, sometimes he needed a good pinch on the back of his arm, but that would only end up with me on the ground and the air knocked out of me. He was like one of those uncles who liked to wrestle with their nieces or nephews.

I kept my steps light as we descended the stairs. We reached the door, but it started opening before we had a chance to do it ourselves. I flattened myself against the wall next to Dodge behind the door, hiding in its shadows. Two Rogues ran out in a rush, no doubt heading toward the explosion. I prayed Dylan had found a safe place to hide.

Dodge grabbed the door, and I was on his heels as he entered the basement. The first part was empty, and it was eerily silent. My skin crawled from the negative charge in the air and the dread of what was around the bend.

I rounded the corner, almost running into Dodge as he halted. I took in the scene before me, my heart freezing, my teeth grinding, and my power threatening to burst out of my chest. Miles' cold, dark eyes left Krauss, flitting to me and taking in my very reaction while next to him, Liam glared at Krauss with another Rogue at his side. And at the Rogue's feet was my mom.

The door behind them was open and the dark black cord around Krauss' neck laid unhidden against his dress shirt, exposing the key at his neck. Sweat dripped down my spine as I swallowed. Every scenario I could think of crossed my mind, but it only ended with the knife the Rogue held piercing my mother's neck or a nuke going off.

Part of me wondered why Miles hadn't disarmed him. No one else was down there—surely he could have gotten my mom away. Krauss grinned, looking like he was about to give a speech. That's when I saw it. A small black fob rested in Krauss' hand and his thumb held down a button—my first thought went to Miles. Krauss tracked where my eyes were looking and lifted his hand.

"Always have a backup plan." His sly voice rattled my insides, and I wanted nothing more than to wipe that smug expression from his face. "If my thumb releases this button, it will send a signal to dear Barbara, who will then send a message to a Hybrian who is currently a guest at your house."

"Signals don't reach far down here," I said.

"This one does." Krauss lowered his hand. "We made sure of it. Your stepfather has been such a gracious host since we took your mother—I would hate for his company to have to kill him."

The blood drained from my face. How had that been possible? No one was stationed there, but the camera that had been installed on the streetlight outside my childhood home was monitored. Surely it would have picked something up. To get my mom there from Canby, they would've had to take her sometime that night after I had visited, or shortly after.

"Did they hurt you?" I looked my mom in the eyes, trying to gauge her broken expression. Her hair wasn't a tangled mess and her clothes weren't covered in dirt or grime. She looked like she had just gotten ready for the day.

Her gaze went from Krauss to me, and then she shook her head.

"Are you waiting for an appraisal?" Dodge laid the sarcasm on thickly. "What do you want?"

"And who are you?" he asked.

"Dodge. Now that we are past the introduction, what are you doing with the bombs?"

"It's a pleasure to finally meet you." Krauss smiled. "I've heard so little about you. Avery had only heard your name—she had never seen you."

"Get on with it," I bit out.

"Patience." Krauss waved the fob in the air, and my body tensed even more. "Dodge. I heard a little rumor you were chasing something that supposedly doesn't exist."

"If we leave, will you let her go?" Dodge asked, meaning my mom.

"That depends on your cooperation." Krauss coughed and hit his palm against his chest. I had been too occupied by the knife at my mom's throat that I had failed to notice his sickly pale face and the beads of sweat lining his forehead. Instead of looking forty, he looked seventy. He was dying—the same way his mother had.

"This basement is lined with lead, so it will act as a containment system." Krauss motioned to the walls around us. "Chances are it will burst into a million little pieces and be vaporized will that many bombs. One bomb? It will probably contain some of it but still level this building, and even if it's locked away in this room and not that one, it will be potent enough for a chain reaction. I perfected these to range a mile radius, but all of these will instantly kill anything nearby."

"The desert—that wasn't the only reason you chose that location," I said. It was a perfect place to experiment on bombs. The shaking I felt, that wasn't in my head. "What do you plan to do with them?"

"To create a better governed society for those insignificant to the government and the one percent that are unheard in a democracy. Nothing gets moved through parliament—the process is slow. This is a worldwide problem."

"So you're looking to control everything. For the world to be Totalitarianism? And you think ten nukes will change that." Miles voice was heavy.

"Not Totalitarianism, but Communism. The people themselves can decide their fate. And ten well-placed bombs will pave the path to the beginning," Krauss said.

"That's asking for war." Dodge took a deep breath. "Pure communism can only exist in philosophical thought."

The conversation was starting to go over my head, but there was something I realized. Their fate. Krauss was dying, so why would he care to change the world? He hadn't found a cure, and who knew how much time he had left. He had watched his mom die—something that he couldn't do anything about. The article had stated families couldn't move due to cost. He had been stuck in this town.

"You're trying to make it so others won't end up suffering like your mom. Like you are now." My voice had softened at the image of a young boy watching his own mother suffer. "You're looking for utopia"—I knew what that was, at least—"but a perfect world doesn't exist. I'm not saying anyone that lived in this town deserved what they went through, but the path you're on is going to kill thousands."

Krauss' mouth fell open for a mere second before he clamped it shut.

"That's how you found me," he said after a few seconds.

I nodded.

"You didn't give me answers to my own problem—a cure—and my only hope left had been killed." Krauss glanced at Miles, and a muscle in Miles' jaw ticked. His hope had been my dad. "Everything is set. This can't be undone."

I went to say it wasn't too late, but the Rogue's hand tightened on my mom's shoulder. The energy surged inside me, but it also picked up something else I hadn't noticed before. I traced the invisible strand tugging me toward the hint of electricity flowing through the thick, tainted air. It led to the back of the Rogue's neck while another led to the back of my mom's.

I stifled my gasp and hid my shock. No freaking way.

The door opened around the corner, and all of our heads swiveled toward the bend. Elias came around the corner, limping as he used a rod like a crutch. His gaze pinned me as if he was picturing a thousand ways to kill me.

"Elias, dear boy, I suppose I don't need to ask what happened." Krauss' gaze moved to me. "The plan will not be stopped, and I'll take my Miles back."

"Don't you dare." I growled.

"We can't have his speed against us right now. As soon as we clear this basement and seal it, I will tell my acquaintance at your home to stand down. *Der Himmel ist blau. Das Gras ist grün. Der Wind ist warm. Die Erde ist hohl. Die Atmosphäre ist leicht.*"

I stood there, helpless, as Krauss began saying Miles' trigger words. I held Miles' gaze. I will get you back. I willed to him as if whatever bond we felt could pass words through it. He gave me a curt nod, as if sensing my hope. The vein on his neck stuck out as his muscles tensed the closer Krauss was to finishing the words, and I noticed he had the ear buds in his ears. Could he still hear him?

"*Drei. Zwei. Eins,*" Krauss finished. Miles relaxed, but his eyes weren't glossed over.

CHAPTER FORTY-TWO

"**T**HERE HE IS. I need you to keep an eye on these three while we prepare the trucks," Krauss ordered Miles.

"Isa Westbrook had time alone with the trucks. Chances are they're not in working order," Miles stated. Krauss looked at Elias for confirmation.

"The van with the bombs are gone, but the other two are still there." Elias looked away. "I didn't check them."

"I guess we'll assume they're not working." Krauss assessed Elias with a cold glare.

"This may help." Miles pulled out something from the inside of his jacket pocket and tossed it to Krauss. "It's hidden in the upper left of the compartment. Twist the wires back together and the helicopter will fly just fine."

"Devious." Krauss twirled the cut wire in his hands and looked at Elias. "Aid him and Miles in watching these three. I'm going to send down our help to carry these aboard."

Elias was in no shape to fight, and I had a feeling it was punishment for not checking the vans.

"Wait!" I yelled out. "This might be the last time I see my mom." I glanced at the room with the nukes. "I'm not sure if you got to say goodbye to yours, but I'd like to get the chance to say goodbye—to get one last hug."

Krauss glared at me, and a small grin appeared before disappearing. "Fine. Don't try anything." He held up the fob.

If I was wrong, my mom probably wouldn't forgive me for this. I also had to be really careful if I didn't want to blow us up. I slowly strode toward her as the Rogue released the knife from her neck and kicked her in the back.

"Mom?" I said as I knelt down. She didn't say a word, but her eyes glistened with tears and it almost broke my heart—almost. She was a good actor. But it wasn't real.

I hugged her, my hand finding the back of her neck, where my answer laid. They wouldn't have turned her into a Hybrian this quickly, and the mom I knew would have had her say with Krauss by now. I closed my eyes and focused on channeling the energy to my palm, using the chip as a targeting beacon.

My eyes flew open, facing the room of nukes, where no one could see them glow. I sent a stream of energy toward the chip. My mom—the impersonator—shook in my arms. The room in front of me stayed quiet and the air stayed stagnant as I sighed in relief. The nukes were still intact. I summoned the energy back to my core. When the impersonator stopped shaking, something moved underneath my hand. Gross. Was that skin?

I dropped the Rogue, eyes wide as they morphed into a completely different person. They still wore the same clothes, but nothing else was the same. The Rogue above me moved, and I stood, grabbing his wrist and twisting until his hand loosened. I grabbed the knife and then twisted him around so I now held the knife to his throat.

"That was bold." Krauss nodded at me...in approval? "Officer MacLand. Make sure they don't leave." He pivoted on his heel and headed for the exit.

"You're going to leave while she has a knife to my throat, Elias can't even walk, and the room next to us is full of bombs?" The Rogue said angrily.

"You'll manage," Krauss called over his shoulder.

"See, he's trying to make the world a better place," I said. "He doesn't care about his minions. I even told Avery that. This vision of his, he's trying to protect the future children, but this will only doom them."

Krauss halted.

"The phrase this is for the greater good?" Krauss turned back around. "This is its definition."

He started walking away again. I pulled back my arm and threw, the knife planting itself in his calf. He grunted and fell to the ground as the Rogue elbowed me in the gut. I had to trust this entire thing was a ploy as the fob in his hand went skidding across the concrete—that my mom and Joe were not in danger. The Rogue pulled his gun, but I disarmed him and aimed the barrel at his chest.

I glanced over my shoulder at the others. Miles stood with his arms across his chest, eyebrow raised, as he assessed me. I felt the warmth in his gaze, but I also felt something extra—admiration? Triggered Miles was admiring me—and I could feel it?

Dodge braced himself for a fight with Miles. Elias had backed up, realizing something was wrong as Liam grinned—he knew what I knew deep down. Miles wasn't triggered.

"You could have ended this before I almost blew us up by chancing the use of my powers," I said to Miles.

"I was waiting for the right moment." He glanced at the Rogue who had imitated my mom. "And I didn't know that wasn't your mom."

With the other Rogue detained and Elias wounded, we had everything under control—until more would eventually come.

"I need to get out of here." I could feel my skin prick and the pressure in my chest building. Using my power had made me crave more with being so close to the nukes.

"Harper, get topside," Liam said and then glanced at Krauss. "You're going to help us end this."

A hazy wave of dizziness washed over me, urging me to follow the tainted energy.

The Rogue moved, and I saw his intentions too late as he reached for my gun. The haze—almost like brain fog—vanished as a bullet whizzed by my face. Miles had moved me just in time to prevent the bullet from hitting me square between the eyes and disarmed the Rogue.

A clank thudded from inside the other room, and we all turned toward the noise as a beep went off.

"It looks like my time is up sooner than I had thought." Krauss laughed from his spot on the floor.

The bullet had ricocheted off the wall behind me and hit one of the cases.

"How do we stop it?" Liam demanded.

"You don't." Krauss laid down flat, staring at the cement ceiling like it was a clear night sky. "You have ten minutes before it goes off. There's no built-in safe, and if Isa uses her powers to stop the timer... boom."

Miles pocketed the gun and blurred over to Krauss, lifting him off the floor and against the wall by his expensive tie.

"There's always a failsafe," Miles gritted through his teeth. "You always have a backup plan."

"I do." Krauss' feet dangled as he stared straight into Miles' eyes. "My backup plan was to not let anyone disarm the weapon once it went off. I'm running out of time regardless. There was no point in installing a failsafe."

Miles let go and Krauss crumpled to the ground, coughing. Liam had already entered the room and had the case opened. I ran to his side, studying his distant face and the way his hand rested on the nuke.

"Watch them," Miles told Dodge from outside the room.

I placed my hand next to Liam's, palm against the smooth green metal shell. The heat searing my palm and the urge to draw out its energy like I had the van batteries, was strong.

"You can feel that?" Liam glanced at me.

"I feel something, but I don't know what it is," I said as Miles' hand landed on my shoulder. As soon as it did, the energy in my chest intensified yet the edge was taken off, more focused.

I heard a whack outside the door and pulled my hand from the bomb, turning to see what had happened.

"I don't have time to babysit," Dodge said as he entered the room and pushed Elias to the floor.

Behind him, the Rogue lay on the floor, eyes closed. Krauss wouldn't get far, the shifter Rogue was unconscious, and Elias wasn't in the best shape. Dodge's eyes widened when he saw the bomb. We had seven minutes.

"I think I can stop it," I said, glancing back at the bomb. "It's like it's calling to me." I didn't have time to explain it to Dodge, and Miles and Liam knew I could draw in energy.

"No." Miles' voice was sharp. "This is nuclear, not electrical."

"I have to try." If I didn't, everyone there would die—Dylan, Maya, and Adam too. "The fallout shelter can help—you heard Krauss."

"If this bomb goes off, they all explode." Miles' lips were pressed in a thin line.

"I don't know how, but I can help," Liam added. "I can feel it too."

"Liam, no." I looked at him, his expression told me his mind had already been made.

"I'm not going anywhere," he said. "Even if I were to leave, I would still be dead if they went off."

I didn't like the idea, but I was starting to think this was the only option. And we were running out of time.

"We don't have time to argue." I grabbed Miles' hand. "You and Dodge need to get out of here."

"Not an option. You're leaving with me." Miles reached for me but Dodge put out a hand to stop him, and I swore Miles was going to rip his arm off.

"Calm down." Dodge lowered his voice but spoke quickly. "They might be right. I don't like it either"—Miles growled at him—"but Harper has more than electrical properties. Same with Liam. They differ, but Harper's blood contains uranium—what's the element in a nuclear bomb? Uranium. Both of them have been exposed to gamma radiation. If Harper can absorb electrical energy, maybe she can absorb that too—same with Liam. Once you meddle with it, it will probably go off and your best bet is to absorb the blast."

Is this what my dad had meant by we still had a lot to catch up on?

"That's why I can feel it?" Liam asked. "But what about the others?"

"We don't have time for details." Dodge looked between Liam and me. "Do you think you can do it?"

"Yeah, sure. I've totally absorbed the energy from a nuclear blast before," I quipped. Dodge went to say something, but I cut him off and glanced at Miles. "We need to do this now. The two of you need to get out of here, now."

Miles rubbed the back of his neck. "I'm staying."

"Miles... what if your body can't stand the radiation we can't absorb? We know nothing about this." The thought clawed at my heart.

"I can sense the energy through you—like I did outside. It calls to you, and when I touched you just now, I felt it. When Krauss transformed me, our blood mixed and we already had a connection. What I've been feeling, it's a joined bond. I can help you."

All I could do was shake my head.

"I'm not leaving either," Dodge added.

"Yes you are. You need to get the others out of here." Despite hating their guts, it wouldn't be right to leave them down there where they can burn. "At least out of the basement."

Dodge paused and grumbled after a split second. He went over to the door where Elias had slowly crept to. He shoved him out and closed the door.

"Miles..." I couldn't get out the words. He gently cupped the sides of my face.

"Together," he whispered, and I nodded as he wiped a single tear away from my cheek.

"Not to interrupt, but I'm interrupting. We have less than two minutes." Liam glanced at the bomb's timer.

I reached my hand out and grabbed Liam's, giving a hard squeeze.

"Since the beginning, sunshine." Liam smiled.

"Since the beginning." I nodded. "Let's do this."

A nuclear bomb counted down to our vaporizing death. I've seen enough horror films with Dylan to see how this ended.

CHAPTER FORTY-THREE

Molten burning lava encased my hands and trailed up each vein and nerve in my arm—at least that's what it felt like as I attempted to draw the energy from the nuke.

Twenty seconds.

"That's not working. We need to back up." Miles clasped a hand over mine, tugging me backward.

"This close might incinerate our hands," Liam agreed.

The three of us took a step back, bracing ourselves as we stood between this single bomb and the others. Miles hadn't dropped my hand, and I reached for Liam's. If we were all going to get through this, we had to join forces. There was something that made Liam and me different from the other Hybrians, and I was going to get answers from Dodge if—when—we got out of this.

Miles and Liam summoned their beast and so did I—I guess it didn't matter if I set off any bombs now.

Boom.

That's when I felt it—not just the uranium inside waiting to react, but the entire energy it yielded when it combusted. It was like I could sense the amount of power inside its shell before combustion. The air vibrated, and the first wave happened so quickly, like an electric force entering my body—and I absorbed it all.

Time stood still. The EMP at the run-down library was strong, but this hit differently, more powerfully. Miles' hand branded heat into mine, and I could feel him—his worry, his fear, his love for me. An invisible rush of something that was so new yet felt so familiar soothed the static that was surging out of me. Liam glanced at me, his brows creasing as if he couldn't feel anything.

There was no time to communicate as the second wave hit, the entire room shaking. The second wave seemed delayed and who knew if maybe we had absorbed something after all before it exploded. Liam's hand crushed mine, and this time I knew he felt the searing pain. Hot. Extra spicy dipped in the core of the earth.

Each nerve ending and vein was on fire and my skin radiated blue. The three of us had drawn the blast toward us, and out of the corner of my eye, I could make out glowing amber etched in bulging veins in Liam's arms.

A scorching pain in my chest caused me to keel over as each bone in my body felt like it was going to snap. Miles' grip tightened around mine, and some of the pain lessened, but it felt like I was about to explode. My body involuntarily straightened, arching backward, as the energy burning through me released. The pain ceased and static blanketed my body as power seeped from every surface.

The blue haze I had never been able to control encased the three of us. Static fizzed inside the orb as blue and black bolts sailed, not touching Miles or Liam. They stood next to me, hands still gripping mine.

It started to get hot inside the orb and black flares started flying from the sphere's rim and hitting the walls in the room. If they didn't stop, one of them would hit another bomb. I couldn't do this again. The pain started in my chest again and my brain felt like it was about to burst—I couldn't contain it anymore. The blue haze imploded into me, like reversing the video of dropping an opened water bottle.

White-hot heat slammed into my chest, and I could feel it twisting inside, like it was being altered. My veins still glowed blue as each static particle traveled to my chest, containing the ball of churning fire deep within. The searing-hot churning stopped, and when it did, the bright blue—no, black—burst outward from somewhere deep inside my chest.

My ears rang and my vision blurred. When the ringing stopped, my knees gave out, but I was supported on each side. I wasn't sure if my heart was beating—I couldn't feel it. My legs and arms were numb as someone laid me in their arms.

"Harper?" a worried voice said. "Harper, can you hear me?" Miles. It was Miles. "Let's get her out of this room."

The ceiling moved as strong arms lifted me to their chest and carried me out the door. A door shut behind us and someone appeared next to Miles.

"Harper? Can you hear us?" He called me Harper—not sunshine. Liam was worried too, and I strained to focus, picking up the exhaustion riddled over Liam's face, which was dripping in sweat.

A finger gently stroked my cheek, and I leaned into the soothing touch.

"Why did you give Krauss the helicopter wire if you weren't triggered?" I asked the first thing that had come to mind, and I had no clue why it had been that.

"That's what you ask after all of that?" The chest my head rested on vibrated with a deep chuckle. "I needed him to trust me."

"Why didn't it work?" I wanted to add that it was good Krauss' trigger words hadn't worked, but I couldn't get anything else out.

"I had someone else to focus on." Miles kissed the top of my forehead. "I also had Queen on my side."

I felt the tug of his lips against my forehead as he smiled, and I sighed into his chest. The headphones had helped then.

CHAPTER FORTY-FOUR

I FORCED MY EYES to stay open, straining against the dryness that stung and the throbbing in my head and chest. Miles carried me toward the stairs, and I wanted nothing more than to stay in his arms, but I needed to walk out of there on my own. I tapped him on the shoulder to set me down. His brows furrowed as he nodded, understanding my intent.

He slowly set me down. My feet reached the ground and my legs wobbled like a newborn foal's—or so I've heard the saying, and I was pretty sure this was close to it. I started walking with Miles' arm wrapped around me for support. The thought of the stairs behind the door was dreadful despite the need to do this myself. I glanced at the elevator as we passed. It wasn't in working order after Miles had punched the panel, and I doubted it would be trustworthy after the foundation had shaken.

We made it through the door and I took a moment to despise the number of steps in front of me. They seemed like a lot less when your body hadn't felt like it had been kicked in every area so many times.

Neither Miles nor Liam spoke while we slowly ascended the stairs. Miles didn't offer to carry me, and I had appreciated that—he knew I wanted to do this myself and would ask for help if I wanted it. After what felt like the longest time ever climbing up only a few flights of stairs, we finally made it down the hallway and outside into the back parking lot.

"—already shook. If there were more, it would have happened by now," Dylan said.

"If the entire collection went off, this entire area would be obliterated," a voice replied. I wanted anger to flare inside me at the sound of that person's voice, but I was too weak for anger.

Barbara kneeled—no doubt ruining her expensive dress pants. Barbara's hands were on the back of her head as she looked at Hannah, who stood with her arms crossed and beautiful soft wings folding at her back. Next to them lay Toad, still unconscious.

The air felt charged and I wanted to reach for its power, but the small voice in the back of my mind said to leave it alone. Each weak nerve ending knew it was mine and there was a reason I had let it go—I couldn't hold on to it.

"You guys are alive!" Dylan shrieked as he ran toward us, stopping once he reached us. "Wow. You don't look so good." He looked from me to Liam. "Neither do you."

Liam was pale and Miles didn't look so hot either—but better than us.

"What's going on here?" Miles glowered at Barbara, who studied the three of us like we had just arrived through a portal.

"Oh, uh." Dylan glanced over his shoulder at Hannah, who hadn't taken her eyes off Barbara. "I sort of made an explosion, but I also found Hannah. When I called her out for running, she said she was on her way to capture Barbara—who was evidently hiding out in Krauss' old home. We brought her back here when everything started shaking."

"That's not possible," Barbara stammered, her pink, plump lips slightly parted.

"What's not possible?" Liam asked as he walked over to her cautiously, and I slowly followed.

Barbara dropped a hand and looked at her watch, but hastily brought it back behind her head when Hannah extended her wings behind her in warning.

"The air is charged—almost like a nuclear weapon was activated, but without the radiation fallout. Unless, unless it's from you." Barbara looked at me. "Your bodies clearly indicate something happened. How many detonated?"

I scoffed and swallowed, my throat dry. "Maybe ten or maybe zero. You will never know what happened."

Liam moved, heading over to Toad and standing above him. His fists clenched at his sides and though I couldn't see his face, I knew he was enraged. He grabbed something from his pocket and plunged it into Toad's shoulder. I went to call his name when I realized it was just an inhibitor.

"Have you seen Dodge?" I asked Dylan.

"No. He's here?" Dylan glanced around like he would spot him.

"He was," Liam answered.

"Where's Krauss?" Hannah's voice cut in as she knelt in front of Barbara, the anger in her voice directed at her.

"With Dodge." I pushed off Miles, chancing my ability to carry my own weight as I walked toward Hannah. "Is he threatening someone you love?"

Hannah's emerald eyes shot to me, her pupils dilating. He was.

"We'll find them," I told her.

"He wasn't the only one." Her eyes flicked back to Barbara.

"Are they still in danger?" I asked, slightly wavering on my own two feet.

"I had her call them off." Hannah's suggestive tone made it sound like there was a little threatening involved.

"If she called them off, they could still be in the area," Miles said.

"As soon as we can, we'll send the closest team—"

"No," Hannah interrupted Liam. "I'll go myself."

Liam nodded just as the sound of an engine grew louder. The nose of a jet—our jet—rounded the corner of the hospital, rolling across the grass and onto the pavement.

"How's the jet working?" Dylan asked.

"They must have been out of range." Miles came over and put an arm around me, and I raised an eyebrow.

"It's like an EMP went off. Nothing's working," Dylan answered my look.

I glanced at Miles, but he was watching the jet.

"Jer," Dylan said, his voice dipping. "We have to find Jer."

"He's okay," I nodded at the jet. "He's with Frank."

I leaned into Miles as the jet came closer and halted. Maya came out, followed by Adam, who pushed Krauss down the stairs in front of him. My body was weak, but somehow it managed a low snarl at the sight of him. I started toward him, my legs getting new strength.

"Harper..." Miles warned from behind me.

I ignored him. My exhausted beast came forward, and I welcomed her. Krauss' widening dark eyes, contrasting against his pale, thin skin, told me he was afraid as I strode toward him. I stopped a few feet away, fully aware my eyes were glowing. My beast wanted nothing more than to use the charged tainted air around me to fry him.

"You killed my father, you tortured Miles, you tortured me, threatened my family, and hurt countless people." My voice was laced with hatred.

"I also know how to alter Officer MacLand at my very own choosing, unless you kill me yourself." Krauss' fear vanished, and that was when I saw it— he hid his fear and sorrow behind his snarky grin. But this time, he was ready for it to be over.

I raised my hand, smoke trailing from my palm. The sight flashed me back to my nightmare—the one where smoke trailed my loved one's bodies. Even though Krauss wasn't my friend, I had never wanted to turn down that path.

"You're sick. You're going to die the same way your mother did—I don't need to kill you." I almost felt pity—almost. His actions weren't justified by the terrible suffering brought to his mother—or to the downfall of this town and its people. "I am sorry about your mother and for the people of this town, but that isn't a reason to hurt innocent people—even if you don't think some of them are."

What if he believed some of the delusions he had instilled in Miles? The ambassadors he had Miles target had been considered evil in Miles' eyes. If the person brainwashing you believed it too, it had to have helped with the process.

"I'm not going to kill you," I said, letting my beast fade and ripping the key from his neck, sending Krauss into a coughing fit. "You will die in a cell, and hopefully you will think about all of the wretched things you have done."

I had wanted nothing more than for Krauss, Toad, Elias... all of them... to face unimaginable pain, but that wasn't who I was. My soul—and my beast's soul—was something I wouldn't let be taken from me.

"Let's go home." I glanced past Krauss and to the jet, wanting nothing more than to claim a comfy chair.

Dylan ran up the stairs and past Dodge and Frank, who stood in the opening. Elias and the other two Rogues were no doubt already aboard and cuffed.

"We have to wait for my friends in Interpol to arrive before we can head out, dearie," Frank said.

I guess we couldn't just up and leave.

CHAPTER FORTY-FIVE

I SAT ON THE gym floor at headquarters, staring at the photo of my father. Flipping it back and forth had revealed nothing, and Dodge hadn't asked about it since we had arrived. He had only asked to meet in the gym along with the photo.

Krauss, Barbara, Avery, and the other Rogues had been transported to a secure facility, which was apparently impenetrable, unescapable, and had heavy surveillance under the Alliance. Liam had made sure he saw them locked away before getting back to headquarters—he even sent me a confirmation video.

My body was still recovering from Germany a couple days ago, but I was almost back to full strength. Liam had recovered more quickly than I had during the long flight. The jet had been out of range from the EMP I apparently put out. Lead was a conductor when pure, but not the best, and the waves had traveled through the basement walls and ceiling, affecting anything electrical in the town—according to Frank. Once Krauss and the others were gone, he had so many questions, but so had I, so I pushed through the exhaustion to get answers.

Frank was most amused by the connection Miles and I had. He thought it was due to our blood being mixed together. His blood flowed through me and mine did flow through his. Miles was my catalyst—much more potent than the river back at the cabin had been a long time ago.

The EMP had hit Dodge, who had the others in his Audi R8. When Frank drove the jet, he had picked them up along with Maya and Adam. Frank was working with Interpol to make sure the bombs would never end up in the hands of anyone.

"Thank you for coming," Dodge said as he walked through the gym doors.

"You're not here to train me." I glanced at his tan cargo pants which he would often train in, but the serious expression on his face said he was there to just talk.

"No, I'm not." He took a seat beside me. "I asked Liam to join us."

"What's going on?" I faced him, unease stirring in my gut.

"I wanted to tell you about the picture." He pointed to my hands.

"The truth?" I asked.

Dodge nodded and reached out a hand. "May I?"

I handed it to him as Liam walked in, his brown hair disheveled like he had just woken up. Dodge waved him over to have a seat. The three of us sat in an odd circle like we were in kindergarten, but if Dodge was going to give me answers, I was going to listen.

"This stays between us." Dodge glanced at the both of us.

"What about the cameras?" I asked.

"They're taken care of. Do either of you know what this is?" Dodge held up the photo of my dad, and part of my heart clenched. It was someone I would never get back.

"It's a recipe—in a way," Dodge continued when neither of us answered. "Both of you are made a little bit differently. Harper, your father never shared what else he used to make your serum. It was made with uranium and was also exposed to gamma radiation—carefully. I don't know the process, but I'm assuming that's how you were able to absorb the energy. Nuclear bombs are made up of uranium or plutonium. Seeing how you were reacting to the bombs, there was a high chance you could absorb the gamma rays much like you can with electricity."

"How did you know I can absorb electricity?" I questioned.

"You did during our training—you just hadn't realized it. Your dad assumed this too." Dodge sighed at the mention of my dad's name. "This is one of the reasons your father believed your chronic illness was cured and not the other Hybrians with medical issues, but it's not something to mess around with, and we both made a promise to never let that happen again. Its survival rate is less than two percent, and the rage is unpredictable—it's not meant to be. Your father knew you were strong and had faith that you would overcome it, but he later knew it needed to never happen again—no matter who it was or the situation."

I shivered. Good thing Krauss didn't have the formula—he would have killed so many.

"Why wasn't it detected—how did Krauss not know?" Krauss had experimented and researched every cell and DNA in my body.

"I'm not sure." Dodge shrugged. "Maybe it's undetectable. Frank couldn't detect it either."

"And what about Liam?" None of this made sense—all I knew was what I had felt. Liam had felt something too, and we both had somehow absorbed that bomb.

"Your serum wasn't the same as other Hybrians." Dodge's eyes fell on Liam. "It contained radiation—it wasn't exposed to it. Neither Frank nor I knew who you were for sure until I saw how you reacted with the bombs."

"What do you mean?" Liam asked.

"Your Hybrian DNA was passed down through genetics."

"Genetics?" Liam stiffened, his arms still resting on his bent knees.

"Your father was a Hybrian—and not just any Hybrian. He was the first one."

CHAPTER FORTY-SIX

MY BRAIN TRIED TO process the millions of questions running through it.

"No." Liam shook his head and got to his feet. "Not possible."

"It is," Dodge assured. "You were adopted. It was untraceable to your father."

"Frank had said the first Hybrian had morphed and couldn't morph back—he was full of rage and killed people. There's no way Liam is his son," I attested for Liam.

"He apparently had a kid." Dodge stood. "That's why I've been traveling. I've been trying to find answers, but I'm coming up short."

I heard a little rumor you were chasing something that supposedly doesn't exist. Krauss had said those words.

"Krauss knew?" I asked.

"That man always seems to know everything," Dodge said. "I don't know what he knows, but he doesn't know about you, Liam. For all he knows, you were made differently. If anything, this gave him suspicions of what both of you had inside you, but he is locked away until he dies. I can guarantee it."

"So I was adopted and my family never told me?" Liam asked but obviously knew the answer. "Is he still alive?"

"I have a suspicion he is, but I don't know for sure." Dodge held up the photo, turning it around to the blank back. "This has the key ingredients that created the original Hybrian hidden on the back."

"If you both swore to not let anyone ever do that again, then why keep it somewhere?"

"Your dad was cautious. He wanted his own failsafe for you—a way to make an antidote. He would always remember the formula, but he didn't know if he would always be around." My gut twisted at the truthful proclamation in Dodge's words.

"And somehow my biological father had a child with someone?" Liam had known about the original Hybrian from Frank.

"It sure seems that way." Dodge nodded and waited a second before continuing. "I received a message—before Ben passed." Dodge pulled out a lighter and lit it, holding it so the heat reached the back of the photo. Words and formulas written in messy handwriting appeared on the back. "He wanted me to destroy this. The only ones that know and are living are the three of us. The method is so very specific that one minor mishap would kill someone, as well as kill the person making it. The cells of the person given the serum can attack their own body—even if it's made correctly. It's too dangerous, and if someone like Krauss got his hands on—"

"Many would suffer," I said.

"No one can know about it." Liam glared at letters and numbers written on the back of the photo, his jaw tight.

Dodge moved the lighter closer, the corner catching a flame. The three of us watched as the flames danced along the edges and licked up the sides of the photo. Dodge waved his hand once it reached his finger, the flames diminishing as he dropped the last piece. It turned to ash as it fell. A part of me was sad the photo of my dad was gone, but the other part of me was relieved the information on it was.

"It can never get out, but Ben and I owed the two of you the truth." Dodge glanced my way. "Your dad never wanted anyone else to know, and I was the only one he truly trusted, besides your mother. He trusted Dr. Roulings, but on a certain level. The two of us talked earlier—I didn't mention the photo—and though he suspects what's inside Harper, he would never use anything of the kind."

Footsteps came running down the hallway, and Dylan popped through the door.

"Harper, Miles left," he panted.

"What?" I blurted as I stood. "As in left, left?"

"As in he's gone," Dylan said.

"No," I whispered as I ran, brushing past him and heading toward the studios.

A tear escaped before I even made it past the main area and down the hallway toward the stairs. My heart beat out of my chest and it felt like a weight had been placed there. He couldn't have left me.

The door to my room was cracked open, and it was like I could feel his presence behind it, but I wouldn't believe it until I saw him with my own eyes. I shoved the door open, the invisible weight falling from my chest, but it still hung by a string. Miles stood staring out the window with a bag at his feet.

"Are you leaving?" I asked, finding my voice. Apprehension radiated through the connection.

"I can't stay, Harper." He turned away from the window. "I need time to figure myself out."

"You were going to leave without me—without telling me?" My feet were glued to my spot, my brain not able to communicate anything. I had wanted to talk about the comments he had made about leaving, but we hadn't had time to yet.

"No." Miles strode toward me, leaving the bag by the window. "I want you to come with me—only if you want to."

"Yes," I stammered.

"Yes?" The corner of his mouth twitched upward as he stepped closer, his face inches from mine. "I haven't even told you where I'm going."

"I don't care." I held his gaze. "I want to go with you—no matter where that is."

"I was hoping you'd say that." Miles leaned in and kissed me softly on the lips before pulling away, the apprehension disappearing. "How do you feel about boats?"

"I wouldn't know," I said.

"My dad had a boat that went to me when he passed. It stays up the Willamette River." He moved his gaze from my throbbing lips to my eyes. "I need a couple months to sort through my own thoughts, and I didn't really want to do it without you."

"The one he took you fishing on?" I asked.

"Yes." He had told me stories when we were trapped in the prison.

"I think a few weeks of fresh air and away from everyone would do us both some good." I nodded but bit my lip. "The funeral is tomorrow."

My dad's funeral was in my hometown. It was going to be private and small, but it would provide the closure I needed.

Miles glanced at the ground. "I figured we could head to the boat afterward."

"I think that would be a good idea." I needed to find myself too, and together, we could do just that.

THE CUSHIONED BENCH IN the front of the bow was perfect for lounging and gazing at the vast sea, and there were no cameras nearby to watch my every move. Miles' boat wasn't a yacht, but it was huge by my standards. It had a room, a bathroom with a shower, and a small kitchen. The last month had been amazing, and we had already traveled down parts of the West Coast, going inland when bad weather was reported. Cold weather was around the corner, but we planned to be in before it would affect us too much.

I scrolled through my phone and opened the unread message from Chloe.

Wish you two were here! I miss you both and hope you're having fun.
—Chloe

She had inserted a kissy face at the end. I missed her along with my other friends. She and Brandon had decided to stay in Portland but were going to work for Alcorp at a new stronghold. Brandon had said that after seeing what he had, he wanted to stay in his career path but needed to do more. Frank had proposed having a stronghold in Portland, especially since the Vault closed and Westbrook was still in that location. The new location was already underway.

Liam had been sent all over by Frank, and I still couldn't help but think he was grooming him to take over. After Liam's origins were revealed, he had wanted to find the answers Dodge had been looking for. He had been searching in between missions and no doubt would pounce on the first thing that came up.

Frank and the Alliance were sending operatives inside NATO, trying to figure out who else was loyal to Krauss' plan. Krauss couldn't have done everything alone. The Rogue with cuttlefish DNA—the one that had impersonated my mom—apparently had woken up while we were looking at the nukes and took off. The Rogues were still causing mayhem, but everyone could manage without the two of us for a bit.

Frank no longer created Hybrians and neither did the Alliance—for now. He had admitted the way they went about it was cruel, and he should have used different tactics despite the lower success rate. The future only knew what was to come of any Hybrian making.

Dylan and Jer had finally made their relationship official and continued working for Alcorp, and Maya and Adam usually worked solo on assigned missions.

Once Miles and I were ready, I would help Liam with whatever he needed, just like he had helped me. We weren't planning on being a part of Alcorp or the Alliance, but a mutual third party who answered to ourselves. With a clear mind, I had better control. Same with Miles. The things we had been through would take time to heal, but would also leave scars—just like the ones that littered my body.

As far as we knew, only Elias and Avery had a recording of Krauss saying Miles' trigger words. And as for Krauss? He was dead. Liam had told us the news that he had succumbed to his illness just days after being locked up. I suspected something else had been at play.

"Who's bothering you now?" Miles came up behind me and kissed the back of my neck, sending a shiver down my spine. We had shared many kisses, and that warm fluttery feeling hadn't faded.

"Chloe misses us." I bit my lip, hiding the smile from his touch.

"Is it wrong to say that I'm enjoying this time alone?" He sat down next to me, pulling me to him. My body hummed at his contact.

"No," I admitted. "We needed this."

Miles wove his hand through mine and I rested my head against his chest, hearing his slow, steady heartbeat. Each nerve ending could sense his, and I could tell he was feeling the same responsiveness. We sensed each other in an indescribable way—as if we were one. We centered each other, and once we healed and were back at it, we would be a force to be reckoned with.

Not only was Miles my catalyst, but I was his. And together, we would overcome anything.

I could finally close my door.

THE END.

The Hybrian Series

Hello, there!

Reviews are lifelines to authors, and we love hearing your thoughts!
Please feel free to leave one on Amazon or Goodreads. I would also love
to say hi and meet you. You can drop in on any of my social medias.

You can find everything here: https://www.authorlwood.com/
The Hybrian Headquarters Facebook group:
https://www.facebook.com/groups/thehybrianheadquarters

Acknowledgments

Thank you to my family and friends who have supported me through the entire process—from my husband, parents, grandparents, aunts and uncles, cousins, friends...the list goes on and on. Dad, thank you for inspiring me to use my imagination since I was little. Mom, thank you for always being my number one fan.

To all of my wonderful beta and ARC readers—you are all incredible!

A special thank you to the professional editors and cover designer who helped piece this book together and gave me guidance.

And as always, thank you—the reader—for coming along this journey. If you enjoyed the adventure, please take time to leave a review.

ABOUT THE AUTHOR

L. Wood enjoys living in the countryside of the Great Lakes Region. When she's not writing or working with animals as a veterinary technician, she loves spending time with her family, playing volleyball, hiking, and swimming—much like her dog. And, of course, there's always room for ice cream, no matter the time of day.

Please visit **authorlwood.com** for more.